THE ENEMY WITHIN

THE DEPARTMENT Z SERIES

THE ENEMY WITHIN
DEPARTMENT Z

JOHN CREASEY

OPEN ROAD

INTEGRATED MEDIA

NEW YORK

ISBN: 978-1-5040-9188-6

This edition published in 2024 by Open Road Integrated Media, Inc.
180 Maiden Lane
New York, NY 10038
www.openroadmedia.com

THE ENEMY WITHIN

1

ORDERS

The room was long and narrow, with a high ceiling. The walls, panelled and bare on two sides, were dull light brown, almost yellow. There was one desk, at the far end of the room, and behind the desk were two closed doors. On the wall between them hung a portrait of a man. The face looked pale, but for the eyes it might have been the face of a dead man; but the eyes gave him life. They were a piercing blue. They looked like real eyes placed in the portrait, and made the picture uncanny. Most people would have recognised the heavy features, with the large, dark moustache, drooping downwards at the corners; few would have recognised the eyes.

These were the first things Charles Corliss saw when he entered the room for the first time. He saw them before he noticed the man sitting at the desk; before he glanced about the room. They drew his gaze as a magnet draws steel.

The door through which he had entered closed softly, finally. He was alone with the man at the desk and the portrait —and the eyes. The eyes were the most vital living things in that room. Corliss stood still, and looked at them. Were they real? Was a man standing behind that portrait and looking at him through holes cut in the canvas?

He forced himself to look away but remained conscious of the eyes.

The plain wooden walls had no significance. Because of the length of the room, the far end where the man sat at the desk seemed narrower than this end. The man did not look at him, but continued to read a manuscript on his desk. Except for a telephone and a writing pad, the manuscript was the only thing there.

Corliss saw, for no one could fail to see, the great map which stretched almost the whole length of the right-hand wall, and nearly from floor to ceiling. In front of it were two library ladders, made of the same wood as the wall panels. The map was of the world, and was divided into sections, each section showing a continent. Parts of each, even of the American continent, were coloured bright red—a crimson much more vivid than the red that appeared on British maps and showed the Commonwealth. The whole of Eastern Europe, great tracts of Asia and smaller tracts in other continents, were of the same colour. Dotted about the white, empty spaces of the rest of the map, were crimson-headed pins.

The man at the desk looked up.

"Come nearer," he said.

Corliss drew himself sharply to attention and obeyed, as if he were on parade. The dull, brown, fitted carpet deadened the sound of his footsteps.

There were no windows in this room.

Corliss reached the desk, and stood to attention. On his right was a chair, the only other chair in the room besides that of the man at the desk.

There was no likeness between the man and the portrait.

4

He was sallow-faced and had dark, brown eyes—not beady, not clear; smoke seemed to curl and writhe in them. He had hair of chestnut brown, dark, bushy eyebrows, a long upper lip with a deep groove beneath the nose, a long, narrow, pointed chin. His cheek bones were high and it was possible to imagine that his eyes slanted; a Slav?

"You may sit down," he said. His voice was flat, emotionless and slightly accented.

Corliss sat down—and glanced up again, at those eyes.

"You are an Englishman," said the man at the desk. "Your name is Charles Marvin Corliss. You are twenty-nine years of age. You were educated at a public school and at the University of Cambridge. You are unmarried. You have neither mother nor father living and you have no close relatives. All that is so, yes?"

"Yes, Excellency," said Corliss. He did not know this man's name and had been told to call him Excellency.

The man at the desk was sitting back and speaking as if reciting a well-learned lesson.

"You spent two years with the British Army, in Europe, fighting. You were in the Arnshire Regiment. You speak French fluently, German well, Swedish a little, Italian a little. You have travelled of recent years, representing a British firm of manufacturers."

"Yes, Excellency." Corliss glanced away from the brown eyes to those in the portrait; and both men seemed to be looking at him, appraising every feature, piercing through his flesh and blood and seeing into his mind. Absurd? That was how it seemed to him. He was tense and stiff, numbed and a little cold.

"One year ago, you inherited from your grandfather a large fortune, and since then you have not needed to work. You have travelled extensively during the past twelve months, spending in England only one month or two. All that is so, yes?"

"Yes, Excellency."

"You hate your own country."

Corliss said slowly and with more feeling than he had yet shown: "I do, Excellency."

"You will tell me why."

He did not need telling why; he knew; it was all in the manuscript which he had been reading. That was a dossier about Corliss, and Corliss had seen it before. He had helped to prepare it, had seen other, less important men than this one, writing in it in a clear, bold hand. Nothing was typewritten, everything was set down in ink, and he did not think there was another copy in existence. He knew that it was comprehensive; they had questioned him searchingly, over a long period and in various places. They had often asked the same question in a different guise, and, because he was no fool, he had realised that they were trying to make him contradict himself. He had avoided doing that because he had always told the simple truth.

Yet the man at the desk asked him why he hated his own country. That was because the other wanted to penetrate his thoughts in that uncanny way he had; he was a kind of human lie-detector, who would be able to distinguish a truth from a half-truth and know the moment that Corliss uttered a lie.

"They killed my father," Corliss said.

"So. How?"

"It was during the war. He was a sick man and they knew it, but they sent him on a dangerous mission into Germany, because he could speak fluent German. He was caught and tortured and killed. It was not the fault of the Nazis but of the men who sent him."

"So," said His Excellency. "How did you come to know all

that? Your father, he was an intelligence officer, was he not? He did not talk of what he did, where he was going."

Corliss said: "I was informed of what had happened after his death."

"Who informed you?"

"Some damned little pimp who sat behind his desk in an office while men like my father went out and did his foul work for him. He made me sick! He told me that my father had been a brave man—brave!—he was to be decorated posthumously." Corliss fingered his waistcoat pocket. "I have the decoration here."

"Yes. How did you know that your father was a sick man?"

"We had shared a week's leave together, just before he left. He told me he was going on a special mission."

"Did he resent it?"

"He was sick and tired—and afraid. He did not want to admit that he was afraid, and so he went. They killed him."

"Yes," said His Excellency. "How did you learn of the fact that he had been tortured?"

"The officer who told me hinted at it."

"Hinted?" The man at the desk repeated the word as if it were unfamiliar.

"He told me enough, I could guess the rest."

"I understand," said His Excellency. A note that might have been one of sympathy crept into his voice. "It is true that your father was a brave man, Corliss, and I am told that you have also proved to have courage."

Corliss did not speak.

"That you, also, were decorated for a brave deed, when single-handed you took control of an important bridge, over a small German river. That is so?"

"I suppose so," said Corliss.

"Suppose?" the other barked.

Corliss started. "Yes—yes, of course. They made a big fuss of it, it was really nothing much." He had relaxed and seemed much more English, now.

"Is this the only reason why you hate England?"

"The chief one," said Corliss. "I hate the whole rotten setup. All this sham talk about democracy and freedom. It's *all* sham. The politicians are liars and the statesmen fools. They give an idiot who sweeps the roads the same vote as they give me, and call it democracy. I've no time for the rabble. I've read a lot, and I've come to the conclusion that there's only one man who knows how to rule a country."

He glanced up at the vivid eyes in the portrait, and this time could not look away. The whole face now held him fascinated; although it was a painting, it was as if he were sitting in the presence of an omnipotent being.

His Excellency's voice was very gentle.

He handed an envelope to Corliss.

"Have you seen these?" he asked.

There was nothing to see but a plain white envelope.

"What are they?"

"Look at them," said His Excellency in the same soft voice, and he sat farther back in his swivel chair, his hands resting lightly on the arms.

Corliss pulled up the flap of the envelope and drew out three shiny photographs. They looked old. The corners were creased and worn, the edges were yellowing. They were pictures of a man—and Corliss stared at them, horror springing into his eyes. His hands did not tremble but the fingers seemed locked to the photographs.

These were pictures of his father; a man, dying; and of a man who had been damnably tortured. The marks were there.

His Excellency said gently: "Your father penetrated into Berlin, Corliss. Had we arrived a day earlier we should have saved him. We were too late. He was brave, as you have been and will have to be."

Corliss put the photographs down on the desk, but didn't speak. His nostrils were distended, his lips parted, and he breathed as if he had been running.

"You will serve?" asked His Excellency, and turned in his chair to look up at the portrait. "You will serve him?"

Corliss licked his lips.

"*Yes.*"

"I will be frank with you," said His Excellency. "For more than a year, we have been questioning and watching you. We have a task which you can do, but we had first to be sure of your reliability. We had to be sure of your hatred for England and your willingness to hurt her present rulers."

Corliss said: "You can be sure of that, all right."

"Yes," said His Excellency. "I was sure, before you came in here. I am to give you your instructions. You understand that if you should try to betray us—betray *him*—you will convince no one. You might talk of this interview but it would be proved that it did not take place."

"I shan't talk."

"We will say that I am joking," said His Excellency, and for the first time, he smiled. It was a slow smile, a slight curve of thin lips, and he did not show his teeth. "You have heard, Corliss, of the organisation in England knows as Department Z, which is actually a branch of Intelligence and which has the special task of countering espionage in this country."

Corliss nodded.

"You will know the little that the public knows about the organisation. What would you say the public thinks about it?"

Corliss laughed; the sound wasn't mirthful, but ugly and harsh.

"They think it's wonderful! It's almost legendary. No one

knows who runs it or who the agents are, but—well, they think it's foolproof."

"Yes, they think that," said His Excellency, "and in some ways, let us admit, they are right. It is a remarkable organisation. It is led by a middle-aged man, one Gordon Craigie. He has many assistants—some we know, some are unknown. It is charged with making sure of the security of the realm. Like us, it has cells, dotted about the country. The most unlikely men and women serve it. All are loyal. It has achieved some remarkable results—what is the proper word?"

"Spectacular," said Corliss.

"Yes, yes, spectacular. But like all espionage organisations, its most important work is done without sensation, quietly and day by day. Now! I can tell you this. The English are not fools, they are clever, shrewd and proud. They permit the political activity of the Party, because that is democratic." The faint, sardonic smile curved his lips again. "But they are aware of some of the Party's non-political activity. They know that we have, in England, strong cells of people who, when the time comes, will act swiftly against the Government. These are men and women in key positions in industry, commerce, the Civil Service, the Armed Forces. They know, or at least suspect, the existence of these inner cells. They are seeking them out. Craigie and his Department now have that task. At the same time, Craigie is strengthening his own organisation. For—and remember you English are not fools—they take into account the possibility that one day this country may be occupied.

"If that day comes, they must have their underground forces, which will work against us.

"So, Craigie has two tasks: to find where we are strongest; and to prepare against the day when we might become all-powerful here. But although we know these things, Craigie's organisation is strong, secret, and cunning. We know a little. Our agent, who has informed us of these things, has disappeared. He must be replaced."

Corliss said softly: "By me."

"And not only must he be replaced, but the man who takes his place must become one of the Department," said His Excellency evenly. "Its members are of two kinds. Those in the cells, who are numerous. It is known, for instance, that the owner of a small garage near London is one; a postmaster at a village shop, another; the manager of a large cinema in a Midlands town, a third—and there are many like them. They will form the background of the resistance, at a later date. Few of these do any active work for the Department today. The other members are not in the cells but are attached to the Central Office. That Office is somewhere in Whitehall, but I do not know where. The members are nearly all young or young middle-aged men, and there are one or two, but very few, women. These people are responsible for the spectacular successes which the Department has had. They are, I am given to understand, strange men. They have the British habit of being flippant in times of acute danger—they appear not to take any matter seriously. I need not tell you more about that."

Corliss said: "I know the type of idiot pretty well."

"Be careful not to under-rate their ability," said His Excellency. "There is a great difference between the man who is a fool and the man who simply appears to be one. These men, however, have one thing in common—distinguished war records and a sound background according to Whitehall estimates. *You* have that background. You will, shortly, be given an opportunity to be on the scene when one of these agents is injured. Thus, you will be put in touch with the Department. There can be no guarantee that you will be drawn into it, but it is known that Craigie has great difficulty in recruiting his agents. The right type of man is scarce. The Department continually suffers losses, of men who take up dangerous work and are killed. It is known that several recruits have been enlisted, from ordinary people—like you. It is also known that before any man is taken into the Department, the most painstaking research is made into his past. That is why we have always been at great pains not to interview you in suspicious or noticeable circumstances. That is why you were brought to this house, from the country, in a closed car with the curtains drawn. That is also why you will be taken back in the same way. You will not be seen. You will return to your hotel, your inn, and stay there. Soon, you will have a visitor. He will call in most unexpected circumstances, and will say to you: 'You are to act now.'"

Corliss said: "Yes."

"You will kill that man," said His Excellency. "You will break his neck. You know how."

Corliss looked down at his hands.

"Yes."

"Afterwards you will act on your own initiative, knowing that by then you have had an introduction to the Department."

"Yes, Excellency."

"You will get in touch with us only on important matters. We shall often get in touch with you. The envoy will show a card or a metal symbol—like this." The man held out a small badge, of a hammer and sickle. It was polished; and at the edges were two tiny flaws. Similar flaws showed in the printed sign. "A hammer and sickle with two flaws," said His Excellency. "Is that clear?"

"Yes, Excellency."

His Excellency leaned forward and pressed a bell-push fitted to the side of his desk.

"Good," he murmured. "You will, of course, remember my joke."

Corliss said: "I'm with you, all the way. Just give me the chance of getting inside this Department, and—you'll see."

His Excellency nodded. Then he did an unusual thing—and this was noticed by the man who stood, outside the room, and looked in through a narrow aperture in the wall. He stood up and shook hands with Corliss, who backed three paces, saluted smartly, turned and stepped briskly away. As he reached the door at the far end of the room, it opened. No one appeared at the doorway. Corliss knew of no way in which he could be observed; but he felt, all the same, that he had been watched.

He turned.

He did not see His Excellency, who was at his desk again, and reading, but he saw the vivid, luminous eyes in the portrait. They seemed to hold his gaze; it took a physical effort for him to turn away and go out of the room. The door closed behind him. A dark-clad man stepped from the side of the passage and, without a word, accompanied him to another part of the building.

As that door closed behind Corliss, another opened—on the right of the wall behind His Excellency. A small, thin-featured man wearing thick lensed *pince-nez* stepped silently into the room.

2
THE INN

His Excellency did not look up, did not turn his head. The small man rounded the desk, without making a sound, and stood in front of it. He hardly appeared to be breathing, and did not take any notice of the eye in the portrait. He waited, with the patience of an automaton, until His Excellency looked up.

"You heard and saw us, Pera?"

The other answered in Russian.

His Excellency said: "We shall speak English, it is good practice—they are the instructions, you understand."

"Yes, comrade," said the little man. His voice was flat and monotonous, but his sharp featured face was restive. "I heard and saw you."

"And what is your opinion now?"

"There is no reason to change my opinion." The newcomer's English was good but more heavily accented than His Excellency's. "Corliss will be quite reliable. He is a psychopathic case. His hatred is real. He has a hate motivation, because of what happened to his father. He had great love for his father. That was because, early in his life, his mother died. All his affection was diverted to his father, a good man by English standards. The loss of his father shocked him and he sought for someone to blame. He blamed the authorities and that has developed into hatred for his country. You know, of course, that we have worked on him for some time increasing the strength of that emotion, feeding it, making it more bitter, more real. He has, now, a positive motive in life. Whatever he does is to avenge his father. We have helped him to choose a certain way. I have no fear that Corliss will betray us."

His Excellency said: "Good. He will, of course, be watched."

"That is necessary. It is also necessary that he should soon be given an opportunity for action, he will become restless if that is delayed too long. Should he become restless, he may decide that we have merely talked, that we meant nothing. The stimulus will be needed, soon."

"How soon?"

"In two days, perhaps? No more."

"In two days," said His Excellency.

The powerful closed car pulled up in the darkness of a country road. It was past midnight and there was little traffic. Far away, on the horizon, the misty glow of another car's headlights made the sky pale. Above, light clouds hid the stars but drifted here and there, and showed a few dimmed spots of light.

Corliss got out of the car.

The driver said: "Good night, comrade."

"Good night."

The car moved off, slowly at first, gathering speed but making little noise. There were trees near by, and a dark shape of a haystack loomed close to the high hedge near which Corliss stood.

It had been warm in the car; it was cool out here.

Corliss wiped his forehead, breathed deeply, and walked slowly along the road. The distant glow had changed, was nearer and brighter. He stood in the shadow of a tree as a powerful car hummed past, bathing the road ahead in its bright light and leaving that behind it in blinding darkness. Corliss waited until the sound of its engine had died away, then moved again. He turned through a five-barred gate into the field where the haystack stood. Behind the haystack was a powerful, low-bodied car with sleek lines. He took the wheel, started the engine—and in two minutes was driving along the road, carving a lane of light which lit up the fresh, young leaves of Spring, their green glittering in the headlights. Telegraph poles showed grey, the wires glistened. He drove at high speed through a small village and a mile beyond it, slowed down.

The glow now shone on a thatched roof and a whitewashed building. A painted sign stood near the road outside the inn, and the light was good enough for Corliss to read: *The Fiddlers' Rest;* he could even pick out the three fiddlers painted on the sign. A sign-post, pointing across the road, bore the one word: *"Garage"*.

There was a gravel yard outside the garages—four in all. Corliss stopped by the first, and switched off the headlights. He put the car away, jingled the keys in his pocket and crossed the dark road. In the gloom the whitewash showed up clearly.

So did a light, shining from one of the first floor rooms. The light was dim and yellow, and just showed the branches of an oak tree which grew close to the inn. Corliss stood and watched, then glanced at his watch; it was nearly one o'clock, late for anyone to be up at *The Fiddlers' Rest.*

He went to the front door, and unlocked it—mine host was generous with his keys. He closed the door, firmly but quietly. Then he walked briskly across a carpeted stone hall and up a narrow, twisting staircase.

The light was on in the room next to his. He did not know who was in there; he had thought it unoccupied, and knew that no one had stayed there the previous night. He felt on edge; memory of those vivid eyes and of the interview was deeply imprinted upon his mind.

He opened and closed his own door, but did not go into the room.

He had been trained, taught the kind of work that was likely to be expected of him, told to act always as if he were at work. The window of his own room was in a different wall from that of the next. He crept downstairs and went into the dining-room; the window here was immediately below that from which the light shone.

The dining-room window was closed.

White-clothed tables showed ghostlike in the darkness which was only slightly relieved by the light outside. Cutlery glistened, and rang slightly as he crossed the room. He avoided the tables carefully and reached the window. He could see the lower branches of the oak tree. He unlatched the window, careful to make no noise, then pushed it open an inch; there was no sound. He knelt down on one knee, leaned against the window ledge and listened.

He heard a man say: "It's all safe."

"Yes," someone whispered, "he is in."

"He couldn't have seen me."

"No, darling, you need not worry."

"Good night, my sweet."

"Good night, precious."

Corliss's lips, well-shaped lips, curved contemptuously. He

watched as a man appeared, just a vague shape, outside. A little light shone on his head and face. He was staring up at the window. He put his hand to his lips and blew a kiss; the contempt in Corliss's smile grew deeper. Then the man turned swiftly and walked away, out of sight.

A window closed, upstairs.

Corliss went up, soft-footed, crept into his room and closed the door silently, and then moved about so that he could just be heard by the woman next door. He looked at the dividing wall. He saw a faded wall-paper sprawled over with large red flowers, and a single picture—of Christ on the Cross. It was an old print, speckled with browny-yellow stains, and the glass was heavily fly-spotted. It wasn't a good picture, but as Corliss glanced at it, the eyes seemed to be touched with something of the vividness of those of the man whose portrait had been above His Excellency.

He looked away quickly.

He could hear the woman walking about, but that soon stopped, and the springs of the bed creaked; so she had been ready for bed. What had he interrupted? The obvious seemed the likely thing; she had received a lover, and he, Corliss, had arrived just as the man was climbing out of the window. There was nothing more in it than that. They had talked about him only because he had been in a position to discover what they were doing. The man was probably scared of his wife finding out how he had spent that part of the evening.

But—

Could there be a deeper significance?

He had been taught so well; suspect everything, suspect everyone; never assume that the obvious is the true explanation. Watch; be wary; be suspicious all the time.

He heard a slight click; the woman had switched out the light in her room.

Corliss turned to his own bed. It was high, had a box mattress, but comfortable. Except for the old and stained print and the wall-paper, there was nothing much the matter with this room. The furniture was antique, some of it three hundred years or more old, there was a thick Indian carpet on the floor. In one corner, concealed by a carved oak cupboard, was a hand basin with hot and cold running water. *The Fiddlers' Rest* was a good and expensive pub—old-fashioned even to the excellence of the food and the service. He had heard about it, before he had been told to come and stay here for a week. There was good hunting and fishing near by, the man who liked a country holiday in luxury couldn't choose a better spot.

But Corliss wondered why he had been sent here; and then wondered if he had interrupted the last stages of an illicit *affaire* or whether there was a deeper, menacing significance.

Once or twice, he thought he heard the woman turn over in bed. He lay thinking about her—as she was, as she had been perhaps an hour ago. He grinned to himself as he undressed and got into bed. The grin lingered even after he put out the light.

It was dark; the stars were completely obscured now. He could just make out the shape of the window and the grey of the sky beyond. He looked at it. He knew that he wouldn't be able to get to sleep quickly; he never did, but he usually slept well into the morning, and there was no reason why he shouldn't tomorrow.

Tomorrow—would 'it' happen then?

They had warned him time and time again against impatience, but he was impatient. Every day that passed without action, irked him. Irked was hardly the word; it drove him sometimes to the point of desperation. He wanted to strike and to hurt the men who had killed his father.

Only one figure loomed in his mind's eye when he thought about them; that was the little pimp in khaki who, in a hushed but still hearty voice, had told him what had happened to his father. When he had sat there, listening, he could have got up and put his hands round the plump neck and strangled the life out of the man. He'd felt something like that from the time he had been told that his father was dead; he'd felt hatred. But until he had seen the pimp, there had been no flesh and blood to hate; so, his hatred had turned towards 'them'. Gradually they had grown into his consciousness. He included all politicians and Service officers who had been superior to his father, all who had been responsible for sending his father, by parachute, into Germany. It had gradually turned to hatred of everyone even partly responsible; to hatred of the system.

He did not realise that it had turned him into a psychopathic case. He felt normal; except for the one obsession to hurt everyone and everything that had been responsible for his great loss, he was normal.

He lay thinking of a talk he'd had with a little man on the veranda of a hotel overlooking Lake Geneva. Thinking back, it was easy to realise that the man had known who he was, and something of what he felt. The man had started to enlist his help for His Excellency and the man with the vivid eyes, even so long ago. Corliss remembered the various stages which had followed. He wasn't a political fool, but had been attracted by the philosophy and by the actions of the rulers of half the world.

He even had the clearsightedness to know that it was a philosophy of hatred; that was why the ideology appealed to him, for it seemed to him a cleansing, virile emotion. He hated those responsible for what he called a crime, and hated the masses of the people with whom he had to live.

He hadn't always felt like that.

* * *

He woke earlier than usual next morning; it was just after half past eight. He didn't know what had disturbed him at first; then he heard the woman in the next room, humming; she had been moving about for some time, of course, the unaccustomed noise had disturbed him. He stared at the wall; while in bed, his eyes were not on a level with the crucifixion picture and so he didn't notice it. He tried to imagine what the woman was like; all he had to work on was her whispered voice, which had sounded pleasant, and the fact that she was amorous. He knew that her night visitor had been young, too—young and good looking.

He wanted to know what the woman was like.

On the two previous mornings, he had breakfasted in bed. This morning, he decided to go downstairs. Should he bath first? Breakfast was served from eight until ten o'clock, there was good time, if the bathroom was free. He rang for the maid, a middle-aged and faded woman with a slightly humped back.

"Breakfast as usual, sir?"

"No. I'll get up. Bathroom free?"

"I think so, sir. Do you like it hot or cold?"

"Tepid."

"I'll run it, sir," said the maid, and went out quietly.

Corliss got up, brushed his teeth and shaved. The woman next door was still humming; so she was happy. Ten minutes later he was in the bath, and he wasted no time—the woman would probably be down early. It was a small dining-room, he could make sure that he was sitting close to her. He couldn't understand why he was so anxious—and told himself that it was because he wanted to make quite sure that there was no greater significance than he imagined, in the incident of the previous night.

21

Hugging his silk dressing-gown round him, he walked from the bathroom towards his door. The one next to it opened and the woman stepped out.

She was young; radiant; beautiful.

She saw him and started; she seemed almost alarmed. She averted her gaze quickly, made as if to go back into her room, changed her mind and came forward boldly towards the head of the stairs.

"Morning," grunted Corliss.

"Good morning."

She hurried downstairs, and he watched her from his doorway. She moved quickly and with grace; true grace was a rare thing in a woman. He went into his room, and dressed hurriedly; he was more than ever anxious to be near enough to talk to her. If she refused to talk, if she showed further signs of nervousness, he would know that he had disturbed something more than an *affaire*. Why had she been so nervous of him? Had it just been a guilty conscience?

He paid careful attention to his dressing; that wasn't unusual, but he took extra care this morning. He wore a well-cut, smooth-textured sports jacket and flannel trousers; all his clothes were exceptionally well tailored. He could wear them well, too; he had the lean figure and the slim hips which helped. As he put the finishing touches to his collar and tie he studied himself in the mirror.

He was like his father, and his father had been one of the most handsome men he'd known. He didn't care for his own looks, as such, just accepted them. He was aware that he caused many a flutter when he met young women and girls for the first time. It was hard to put a name to his attraction for them—whether it was just his looks, with the almost rakish air which went with them, or whether it was his freshness. He was fair; his hair curled a little but he kept it severely cut and it was never wavy. His mouth, nose and chin were good; and he had, above all other things, his father's clear grey eyes.

He kept thinking of the interview with His Excellency, and suddenly he remembered being given the photographs. He clenched his teeth. The pictures were as vivid as when they had been in front of him.

This was fate; what else could it be? The Russians had even discovered his father, before his death. It was as if fate had pointed a finger at him, and he had been irretrievably drawn into the vortex of great affairs. Of course, they had discovered the name of his father, had traced him, had worked slowly and carefully before approaching him, had been quick to realise how he *hated*.

He shut the pictures out of his mind.

At the door, he discovered that he had just lit a cigarette; he hadn't realised what he had been doing. He squashed it out in the ash-tray on the table outside the dining-room, and went in.

The girl had been looking towards him; now, she turned her head away quickly. The room was full and there was no empty table, but several with a place free.

The elderly waiter came up, smiling, eager.

"Good morning, sir."

"Morning. Is there a seat by the window?"

There was only one, at the girl's table. She heard the question and he saw her start.

3
THE GIRL NAMED HILDE

Corliss inclined his head and smiled at the girl as he approached with the waiter.

"This gentleman would *very* much like a window seat, Miss Hansson—" the waiter broke off.

Corliss said quickly: "Oh, no, I'm sorry. I didn't realise this was the only place vacant. Anywhere will do."

He spoke clearly. Most of the people in the dining-room looked at him; two couples exchanged glances. A nondescript little man, who always walked with the aid of a stick, grinned. There was nothing surprising in a handsome young man angling to sit at breakfast with a lovely young woman. Corliss had that all worked out; it would attract attention but no one would really be surprised.

The girl said: "Please, you are welcome."

She wasn't English.

"If you're sure—"

"Please," she said. Her smile was strained, but it lingered as he sat down.

The dining-room had oak beams and rafters; the walls and

ceiling were washed a pale cream. The wide window was fitted with leaded diamond-shaped panes. Beyond was the small back garden of the inn—and there was a square of perfect, close-cut lawn and three beds of daffodils in thick clusters. A gentle wind stirred them as it stirred the hedges and the trees beyond. The great oak spread branches near the window; the leaves were only half unfurled. Early morning mist had cleared but hung in a hollow seen through a gap in the hedge, a pale gossamer cloud.

"I think we're neighbours," Corliss said, and smiled. "It was you whom I met coming out of your room just now, wasn't it?"

"Yes." Her smile was mechanical. There was a half hidden quality about it which he saw and understood; she was afraid; but of what? Was she still worried about having been noticed the night before? Or *was* there something else?

He had been told to come to *The Fiddlers' Rest*, surely he would not have been sent to a place where there was danger, where he would be suspect? Nonsense! No one suspected him; the use of the word was absurd. He had stumbled. He had stumbled into an *affaire*, and the girl was on edge with a guilty conscience.

She wasn't beautiful, after all; her features weren't regular, certainly not classic. She was a good Scandinavian type, fairer than he, with open features, clear grey eyes and a quality of freshness which lent her the appearance of loveliness. Her clothes were good, her make-up was excellent and not over-done. Her hands were long and slim—a little too long. There were no rings. The long, well-shaped nails were varnished a pale pink; she was dressed in a light grey suit, with a cream silk blouse—plain, neat, simple.

"It's going to be a lovely day," said Corliss.

"Beautiful."

He wasn't making much progress.

There was little chance, for she had reached the main course, of bacon and eggs—the inn managed to supply that most days—and he was eating stewed fruit. The waiter kept fussing about them. Two or three couples went out, others came in. No one now took any notice of Corliss and the girl, except the waiter. Corliss ate quickly, so as not to be too far behind her. He expected her to jump up, as soon as she had finished, and leave him alone. Instead, she lingered; as if she had managed to quieten her fears. She opened her handbag.

"Please smoke," said Corliss.

"Thank you."

He finished eating, lit a cigarette for himself and leaned back in his chair.

"Good place, this. Are you going to stay long?"

"I do not know," she said, quietly, "it will depend on my friends." She meant, on the boy-friend.

Corliss nodded understandingly, and then the waiter came in with the morning papers and the post. There were two letters for the girl, and Corliss read the name on the envelopes. They were addressed to 'Miss Hilde Hansson'. One was typed, the other written in sloping writing, and purple ink, and the postage stamp was foreign. She murmured: "Excuse me," and tore open that letter first; there was only a brief message inside. She did not trouble to open the other, but put both in her handbag.

"Perhaps I see you again," she said, and stood up immediately and went off.

He was struck, again, by the easy grace of her movements; her face might not be really beautiful but her figure certainly was. He had not spent much time thinking of women, recently; he had been obsessed by his hate and by his sense of loss and of impending action. He was cynical about women as his father had been, although he had never known why.

While he sat at the table, the girl crossed the back garden. She wore no hat, but carried an umbrella, a small thing which swung from her waist. Was she going to an assignation? Corliss shrugged his shoulders, and went out. Beyond the garden was a meadow, and on the far side, a stile; the girl was climbing it. She didn't look back.

Corliss felt an impulse to see where she went.

He hurried out the front way, along the road, and to the stile from a different direction. The Hampshire country around was undulating and wooded; there were some meadows clear of trees, but most had a copse in them. He saw the girl entering one of the copses; beech leaves had not yet come out, and the copse looked a brown and spidery mass. He could follow her movements easily. She came out on the other side, then turned towards another field. A man was waiting there.

They met; Corliss expected them to hug and kiss each other.

They did not even shake hands.

So it wasn't the boy-friend.

Puzzled, Corliss walked back to the inn. He imagined that he knew, now, why he had followed the girl and taken such an interest. He was bored. Worse than that, he was waiting with the knowledge that he would soon have a job to do, and he was boiling up to the point when he couldn't wait patiently any longer. The interest in the girl gave him something to think about; so did the possibility that she wasn't exactly what she seemed.

The maid was coming out of Hilde Hansson's room.

"Finished mine?" asked Corliss.

"Yes, sir, all these rooms are finished." The maid went off

along a narrow, twisting passage. There were three rooms in this little corner, the two singles and a double room occupied by a middle-aged couple who were out most of the day; the man was a naturalist judging from the equipment he always took out with him.

Acting on impulse, Corliss tried the handle of the girl's room.

It wasn't locked.

He slipped inside, swiftly, and stood with his back against the door, breathing hard. There was no need to be alarmed, the maid had made it clear that she had finished, and yet—his heart beat fast. He would have to learn to get used to danger; to acting like this. He had not yet fully seen the implications of what he had committed himself to do. Well, he could learn with the next man, and this was a good chance to start.

The room was almost a replica of his, and as clean as a new pin. There were a few make-up oddments and a silver-backed brush and comb on the dressing-table, a bow-fronted Queen Anne period piece. He opened the wardrobe; the few clothes hanging there were of good quality. There was another suit, two blouses on the same hanger and a light coat on another; in none of these was there any maker's name-tab, and that was unusual. He turned and went through the clothes in the drawers of the dressing-table. There was no maker's tab on anything—no indication where these had been bought. The lingerie was all pale green, of silk or satin; beautiful stuff.

Corliss opened a top drawer.

There were handkerchiefs; some oddments of jewellery which he knew weren't really good—and, the last thing he had expected to find, a man's handkerchief. It was folded, but had obviously been smoothed out, it wasn't freshly ironed. He grinned. The fellow had left this here, the night before—careless of him. He turned the handkerchief over—and then started back, as if he had been struck.

Marked in pencil in one corner, grey and very small, was the letter 'Z'.

Corliss felt a chill run through him; a physical tremor. He put the handkerchief back the way he had found it and hurried out of the room. He forgot, for a moment, to look outside and make sure that no one was coming. He wasn't seen, but it had been careless; carelessness might one day lose him his life and also any opportunity he had for vengeance. He shut himself into his own room, and sat on the bed, staring at the wall, imagining that creased handkerchief with the single letter on it. This couldn't be coincidence.

He felt stifled.

After five minutes, he went downstairs. He had definite instructions about what to do, if he needed to make a report; he had to telephone a certain London number and leave a simple message. The telephone kiosk was in an alcove off the front hall. He turned towards it, as a man said:

"Mr. Corliss."

He started violently, and turned around. This wouldn't do; the slightest unusual thing threw him off his balance.

The man was the manager, a tall, heavily built fellow whom Corliss had never seen wearing a coat. He was by the desk, the sleeves of his striped shirt were kept up at the elbows by green rubber circlets; he held a letter in his hand.

"A letter for you, Mr. Corliss." He came forward.

"Oh. Thanks."

Corliss nodded as he took it, then went outside.

He hadn't expected a letter. Except for the Russians, no one knew that he was staying here. But this was addressed to him at the inn, and—it hadn't been posted, it had been delivered by hand.

He tore it open. There was a single sheet of folded paper inside and a brief typewritten message. There was neither address nor signature. He had received messages like this before, and they had always been to the point.

The wind rustled the paper in his hand as he read: *Do not become too friendly with H.H.*

The wind had a sharpness; it seemed to cut him, like a knife—and like this message. It was uncanny, unreal; as if 'they' knew what had happened in the past hour and a half, could see not only into his mind, but through brick walls and over great distances. This was not the first time he had been affected by their prescience; it was frightening, but at the same time, gave him courage; who could fail when protected by such powers as these?

He forced a laugh.

A sudden gust of wind sprang up and carried the paper out of his hand. It curled and whisked its way across the cobbled yard towards the gaily-painted sign of the three merry fiddlers. Panic swept into him, like the wind. He rushed towards the paper; his instructions were to destroy any message so received, at once. If anyone read this they would know immediately that he was working for someone else. The sun glinted on the white sheet and made it shine as it hit the oiled post of the sign. Then it dropped to the ground. He raced after it and bent down—and another gust of wind whisked it away again. He heard a sound in the distance, without realising what it was, and ran into the road.

A man shouted in alarm, from behind him.

A car loomed up, only a few yards away; the roaring engine was the sound he had heard.

He leapt forward, heard the brakes squeal and out of the corner of his eye saw the car pass behind him. He thought the wing touched his coat, but it may have been the wind of its passing. The car stopped. The paper lay against a bush, near the gravel parking space outside the garages. He picked it up and slipped it into his pocket.

The car was a sleek sky-blue monster; only a man with money could own such a leviathan. The driver stepped out. He was tall and rugged looking, brown haired and hatless. He had his head on one side and looked at Corliss with an expression which was half smile, half scowl.

It was the man who had come away from Hilde Hansson's room the previous night.

He called: "There are easier ways than that."

Corliss moved towards him.

"Easier ways of doing what?"

"Committing suicide."

"I didn't see you. Sorry."

"It's a damn good thing I saw you," said the motorist laconically. "Are you all right?"

"Yes, thanks."

"Good. Let me know, if you ever want running over in earnest." The man turned, got back into his car and drove off. The sky-blue monster disappeared round a corner. Corliss, vicious with himself for his own folly, went back to the inn. Lewis, the manager-owner, his billowing shirt-sleeves rippling in the wind, stood at the open front door. The nondescript man limped into sight with his stick, but didn't speak.

"I was afraid you'd caught it, Mr. Corliss."

"Yes—lucky thing the driver was good."

"Saved *your* life," said the manager. "Sure you're all right? It looked as if it hit you."

"No—my lucky day."

Corliss forced a smile and hurried indoors and upstairs. He had succeeded in making himself noticeable; the manager wouldn't forget the way he had behaved. The man might even suspect the importance of that letter. Nonsense? Corliss struck a match and set light to one corner of the sheet of paper, waited until it blazed up and stung his fingers, then tossed it into the empty fireplace, which was shiny black, with polish. It flamed up and then slowly crumpled into a whispering black mass. He broke it into dust and fragments with the poker, washed his hands and looked out of the window.

He could see the side garden and the countryside beyond, but not the copse where the girl had been or the stile where she had met the man in brown. Certainly it hadn't been her boyfriend; he was dressed in light grey and had come from the other direction.

Why had the boy-friend returned?

Did that marked handkerchief belong to him?

Questions; nothing but questions; and the certainty that he had made a fool of himself. He must go out—walk across to the nearby stables and take a hack out for a couple of hours. He had been told that he must do that, as well as some fishing and walking, to give an ostensible reason for staying at *The Fiddlers' Rest.*

Should he telephone the message now?

He had been told, frequently and insistently, that he must rely on himself as much as possible and avoid telephoning that secret number except in real emergency. Could this be called an emergency? 'They' knew that the girl was important, that an agent of Department Z was interested in her; why else should he have been warned not to get too friendly with her? The only reason for telephoning was to report that handkerchief with the pencilled 'Z'.

He decided not to make the call.

The girl was not in for lunch and he did not see the man at the wheel of the sky-blue monster again that day. But he remembered him well—the rugged features seemed to grow on him. Six feet tall or more, broad, with straight hair and a droll face—not really good looking but one with an undoubted touch of quality—quality, or breeding. The look was as unmistakable as his manner. He'd made no fuss, indulged in no cursing, just made sure that Corliss wasn't hurt and then gone about his business.

Was he a Z agent?

If so, what was his business with Hilde Hansson?

Corliss remembered another lesson he'd been taught: don't guess, don't speculate. Assemble facts and pass them on to others. The whole routine and discipline of training which he had received over a period of nearly twelve months before meeting His Excellency pressed heavily upon him. He had not known for what he was being trained, except that it would be work for 'them'. Now he knew what work, and also knew that there was a world of difference between theory and practice. Theory had not told him how to control the thumping of his heart when he had broken into the girl's room; when he had found the handkerchief; and when the letter had nearly blown away.

Had he shown his alarm to Lewis, the owner of the inn? Or to the man from the sky-blue monster?

After lunch, he changed and hired a spirited mare from the nearby stables and rode across country. He had a good seat but knew that he was only a moderate rider. He wanted to gallop, craved for speed. But whenever he let the mare have her head, he thought of the narrow escape on the road, and pulled her in. It was an unsatisfactory afternoon.

The girl was in to dinner, but not alone. A man dressed in a brown suit, with dusty shoes and tired eyes, was with her. They had a secluded corner table; it was the only table in the room where they were free from neighbours and out of earshot. Corliss sat at the window table next to an elderly woman who read a book so thick that it looked as if it had a thousand pages.

After dinner, he went for a drive. The easy speed exhilarated him, he forgot the warning of the morning. There were long straight stretches of road, little traffic and the dark coolness of the night for company. Once, the speedometer needle of the car touched a hundred. He slowed down at a bend and was surprised to find himself laughing. He was still waiting, but had a greater sense of expectancy than ever before. He felt that something vital would happen tonight. It was useless to warn himself that this might be wishful thinking. Speed and the lonely darkness filled him with a sense of certainty which brought exhilaration.

The exhilaration was tempered, suddenly, by wariness.

A motor-cycle caused that.

He had passed it twice, on the road; once when the driver had been bent over the engine, as if doing a running repair. The man hadn't looked at him and Corliss hadn't seen him clearly. For ten minutes or more the motor-cycle remained behind him, and although Corliss slowed down, it didn't overtake him. He turned off the main road suddenly, and drove slowly for a mile. At the breast of a hill, he pulled up and looked round; the single headlight of the motor-cycle was still behind him. He took a circular route back to *The Fiddlers' Rest;* the motor-cyclist passed the garage as he was putting the car away.

So he had been followed.

It was a little after ten o'clock. He passed through the lounge, where two couples were playing bridge, and went into the public bar, where a dozen local people were drinking and talking in desultory fashion. He had a whisky and soda, found no one of interest to talk to and went upstairs. Even then, he felt that he was being watched, put it down to imagination, but stood close to his door after going into the room, and listened. He heard footsteps pass his door, light and swift. They did not stop at the girl's room, but went straight along the passage.

The girl came up half an hour afterwards. He was reading. He put out the light and waited by the open window. Her light shone out, catching the long branches of the oak tree which stretched beyond the corner. He wondered if she would have her nocturnal visitor again and where the brown-clad man with the tired eyes had gone.

Nothing happened.

Her light went out.

So there would be no excitement next door. But something must happen tonight, he couldn't stand this strain any longer. If 'they' didn't fix it, he would begin to think that they had been fooling him.

Who had followed? A man from Headquarters or a friend of the driver of the sky-blue car? He couldn't be sure; he did not want to believe that Department Z agents were watching him. He didn't feel like sleep or undressing. He sat in the darkness, knowing it to be folly, but waiting; it *must* happen tonight.

A clock, a long way off, struck midnight sonorously. The inn was quiet, most people were asleep. There had been no sound from Hilde Hansson's room. He'd have to give it up, but the thought of going to bed stifled him. He would creep downstairs and have a walk, it might settle his mind.

He actually stood up, with his body turned towards the door, when he heard a rustling sound outside. He stood stock still. Imagination? A stirring of wind? No, this was neither; there *was* a rustling sound, as of someone moving stealthily. Then it faded. He leaned out of the window, and could hear it again.

Was the girl's caller there? Would he next hear a rattle of stones against the window?

He heard little for what seemed a long time, but into the silence there came an occasional creaking noise. It was outside. He listened more intently, but couldn't place it. The noise stopped. Silence seemed to last for an age but was actually only a few minutes. Certainly no one had gone in to try to arouse the girl.

Then, she *screamed.*

4

KILLER

She screamed just once. In the cry was splintering horror. It was a call not of life but of death. It pierced the quiet of the night like the swish of a thousand swords. After it came deathly silence.

Corliss recoiled from the window.

He stood gripping the frame, icy cold, heart thumping; but his mind began to work. This was *it*. He did not try to force himself to act until the frigid paralysis which had caught him slackened. Then he could both move and think clearly—and he could hear.

There were voices in the hotel, but he could not catch the words.

There was another rustle of sound, outside.

He climbed up on to the window-sill, turned round and lowered himself. He clung to the sill for a moment, then dropped. His toes touched the gravel, he fell against the wall and recovered his balance. The rustling was much nearer, but did not frighten him. He pressed close against the wall, facing the corner. A door banged inside the inn. There was no sound from the girl's room.

He rounded the corner and saw a shadowy figure, a dark shape in the lesser darkness. Corliss tensed his muscles, to leap at the man—and then out of the shadow came a whispering voice.

"You are to act now."

Corliss was half prepared for the challenge. It had come when there was no time to ponder, only time to act. The speaker, still no more than a shadow, turned. Another door banged; it seemed to be almost immediately above Corliss's head. A man above said clearly:

"The window!"

Corliss leapt at the man in front of him, clutching his throat. The man did not try to struggle, and did not even turn round. Corliss squeezed—and then twisted the man's neck. He had been taught that twist patiently and persistently, and told what would happen—but the result sickened him. He felt the snapping sound; it was not loud, and seemed to come out of the man. He twisted again but there was no other sound, and the neck no longer resisted his pressure. There would be no obvious marks—a slight bruising would show, but no more, and that wouldn't show yet.

A light shore out from the girl's room.

He flung the body away from him as the dark shadow of a man appeared, leaning out of the window.

"There he is!"

Corliss drew back, breathing hard. The game had started and in one clear moment of understanding he realised what this meant—and that the man on the ground had deliberately let himself be killed, had been a willing victim so that he, Corliss, could do what was expected of him. Pain gripped Corliss's stomach, like a cruel hand.

The shadow moved violently. A man scrambled out of the window and then dropped down, not twenty yards behind Corliss. Other lights flashed out. Corliss went down on one knee beside the body of the man he had killed. The victim lay on his face, head cuddled in his arms, as if he were sleeping, but his feet were in an odd position.

Two men appeared by Corliss' side—Lewis and a guest. Lewis was still in his day clothes and without a coat.

"Mr. Corliss," he said heavily.

"Had a nice walk?" asked the other. He was the nondescript little chap who walked about the inn with a stick—yet he had jumped from the window. He took charge of the situation, knelt down and felt for the fallen man's pulse. Lewis stood by, like a policeman on guard.

Corliss said in a flat voice: "I think I've broken his neck."

"Unkind," said the little man. "You've certainly stopped him ticking." He felt the fallen man's neck, and the dark head moved loosely in his hands. "Hum! Quite a grip you've got when you're not thinking. What happened?"

"I heard the scream. I—" Corliss broke off abruptly and turned round towards the inn. "Is she—"

"Let's worry about her later," said the little man. "Okay, Lewis, do some telephoning to the proper authorities, will you? If you can get the crowd to disperse, fine, but I doubt if you will. Offers of free drinks in the lounge might lure 'em." As he spoke, he grinned up at Corliss. He had a most attractive smile, and he no longer looked nondescript. He stood up, showing no need at all for his walking stick. "Bad show, Corliss. Just keep your mouth shut, will you? I'm Special Branch."

He meant, the Special Branch at Scotland Yard.

Corliss said in a thin voice: "You mean—"

"Hallo, hallo, *hallo!*" boomed the little man with a surprisingly deep tone. "All come out to view the corpus. Yes, ma'am, I said corpus—this chap is very dead. It looks as if he broke his neck falling out of that tree. Tried a spot of burglary. Miss Hansson caught him in the act, good thing she screamed."

Several of the guests, all in dressing-gowns, all but one of them men, had drawn near.

"Is she all right?" a man asked.

"I shouldn't worry about her. You know what shock's like. We've sent for a doctor, and he'll order absolute quiet—be good, don't go and worry the life out of her. Also sent for the police," the little man added. "Everything's under control."

Only one of the men argued.

"Are you sure he's dead? I'm trained in first aid, if you like, I'll have a look."

"Help yourself." The little man moved aside.

Another came up to him.

"This is a bad business, Mr. Abbott."

"Yes. Nasty." Abbott poked his fingers through his thin, fair hair. "One of these things. Lewis tells me he had an attempted burglary a couple of years ago, so they don't happen every night. Pity this chap fell on his top-knot, but he knew he was taking risks." Abbott spoke so convincingly that none there would readily doubt that the man had fallen on to his head and broken his neck. "Reached the room along the branches of that stately oak, as they say. Lewis had better have a bit chopped off. Don't tell me that I'm suggesting locking the stable door after the horse had bolted. I know. But there's always a chance of putting another horse in the stables."

He took out cigarettes.

"Smoke?" The case was thrust in front of Corliss, who took a cigarette. Abbott lit it for him. The other men stood in a half circle and looked down at the dead man. The first-aid expert stood up, shaking his head; he'd noticed no bruises or would have said so. Then Lewis came back, taking long strides which looked slow but were in fact fast.

"There's a doctor and the police on the way, Mr. Abbott. We've been asked to leave everything as we found it."

"Ah, yes."

"If I were you, gentlemen, I'd go back to bed," Lewis said, "but there's a glass of toddy in the lounge, if any of you feel like it before turning in."

"Someone ought to stay on guard," said the first-aid specialist.

"I'll do that, sir." Lewis took up his position, hiding the dead man from general view. "The police will be here in a few minutes, I've told them where to come."

"Oh, well—"

They began to move towards the front of the inn. Abbott and Corliss were last and as they stepped into the hall, Abbott whispered: "Take it easy, and don't talk." He followed the crowd, seven in all. One of Lewis's waiters was on duty in the lounge, and stood over a silver bowl which smelt as if it contained rum punch. A tray of glasses was near him, and a glass ladle.

"Anyone care for a drink, gentlemen?"

"Trust me," said Abbott. He went forward—and now, he limped a little! He sipped. "Ah! Almost worth a broken night's sleep!" He put a glass into Corliss's hand and then moved aside, to make room for the others.

In the bright light of the lounge, Corliss studied him for the first time. It was difficult to understand why he had always imagined the man to be nondescript. His clear, blue eyes were shrewd and intelligent. He had small features, but in his way, was not bad looking. His chin was large compared with his other features, he had a most attractive smile, and the night's tragedy did not seem to have affected him.

"Must go and get my stick," he said, to no one in particular. "Trusted my busted ankle too soon. Care to help me upstairs?" That was to Corliss.

"Er—yes."

"Thanks." They went out. Three women were coming down the stairs, and Abbott sent them into the lounge with soothing phrases. Upstairs, all was quiet. Abbott did not go to his own room, but toward Hilde Hansson's. He had a key—so the door was locked.

"Can't be too careful," he said.

He thrust the door open. The light was on, and seemed bright, even on the landing. He stood aside for Corliss to pass him. Corliss sensed that this was a form of test, and he was going to have a shock. He nerved himself and went inside. The other didn't move.

The bed, as he knew, was behind the door.

The girl lay on it.

The horrible part of it was the fact that the bed-clothes weren't disturbed, there was no sigh of a struggle—but for her face, everything was normal. Actually, it wasn't her face which was abnormal but her neck.

It had been slashed.

The pillow and the sheets were crimson.

Corliss felt a wave of nausea, turned and closed his eyes, stumbled against a chair and then stood still, crouching forward. Abbott did not speak, but he shut and locked the door. Corliss opened his eyes and saw the faded pattern of the wallpaper; it was identical with that in his room. Gradually other things came into focus—the wardrobe, the dressing-table and the chair, over which the girl's clothes were draped; lingerie, pale green and dainty, like that which he had fingered earlier in the day.

He schooled himself, turned and looked at the girl. This

time, he didn't turn away. He knew that he was pale, but when he caught sight of himself in the mirror he was startled by his greenish hue. The mirror, for some odd reason, hung on the wall alongside the bed.

He looked down at the girl again.

"The—*swine*," he said. His voice was hoarse, hardly audible. "I'm glad I killed him, glad—"

"Easy," said Abbott. "You didn't kill him, remember? He climbed the tree, fell down and broke his neck. Official story. We'll fix it so that you will not be needed at the inquest. Inquests are nasty, probing things, and always make a lot of trouble. This way, there'll be no need for a prolonged inquiry, the coroner will give a formal verdict and the world will think that the joker got what was coming to him."

Corliss said: "But—"

"You're going to tell me that the police aren't fools and the marks of fingers show up. That will be fixed. Drink up!"

Corliss sipped his punch; it was rum; and fiery.

"Another thing," said Abbott. "The girl is not, officially, dead. That will only cause more of a rumpus."

Corliss saw at least half of the truth. Abbott was a Department Z agent and the Department was interested in Hilde Hansson. There were reasons of security why her death should not be generally known; so it would be hushed up. At the moment, the only person who could make difficulties was— Charles Corliss.

He wanted to laugh, then caught sight of the crimson patches; the laugh was frozen in him.

"I know. Hell of a bad show," Abbott said. "But there will be explanations. Just do it my way, will you? You can tell the police everything, no question of fooling the authorities, only hoodwinking the great British public. You've stumbled into a peculiar business, Corliss. If stumbled is the word, you really jumped!" He grinned; he did not seem to be affected by anything that he had seen. "Now—had enough in here?"

"Yes."

"Why not wait in your room? Then you won't have to talk with the thick-heads downstairs and answer silly questions, and you won't have to listen to people saying that they hope Miss Hansson won't feel the shock *too* badly. Right?"

"I suppose so," said Corliss. Abbott turned to the door, but didn't unlock it immediately. He stood by it, listening; and he was there for twenty seconds or more before opening the door. Then:

"Quick!"

Corliss thought: "I've got to fool him." He didn't move.

"Look here—"

"Hurry!" snapped Abbott. "We want to get this door closed as soon as—"

"Close it, then!" Corliss raised his voice, and Abbott closed the door quickly, almost in alarm. "I don't get this. Who the hell are you? Why should I do what you tell me? How do I know that the police will hush this thing up? She's been murdered. She—"

"And her killer's caught it. Call yourself judge, jury and executioner. He died in much the same way as if he had been hanged, anyhow. Don't be awkward." Abbott took a card out of his pocket with a swift motion, and thrust it in front of Corliss's face. "Can you read?"

The card was signed by the Assistant Commissioner of the Criminal Investigation Department, Scotland Yard; and it said that Abbott was a member of the Special Branch. Only a fool would make difficulties after seeing such evidence.

Corliss muttered: "I don't get it."

"You don't have to. Ready? Slip into your room, and I'll see you afterwards. I'll even bring you a nice policeman in uniform, you won't have to believe what you read."

He opened the door again. Corliss went into his own room. Abbott locked the other door, and then put his head round Corliss's.

"Lie down a bit. Loosen your collar and tie. I won't be long."

He went out.

The door closed on him, and for a few moments Corliss stood in the room, hearing nothing, seeing only that crimson patch and the fresh loveliness of the face above it.

Then he heard a car approach.

He went to the window. He could just see Lewis's white shirt-sleeves, and before long, other men appeared—two of them in police uniform. Abbott also appeared. Although Corliss could hear the voices plainly, they were all pitched in a low key and he caught few words. Someone took flashlight photographs, he knew because he saw the flashes. After a while, footsteps sounded, slow and rather unsteady, followed by the footsteps of several men. That meant that they were carrying the body away.

They were taking away the man he had killed—the man who had known that he was going to die, and who had told Corliss when to act. That man, unknown, had been prepared to die for the Cause.

Corliss felt hot; suffocated.

This was action, and it was not what he had expected it to be.

He tore off his collar and tie and lay down on the bed, but didn't switch out the light. He lit a cigarette, wanting another drink. He had only to go downstairs to get one, but didn't move. He would never be able to do what was expected of him, never steel himself to make such a sacrifice as the dead man had made, if he relied on drink in emergency. He must fight this out by himself. Instinctively, he knew that. His hands clenched and unclenched at his side, his whole body was rigid, although he lay flat.

He heard more voices, downstairs; soon cars moved off. Then two or three men came upstairs. He turned his head towards the door, but they didn't come in here, they went next door. He could picture what they saw.

He saw a different scene, now; of the girl coming out of her room and starting back at the sight of him; of the girl at the breakfast table, so fresh and lovely.

Gradually, he relaxed.

He was quite still and composed by the time the tap came at the door. He knew that he had passed through one crisis, that there was never likely to be a greater one. He was in complete control of himself again; there was nothing he could not steel himself to do.

Nothing?

Would he ever be able to walk into his death?

Why not? His father had.

"The tap came again, and Abbott called in a soft voice: "Okay, Corliss, it's the copper."

There were two policemen in uniform, one a sergeant, and a plainclothes man who had everything anyone could want to prove his identity. Corliss dictated a statement; that he had been at the window, looking out, heard the rustling and then the girl's scream. He had jumped out, seen the man coming from the house and closed with him. The man had struggled and twisted round. Corliss had been trained in hand-to-hand combat and knew exactly what hold to use; he hadn't intended to twist so fiercely.

None of the policemen made any comment, but the plain-clothes man said:

"Thank you, sir. Mr. Abbott is really in charge here, tonight, I'll be glad if you will do exactly what he advises."

Abbott winked.

"All right," Corliss said.

As the policeman went out, the distant church clock struck the half hour; it was half past one. Abbott closed the door on the trio, and then came back, smiling easily, quite composed.

"You see what a power I am behind the scenes! Er—what brought you to this part of the world, Corliss?"

"Does it matter?"

"It could. I'm curious."

Corliss said carefully: "I'm tired of travelling and fed up with London. I thought I could rusticate down here and amuse myself. I didn't dream I'd run into anything like this. If you must know, I'm bored to tears. Have been, ever since the end of the war. I need—oh, forget it!"

"What do you need?"

"I don't know. I haven't been able to settle to anything. My trouble is that I've more money than sense. I'm the kind of fool who wouldn't be sorry if we ran into another war. I—I said forget it, didn't I?"

Abbott gave a comical grimace.

"I know the feeling. You'll get over it. No need to go and look for a war, there's one on the doorstep. Get some sleep. I want to introduce you to some friends of mine, tomorrow. Just remember to keep your mouth shut about Hilde Hansson—and remember the type of gentry this war is against. Her killers."

He went out, without another word. When the door had closed behind him, Corliss grinned, and felt a surge of wild exhilaration. He caught a glimpse of his expression in the mirror; he hardly recognised himself.

5

Z MEN

Abbott said: "Hallo, hallo! Up bright and early." He was at the window table where Hilde had sat the previous morning. Only two others were in the dining-room, and they nodded good morning. Corliss went across to Abbott, who had only just arrived, and whose walking stick stood against the window. "Join me?"

"Thanks."

"Quite a night, wasn't it? I hear that Miss Hansson's been taken to a nursing home—rather bad shock effect. Poor kid. Nothing's been stolen, I suppose that's something. Ah—waiter! Breakfast for two hungry men."

"Yes, sir, whatever you would like."

"They've never heard of austerity here," said Abbott. "There are oases of plenty in a drab world." He gave his order, Corliss did the same, and then Abbott said in a low-pitched voice: "Can you spare some time today?"

"Yes."

"We'll go for a drive, after breakfast. All right for petrol?"

"Not too bad," said Corliss.

"You will receive all you expend in this job plus a handsome bonus," Abbott assured him. "Everything will be on the up-and-up, too. Sleep fairly well?"

"Oh, yes, thanks."

Abbott grinned; he was rather like Punch.

Just after nine thirty they were sitting in Corliss's car. Abbott had limped out of the inn, and apparently he felt confident that no one else had noticed how completely he had forgotten his ankle trouble the night before. A poker-faced Lewis watched them go off. Probably he knew much more about Abbott than he had allowed Corliss to suspect.

"Turn left," Abbott said. "We're going to the Big Smoke which you dislike so much. But you won't have to stay there indefinitely, just have a chat with some friends of mine."

"About last night?"

"And all your tomorrows," said Abbott. "Don't worry about it, let me see if you can drive."

Apparently he did not intend to talk about the project.

Corliss drove fast, for driving was almost second nature. He had plenty of time for thinking. He had little doubt that Abbott was a member of Department Z. The Special Branch, in this case, had a greater significance than it usually carried. Corliss knew that he might be jumping to conclusions, but felt sure that he was on the fringe of great events; and the plan evolved by His Excellency had worked like a charm. The painstaking care of everything that had been done by the Russians greatly impressed him—that, and the ruthlessness; most of all, the willingness of the man to sacrifice his life.

He did not think much about the girl.

"Shall I drive?" Abbott asked, on the outskirts of London. "You've passed the test and I know the road."

"Just tell me."

"Right! Hyde Park Corner, for a start, the route becomes involved after that."

Corliss nodded.

It was nearly half past eleven. The West End was thronged with people and traffic, but Corliss was lucky with the traffic lights. Following Abbott's directions almost mechanically, he turned into Hyde Park, then into Park Lane and, after taking several small turnings, arrived in a narrow street at the back of one of the big squares near Oxford Street. This street was little more than a lane. There was room only for one car at a time. It connected two mews, which had been turned into garages, and there were several narrow-fronted houses at the far end.

"Drive into the mews in front, we'll leave the car there," said Abbott.

Corliss nodded.

They got out, and Abbott turned into the lane. Over the front of the middle of the three houses was a sign; *Hell's Bells* and three girls, quite properly clad, were shown with bare feet—and cloven hooves. Abbott didn't glance up but studied Corliss's face.

"Nice touch," he remarked.

"I thought this was a night club."

"It was. It is. Plus a little something which others haven't got. In fact it's a meeting place for some friends of mine. We are, as they say, mysterious coves. Sometimes we meet here, sometimes in Timbuctoo. We have a big opinion of ourselves, and dislike company. We seldom meet at the same place twice running and have dozens of *rendezvous* dotted about London."

"I didn't think the police went in for that secret service sort of stuff," said Corliss.

"Didn't you?" Abbott grinned as he opened the door of the night club with a key. It was gloomy inside. He closed the door gently. There was a narrow entrance hall, and a flight of steps immediately in front of them with a passage running alongside it. Two signs, *Cloaks,* stuck out from the passage wall, on one a woman was shown powering her nose, on the other a man was smoking a cigarette. "Upstairs," said Abbott.

The first landing was small and narrow. Several doors led from it, and Corliss glimpsed a tiny dance floor with a chromium bar at one end. The light there was good enough for him to see the wall decorations; the belles of the sign outside appeared again; undraped, and with cloven hooves kicking out in great abandon. The walls were covered with them.

"All right, for those as like it," said Abbott. "One more flight."

At the next landing, a door stood open; there were no signs. Abbott led the way into a box-like hall and flung open another door. Corliss had no idea what to expect; he should not have been surprised, but he was.

There were three men.

One, the largest, sat in an armchair with a leg stretched out straight in front of him. He looked bulky and ungainly. His dark hair, showing grey at the forehead and temples, was rumpled. His clothes looked as if they had been slept in for several nights running. He had an ugly face, yet there was something attractive about it. He grinned a crooked grin, and lifted a pewter tankard from the small table at his side.

"Welcome," he greeted in a deep voice.

"Why?" A man of medium height who sat in another chair, nearer the window, put his head on one side and examined the newcomers. He was exquisite, with small, classical features, a smooth complexion, silky brown hair parted in the middle, eyelashes so long and curly that they looked false. His tie, socks and handkerchief were the colour of dark ginger. His suit was light brown, and his shoes gleamed.

"Why not?" asked the third man.

He straddled an upright chair, leaning his arms over the back of it. He had a black patch over one eye. His face was big, the features heavy, and his lips were turned down at the corners in a droll expression; he was a block of a man, with a touch of the sinister. His tankard was in his hand.

Abbott said: "Don't fool. Corliss expects common sense from important people like us."

The big man said: "Poor chap!"

All three were looking at Corliss intently; he knew that, although each of them appeared to try to conceal the fact. They all impressed him as having an unseen strength; a kind of power. It was hard to explain, but he felt that he was in the presence of unusual men. In his way, Abbott was also unusual.

Abbott went across the room to a small beer barrel which stood on a low trestle. Alongside it were several pewter tankards; he drew off two pints of beer, and took one across to Corliss; he did not use his stick.

"Happy nights," he said.

"Plenty of hell's bells," said the exquisite, and grinned.

"Here's how," said Corliss.

He did not feel free and easy; he did not think anyone would when suddenly thrown among these men. He stood awkwardly, still aware of their keen appraisal. He felt that the big, ungainly man stood head and shoulders above the others in every way; he wasn't just physically big.

"Sit down, Corliss," he said.

Abbott nodded to a chair, and Corliss went and sat down. He had been warned not to guess or speculate, but surely there was no doubt that these were some of the far-famed Z men. He put his hand to his pocket for cigarettes; the man with the eyepatch tossed a packet to him, and he caught it deftly.

"Thanks." He lit up and tossed the pack back.

The ungainly man smiled. That made a vast difference to his face; in some strange way he lost the ugliness.

"We're not so daft as we look," he said. "Relax. Don't get annoyed if we ask you a lot of unnecessary questions. Tell us what happened last night, will you?"

Corliss told him the simple 'truth', as he had already told Abbott and the police.

"Hmm." The big man looked at his hands. "You'd better be careful with those fingers of yours, they might do a lot of damage. Ever had an accident like that before?"

"Not in peace time," Corliss said.

"I see. Reserved for war-time purposes only. Perhaps you're right. How long had you been at *The Fiddlers' Rest?*"

"This is my sixth day."

"Why did you go there at all?"

"It was a change. I've told Abbott, I was fed up to the teeth, wandering around aimlessly."

"Man can work."

"I couldn't find a job that seemed worth doing. I'm not an expert at anything—no training, except for fighting." Corliss forced a smile. "I know all the claptrap, work for the good of society, but it's not my cup of tea. As a matter of fact—"

He broke off.

"Yes?" encouraged the big man.

"I'd gone down there to think things over. I'm not a bit sure there's any future in this country. Not for me or my kind. I'd thought of going to one of the more remote countries and kicking around a bit. There's still excitement to be found in the South Americas. Or the Far East, for that matter. I didn't really know what I wanted, but—" he broke off again. A hint

53

was good enough; they would need adventurous young men who found life dull.

"Don't spoil it," said the big man.

"I don't see how this can interest you."

"Everything interests us, especially a nice-looking lad like you with a pukka background, who carries a brand of dynamite in his fingers." The big man laughed. "We're Special Branch. You've gathered that. We can use reckless young men who don't know their own strength."

He almost echoed Corliss's thoughts.

Corliss said slowly, as if mystified: "What are you driving at?"

"The possibility of putting you out of your misery and finding something for you to do," said the big man. He was both spokesman and leader; the others sat idly drinking their beer and watching him and Corliss. "To which end, we have been making what you can call inquiries. Take a look at this."

He pulled an envelope from his pocket, leaned forward and flicked it across the room. It struck Corliss's chest; he caught it. This was so like the interview with His Excellency that it was uncanny; the main difference was in the atmosphere, this ridiculous informality was in sharp contrast to the long room and the portrait.

He opened the envelope; inside were three sheets of close typewriting. At the top left-hand corner there was his own name: *Charles Marvin Corliss.* He read on, glancing up at the big man occasionally, putting up a good show of excitement; that could be expected, for this was a complete dossier. Its thoroughness was as remarkable as its brevity of word and phrase. It covered his childhood, school, university and wartime life; and much of what he had done since. As he read, he felt a shiver almost of apprehension; as they had discovered so much about him in so short a time, had they also discovered other things which were not down here? The names of hotels he had stayed at, and when he had met the Russian agents were there; just the list of hotels and what he had done during his time in the various countries and towns.

He finished reading and folded the sheets slowly.

The big man was smiling, but not simply with amusement.

"Accuracy guaranteed?"

"It's incredible! Why on earth you've gone to that trouble, I don't know."

"Don't you? Think. A young woman was murdered last night. You had tried to scrape acquaintance with her, during the day. Remember?"

"Damn it, I—"

"You aren't being accused of anything, yet," said the big man. The 'yet' came out casually but might be construed as a threat. Corliss's heart began to thump; and there was an unmistakable change in the big man's manner. "It's a fact, isn't it? You forced yourself on to her at the table?"

Corliss said: "Supposing I did? She was a decent-looking girl, and the other old fossils there weren't much in entertainment value."

"Abby," said the exquisite, "you are fossilised."

"Ever since I met you," said Abbott.

"Why did you want to get to know her?" the big man demanded.

"Why shouldn't I?"

The big man said: "That's right. Had you noticed her before that morning?"

The man's grey eyes were smiling, he gave Corliss much the same impression as His Excellency; that he could see things hidden from ordinary men, that he would know if he were told a lie. The tension was almost unbearable.

"Did you?" The question came sharply.

"As a matter of fact, I did."

"When? How?"

"It was the night before. I'd been for a drive. Stayed at a pub, drinking, and then had a flat tyre and a spot of engine trouble. I was back late. A chap was prowling round the hotel and I wondered what he was up to. I discovered that he'd visited the girl."

"Seen the man since?"

He'd soon be caught out if he lied.

"Yes. Yesterday morning, when he drove past the place. I'd dropped a letter and it was blown across the road. If the man hadn't pulled up pretty sharply, he'd have run me down. It was my fault."

"What was the letter?" asked the big man, flatly.

He knew it had been delivered by hand; Lewis would have told Abbott, Abbott would have passed it on. This was one of those factors which made the difference between success or failure, and might eventually mean life or death. Corliss coloured under the steady gaze from the big man's eyes. He felt panic. He must find a satisfactory answer, both to explain the letter and his own reaction now. None of the others spoke or moved; he felt as if he were on trial for his life.

He licked his lips.

"I don't see what that has to do with you."

"Perhaps you don't. The idea, odd though it may seem, is that you are not what you appear to be. What was in the letter, Corliss. It's important."

Corliss snapped: "To hell with you!"

The exquisite stood up. Corliss saw the movement out of the corner of his eye, but didn't do anything about it. The other man moved out of his sight and Corliss knew that he was guarding the door. Abbott broke the tension by getting up and going to the barrel; and increased it, because he had forgotten to take his tankard.

The big man shook his head.

"We may be heading hellwards but you won't quicken the pace. What was in that letter, Corliss?"

"I don't see why the devil it should interest you. It was from a girl. She's been difficult to shake off. She's one of the reasons why I went to the pub. I didn't think she'd find me there."

"I see. We're not a Court of Morals, we just want to establish facts. What's the girl's name?"

Corliss set his lips. The names of a dozen girls passed through his mind, he even considered the folly of blurting out one. If he did, the big man or Abbott would go and question the owner, and prove him a liar. He had never felt more conscious of a tension which existed between him and another; this man filled him with an awe as great as that he had felt with His Excellency.

He said: "If you think I'm going to drag her name into this, you've another thing coming."

"So you won't play?"

"I won't play that tune."

"Young Sir Lancelot or a clever liar, I wonder." The large man spoke as if to himself. Corliss rode the taunt—and then realised that if he took the insult lying down, it would cry aloud suspicion. He jumped up and took a step forward.

"I don't know who the devil you are. I do know you're playing a funny game. I've told you the truth. I didn't know Hilde Hansson, but I'd have like to, she seemed—"

"More attractive than the girl-friend you've let down?"

"That's my business, not yours!"

The big man shrugged. "Pity, but if you feel like that, you feel like that and there's nothing to be done about it. If you change your mind, telephone Abbott." He stood up—levering himself up by his arms. When he walked, his left leg was stiff and awkward; as if it were artificial and he was not yet used to walking with it. "Thanks for coming. Sorry you took umbrage. The fact is, we don't know whom we can trust and whom we can't. That girl was murdered, you know, and there's a simple fact you've probably overlooked. You could have killed her."

Corliss gaped.

The big man laughed.

"Well, couldn't you? And then killed the other man and told your pretty story. Go away and think about it. And if you take my tip, you'll be careful who you mix with; a man can be judged by the friends he keeps."

The menace there could be in simple words!

"Look here—"

"Okay, Corliss," said Abbott. "No need to get worked up about it. We've a job to do and we do it our own way." He came across and took Corliss's arm. His grip was vice-like. Corliss felt another surge of panic. That warning against bad company, the whole trend of the questions, suggested that he was really under suspicion. The big man was right, too, he could have liked the girl. 'They' hadn't done such a good job as he'd expected.

The exquisite opened the door. He was surprisingly tall, and looked almost foppish. Abbott led the way downstairs. He didn't speak until they were at the car; then:

"Take it easy. 'Bye."

He didn't offer to shake hands, but went back to the night club. The door closed behind him sharply.

Corliss sat at the wheel of the car, feeling prickly hot. It was some minutes before he moved away and drove along the narrow lane. Every few seconds he looked behind him, for fear of being followed. He saw no one. He was in Hyde Park when he realised that if the Z men worked with the police, there would be no need for them to follow him, police patrols would watch and report his progress wherever he went. Unseen eyes *were* watching him. He had started so well and finished badly—hopelessly.

Idiot!

Did he expect the Z men to open their arms in welcome the moment they saw him?

He'd fool them, given time, time in which to find out the name of a girl who would say that she had written to him. At last he had an urgent reason for telephoning that special number. He turned into Piccadilly, and was a red painted telephone kiosk. He actually slowed down as he approached it, then put on speed.

If he were being watched by the police, they might report any call he made. He couldn't telephone in the open, like this. But he could from his club or from an hotel—and he had to call that number.

6

FRIEND IN NEED

I f he went to the club he would be recognised, the operator might even remember the number. He drove to the *Mayfair Hotel*, left the car outside and hurried in. He wasn't well known here. The lounge was already crowded, beyond it, one of the dining-rooms was already full; it was nearly one o'clock. He sat down and lit a cigarette, watching the door. No one who came in appeared to be interested in him. He went out of the lounge, after a few minutes, to the telephone booths, put in his number and waited, peering cautiously out of the booth. No one looked towards him.

The low-pitched *brrr-brrr* of the ringing sound went on and on. Wouldn't there be an answer? Couldn't he rely on—

"Yes?" The man who eventually answered had a clear, crisp English voice.

"This is Corliss."

"Yes?"

"I need help urgently, but it might be dangerous to—"

"Lunch at *Cherry's*," the man said, and rang off.

Corliss left the booth and wiped the sweat from his forehead. It had been hot in that booth. He sauntered towards the lounge, trying not to take particular notice of anyone. The instructions had been crisp and sensible. *Cherry's* was one of London's few remaining exclusive restaurants where he might be expected to go. He had often lunched or dined there, it was more club than restaurant, there was seldom room for anyone but habitués. The brief telephone encounter had given him confidence. He took the car to the garage near *Cherry's,* and when he left it, felt more secure. Certainly he hadn't been followed, and he was probably letting his imagination run riot when he thought of being shadowed by the police; all the same, it was better to be cautious.

Cherry's had an inconspicuous entrance in an inconspicuous side street. The small windows were covered with lace curtains, there was no bill of fare, no notice of any kind outside. Inside, it was small, warm and filled with red plush and well-dressed people. The walls were dotted with old prints and caricatures. The tiny bar was packed. He managed to get a drink and stood looking into the main dining-room. After a few minutes, a smooth-voiced waiter came up to him.

"Good morning, Mr. Corliss."

"Oh, hallo." He did not remember having seen the man before.

"I have your table, when you're ready."

He hadn't booked.

"Thanks. I'll come straight away."

The table was upstairs, in a room where there were only three tables, one of them a double, in a corner. He slipped into his seat and the head-waiter moved off. He finished his drink; the other waiter came up, he gave his order and looked round the room. Was he to have a luncheon companion, or was one of the men present the man he had come to see? They were all men; that might be an indication.

Paté and toast and butter arrived, and the waiter who brought it leaned over him and breathed down his neck.

"If you keep your voice low, I shall hear you."

"You—"

"Yes, sir, I think I would recommend that," said the waiter.

Corliss said quickly: "I'm in touch with them. I need a young woman to help. She's to come to *The Fiddlers' Rest* and ask for me. If there's any difficulty, she's to insist on seeing me. Romantic type, I'm trying to get rid of. She sent me that letter about H.H. It was a love letter."

"Very good, sir, I will see if we can arrange that," said the waiter. His warm breath no longer damped Corliss's neck. "You are followed," he said.

Corliss didn't stare after him when he had gone, but reading the menu idly took all his concentration. So it hadn't been imagination; he had been followed.

Suddenly, he grinned.

When he had got used to this, he would enjoy it.

Lewis, his shirt-sleeves rolled up, was working on the hotel car when Corliss arrived at *The Fiddlers' Rest*, late in the afternoon. He nodded politely but didn't speak. Corliss sauntered across the gravel yard. Everything seemed normal, it was hard to realise that two people had been killed here only the previous night. Clouds were blowing up and there was a gusty wind; rain seemed to be in the air. Two or three guests came in, wearing riding clothes. They nodded, that was all. The woman who read the thousand-page book was sitting in the lounge with the book closed by her side; she was dozing. Corliss went upstairs, and was glad to loosen his collar and tie. It wasn't the atmosphere, but something was stifling him. Nothing was quite as he expected.

He had the sense to realise that this part of the game was the most difficult. If he could once break into that inner circle of the Department, he would find the rest comparatively easy. Anyhow, he was doing everything he could; and he was being expertly helped, the *Cherry's* interlude had given him a lot of confidence in His Excellency.

Would 'they' find a girl easily? Would he be able to fix everything he wanted?

He had been in less than an hour when a maid tapped on the door.

"What is it?" Corliss called sharply.

"There's a lady downstairs, sir, she says that she would like to see you," called the maid.

The girl was dressed in a severely cut black suit. She was dark, young, pretty—perhaps more than pretty; and she looked intense. The moment he reached the foot of the stairs, her face lighted up and she took a step towards him. Corliss said in a low-pitched voice which he knew would carry to the man at the receiving desk:

"So you had to come here!"

"Charles, I must—"

"To hell with you," said Corliss. He looked as if he would strike her. As they drew near each other, he saw Lewis entering the hall; Lewis was certainly the man to be wary of here. He took the girl's arm and said in a whisper: "If you cause any trouble here, I'll make you regret it."

She didn't speak, but bit her lips; it was almost possible to believe that she had sought him out, to think that she hated the way he talked to her. She held her head high as they went outside. A few spots of rain were falling. He went straight to the garage, and ran out the car, leaving her in the yard until he was ready; by then, rain was falling heavily.

He leaned across and opened the door.

She got in.

Lewis watched from the inn.

He said: "You're putting up a good show, keep at it." He drove off, westwards, at a good speed. He passed a car parked off the road half a mile farther away and he saw the driver move as he went by; he didn't recognise the man but thought it likely that he was being followed again.

"What is there to do?" asked the girl.

Her normal speaking voice was attractive and yet was curiously empty—like a voice being heard through a microphone. She turned and looked at him. She had dark eyes, and they seemed too, somehow empty. That gave him an uneasy feeling. But there was no doubt about her quickness of mind.

"How much do you know?" he asked.

"All that matters."

"I had a note from them yesterday. It caused trouble. The Z men want to know where it came from. I said it was from a girl who was making trouble for me. They asked me to name her. I wouldn't, but if I'm to make any progress, I shall have to."

"I see." She looked straight ahead of her for a few seconds. "That means, then, that I must be someone whom you have known for some time. They thought of that, I am a member of two clubs you also belong to. What is the trouble between us? Have you said anything?"

"No. I've let them assume it's the usual business—the girl I don't want to marry."

"And you refuse to name her out of a sense of honour." She did not smile, and he wished she had, it would have given her a touch of reality. "That is so easy. I am Hilary Bennett. I live alone at 5 Draycourt Mansions, Mayfair. I—" She named the clubs she belonged to, gave him a few more personal details, and then finished in the same attractive and yet unreal voice: "It is, of course, simple. I am in trouble, you will not marry me, I am trying to compel you. It is better to say that

64

than to pretend I am just chasing you, that might not be believed."

"All right."

"We shall return now," said the girl. "I shall appear to be in tears, and will leave—I came in a taxi, it is waiting for me. Is there any other help you need?"

"No."

"Tell me what has happened."

He told her, and by the time the recital was over, they were near *The Fiddlers' Rest*. It was then that Corliss realised that although the other car had followed them for a few miles, he hadn't seen it for some time. It was parked near the spot where he had passed it before. The moment the girl saw it, she stared straight ahead of her, and dabbed at her eyes. From then on, she lowered her voice, as if it were possible to be overheard while they were in the car.

"I think that is satisfactory. You will not tell them my name, of course, they will almost certainly question me. The *affaire* has taken place at my flat. It has been secret because I insisted on that. You would have married me, you understand, but discovered that I was leading an immoral life. That is all clear?"

"Yes."

"Remember," she said. "A bad memory can be fatal."

He drew up outside the garage. She didn't speak again, but hurried across to the waiting taxi. The driver came hurrying out of the inn, and she climbed inside. She held a hankerchief to her nose—and Lewis saw all that and would be able to report everything that happened.

Abbott came into Corliss's room just after eight o'clock next morning, in a red dressing gown. He grinned as Corliss started up, and put a finger to his lips. He closed the door gently and walked across the room—and it was noticeable that he did not make a sound. Corliss, who had only just woken up, hitched himself up in the bed, and rubbed the sleep out of his eyes.

"I know, I know, we're a dreadful crowd," said Abbott. "But this is quite a job. What's the real trouble with Hilary Bennett, old chap?"

Corliss cried: *"What?"*

"Yes, we've discovered who she is," said Abbott. "Nice girl, if she had anything to feel with. I suppose she has, in a way of speaking. Did you know she was supposed to be on the way to an infant?"

"Now look here—"

"Take it easy," said Abbott. "Loftus told you yesterday that we don't set up to be a Court of Morals." That 'Loftus' made Corliss's heart jump; it was the big man's name, but the man himself had been careful not to give it at their first meeting. Was it a slip of the tongue? Abbott and the Z men were not likely to make slips of that kind. "She's hollow, if you know what I mean. Nice looking piece, but—"

"I tell you I won't discuss it!"

"Look here, you've put up the virtuous young gallant act long enough," said Abbott. "We have been probing into that nymphomaniac of yours. The word is properly used. She can't be trusted. She has tried this little game on several young gallants, and twice pulled it off. It's a form of blackmail plus an unlimited capacity for bestowing favours. On the whole, you deserve congratulations for having stood her up. She asked for it. She isn't likely to give you any more trouble, by the way."

Corliss stared until it hurt; and then the muscles of his cheek twitched.

"Here—" began Abbott.

Corliss laughed; it came out of him like a spurt of water, he could do nothing to stop it. He tried to, pushing his hand against his mouth, but couldn't keep the next burst back. Abbott sat heavily at the foot of the bed and looked at him with his head on one side.

Corliss let himself go.

When he stopped, Abbott said: "Feeling better?"

"I—just—couldn't—help it," gasped Corliss. "It's the relief, I suppose. If—if you'd heard the way she talked yesterday—"

He broke off.

Abbott nodded sagely.

"I can guess. So can the others. I'm sorry to wake you up with the joyous tidings, but I didn't want to wait too long. The fact is, she's no good to man or beast. She won't worry you again. She has been warned off by the police. How long have you been nagged by her?"

"Well, the better part of a year, I suppose."

"Let us draw a veil," said Abbott.

Corliss gulped—and then the maid tapped at the door and asked if he would like some tea. Abbott called: "For two." Corliss nodded and groped for his cigarettes. The interruption had given him the few seconds grace he needed. That laughter might so easily have given him away, and yet it had fitted in with the general picture. Relief! Well, it was relief—that the Russians did the job so thoroughly, that the Z men could be so easily fooled.

He felt quite sure that they had been fooled.

The tea arrived.

"Your health and freedom from malicious lovelies," said Abbott gravely. "I don't wonder you've felt like running away from it all. You can. There's a little job you can do for us, if you're willing."

Corliss frowned. "For the police?"

"A special branch of the police, if you like—not the flat-foots. I am empowered to offer you a temporary post. It won't thrill you very much. On the other hand, you might find that it will break the monotony of life a little. There isn't usually much monotony with us."

"Well—"

"It's entirely up to you," Abbott said, and he sounded almost too serious to be genuine. "You're not a fool. You've guessed that the death of Hilde Hansson wasn't exactly an ordinary murder."

"That was pretty obvious."

Abbott said quietly: "She was a secret service agent. Quite an able one. She was on to something which she wasn't able to finish. She met a man in brown here and he was giving her the gen. He was with the other side but also working with us. One of our boys actually visited her the night before last, on what you thought was an amorous errand but was in fact strictly business. She passed on what she had been able to learn. She was rather worried because you were about that night. Hence our suspicions of you, my son, and we started to collect your dossier then. Actually, you weren't in the deep trough of suspicion. You've quite a good record. We could use you."

Corliss finished his tea.

"Secret service," he said, solemnly; it was difficult not to laugh in Abbott's face.

"That's right."

"It's not exactly my cup of tea, but—" Corliss frowned suddenly, as if at an evil memory. He put his cup down noisily. "I'm not exactly new to it. To tell you the truth I hate the ruddy service. My father—"

"We know all about your father. It runs in the family, doesn't it?"

Corliss didn't answer.

Abbott said: "It's not a big job, for a start. A kind of tryout. You may not be the type for the work. It takes a curious temperament—you have to be mad but not so mad as to be certifiable. Your standards go topsy-turvy. You come across a woman, slaughtered as Hilde was slaughtered, and you turn it into a joke. Well, a kind of joke. This offer is a step, you might say, in the right direction. If you're prepared to have a stab at it, Loftus wants to see you again."

He seemed quite sure that Corliss would want to; and he looked absurdly comical, sitting there with a tea-cup in his hand.

"Well?" he asked.

Corliss forced his voice to sound reluctant.

"I suppose I might give it a trial," he said. "When do you want me to start?"

7
THE START

Only the men and the barrel of beer on the trestle were the same. The house was different, the room was large and luxuriously furnished, and the five men seemed lost in it. The exquisite sat at a pale green grand piano and strummed the keys lightly, making a nonsense medley. It should have proved irritating; instead, Corliss found it soothing.

It was mid-day.

The house was in one of the quite squares which still remain in private hands in London. The branches of a plane tree growing in the green patch in the middle of the square, were bright in the sun. A large bow window was open a few inches at the top, and the room was pleasantly cool.

Loftus *was* the big man. He sprawled in an armchair, bulky and untidy, his leg stretched out in front of him, exactly as at the time of their first meeting. If anything, his dark hair was untidier; a heavy, greasy-looking lock fell over his right eye.

He pushed it back.

"We're all glad you're here, Corliss. We think you have what it takes. Abbott's given you an inkling of that. But before we go any further, I've one avuncular piece of advice to trot out."

Corliss, sitting in a huge armchair, asked:

"What it is, uncle?"

The barrel of a man with the patch over his eye, grinned. Abbott nodded, as if he were fully satisfied. Loftus, easing himself up, placed the tips of his fingers together and looked at Corliss over the top of imaginary glasses. His voice, always deep, became sepulchral.

"Now listen to me, my boy. There is a time and a place for everything. We know that boys will be boys and girls will be girls. It is pleasant to trip the light fantastic and to take shady walks in the sun or the romantic moonlight. But if you play with Uncle Bill, you will have to turn a blind eye to the attractions of lovelies except where they affect the work. That is, when you're working. You won't be, always. What you do with your private life is no one's concern here, but you have to mind your p's and q's. A luscious siren might decide that she can get information out of you, and try very hard indeed. Such things have happened. She will not greatly mind if she appears promiscuous, in order to get it."

Corliss shrugged.

"I've had enough of that kind of business for a while."

"Yes and no. Hilary Bennett gave you a sharp lesson but you were already susceptible to the charms of Hilde Hansson. A different kettle of fish, I know, but you see how insidious the appeal is." Loftus leaned back and his hands rested lightly on the arms of his chair. "Let us put it this way. When you're working, work comes first. We are sly, cruel, cunning gentry playing against other sly, cunning, cruel gentry and they will always attack our weakest link. That makes the job more difficult for a beginner than it is for the old-timers."

"You're making it pretty mysterious."

"It is mysterious. You will never know what it is all about, only what part of it is about. You'll have a job to do, you'll do it and report—if you're lucky. If you're not lucky—" he paused, and the exquisite turned suddenly from the piano. "If you're not lucky," Loftus continued, "you will end up like Hilde Hansson. Follow?"

Corliss nodded.

"You'll work with Abbott and these two, for a start. The tailor's dummy is Reginald Wilson, the old sea salt is Chunky Bray. Abbott you already know. There might, on occasions, be emergencies in which you can't get in touch with any of us. In that case, telephone Whitehall 1212, which is the C.I.D. and ask for Superintendent Miller or one of his staff. He'll know all about you and will be able to help. All clear?"

"Yes."

"One other thing," said Loftus. "It won't be a roller-coaster of thrills from beginning to end, there will be some dull patches. They'll pass. We're on a biggish job and we expect action and casualties. As time goes on, you'll learn more about it. At the moment, you're a neophyte. On occasions, you'll think that we're not trusting you. You will be right. But it won't be doubts about your goodwill, but about your general suitability for the work."

"That's reasonable enough," said Corliss.

"Good! Now, your first job. In that envelope you'll find some photographs, a name and an address. Go to the address and watch the place. When the man whose photographs you have comes out, follow him. Just that, no more. It will probably take all day. He drives a fast car, but Abby tells me that yours isn't exactly slow. Try to conceal the fact that you're following him. At the end of the day, go back to *The Fiddlers' Rest* and give a detailed report to Abbott about what's happened. All clear."

"Yes," said Corliss. He spoke slowly, as if he weren't really satisfied.

"What's the query?"

"Is there any point in going back to *The Fiddlers' Rest?*"

"For the time being, yes. And for the time being, we'll get in touch with you when necessary. You won't know any way of contacting us except through the pub, Abbott and any one of those present. You'll recognise us again. If any other man or woman represents himself as one of us, don't believe him. You will not be contacted by anyone else on our instructions. If there's any change in plans you'll be told by someone you know. That's definite."

"I see."

"Off you go," said Loftus.

He was in!

It had happened quickly, although during the process it had seemed a long time. There was a kind of remorselessness about it; 'they' had planned the thing carefully, and the Z men had fallen for it. It was difficult to blame Loftus and the others—no one could blame them. They'd taken all precautions; no one could have checked his past history more closely; he was obviously exactly the type of man they needed. That was why His Excellency had chosen him for the job. The immeasurable cunning of his real employers made him simmer with admira-tion. It was like playing a game without any chance of losing. The part Hilary Bennett had played had been masterly; every-thing would be masterly.

He was on a winner.

He left Brigham Square, where he had talked with the others, drove round the corner, stopped and opened the enve-lope. There were a card and three photographs of a youngish man. He was shown full face and in profile, both right and left. There was nothing really remarkable about the man, except that he had a round face and his cheek bones were high; but Corliss felt sure that he would have no difficulty in recognising him. Certainly he wasn't English. Corliss studied the photographs for several minutes, then turned the card over. On the back were the words: *André Milanov, 43 Grove Court, W.1.* When he was satisfied that he need not refresh his memory again, he tore the photographs into tiny pieces. Then he got out, dropped the pieces down a nearby drain, and turned back to the car.

43 Grove Court was a tall, narrow house in a long street, which actually made one side of a square. A dozen cars were parked in the street, and near number 43 was a rakish looking Lancia. He had not seen a Lancia for some time. This was old, but the long bonnet suggested power. He felt sure that this was Milanov's car. He parked his own just round the corner, from which he could see the tip of the bonnet of the Lancia. He had no idea whether this was going to be a long waiting job or a short one. Short, he hoped; for his peace of mind he needed to keep going all the time. Once he was used to the job he would be more patient, but now—give him *action*.

He smoked two cigarettes. No one appeared to take any notice of him. A few cars and cabs passed but there was little traffic here and few pedestrians. Once, a policeman walked stolidly by, nodding to Corliss when Corliss said: "Morning, officer." Corliss felt like grinning at the fool. The plodding footsteps faded.

In the square, an engine started up; it had a high-powered, soaring note, almost like an aeroplane. Corliss pressed his self-starter. A moment later, the nose of the Lancia moved. The car came out of the square cautiously, and turned right; Corliss did not have to turn round in order to follow it. He caught a glimpse of the driver's profile; it was Milanov. Identification was easy because the man did not wear a hat. He had dark, rather frizzy hair and a round head. He drove well, and Corliss was glad when he turned into Oxford Street, where it was more difficult to follow him closely but easier to merge with other traffic; he did not seem so conspicuous. Following a man in another car without being noticed wasn't likely to be easy. The man would surely discover that he was being followed. It was like nearly everything Corliss started; at first it seemed full of difficulties, but—they would work out.

He grinned, suddenly; actually chuckled.

Milanov might be working for His Excellency; would know what he, Corliss, was doing; it did not matter if Milanov realised that he was being followed! That was one of the things that he'd overlooked and which Loftus didn't know.

Milanov paid two calls: one at a hat shop at the Holborn end of Oxford Street, another at a newsagent and book-shop in a side street off Shaftesbury Avenue. Then he parked the Lancia near the Crown Theatre, and walked off; he didn't once look behind him.

Corliss left his car twenty yards behind the other's and walked in the same direction. Milanov turned alongside the theatre, and went straight in at the stage door. The door banged behind him. Corliss walked past. The door was of solid wood, he couldn't see inside, and he certainly couldn't take a chance and go in after the man. But he needed *action*. He walked round to the entrance of the theatre and went into the foyer. It looked deserted. Show bills and photographs announced a new play, *Silver Moon*. It had opened only two days ago.

Corliss went towards the stalls entrance, glancing at the box office. The clerk was out of sight. Corliss opened the door to the auditorium. No one was about there and no one stopped him. He stepped inside the theatre. It was dark inside, with only two or three small lights on, but the stage was lighted up, and there were several actors, in daytime clothes, standing about the stage. A little man, with his back to Corliss, was talking in a high-pitched, squeaky voice; the voice didn't carry clearly and wasn't intended for an audience. His last words were clear enough, however.

"Now—try *again*."

Corliss slipped into a back seat. There were several men and two women in the front rows, and no one had noticed him. He looked at each head in turn—and saw Milanov's. He shifted his seat, to get a better view; yes, Milanov sat there, watching the stage.

There were three actors: two men and a girl. At a distance and in the poor light, the girl looked pretty. She was playing a love scene with one of the men; gradually Corliss lost the inevitable feeling of unreality, for this was good acting.

The spell was suddenly broken. The second man, who had been sitting in an easy chair in the modern set, jumped up, disappeared behind the wings and then came storming in. It was an old, old scene—the eternal triangle, the second man being the outraged husband. Quickly, that sense of unreality faded again; these people made it seem *real*.

The man with the squeaky voice suddenly shouted:

"Stop!"

All three broke off in the middle of what they were saying, and turned towards him.

"Better, *much* better," said the man squeakily. "We will have it once more, just once more, and then I think it will be right. Now!"

They played through the scene again. Even at the second performance it gripped Corliss's imagination, but not so much that he failed to glance occasionally at Milanov, who did not move from his seat.

"Stop!" The squeak came again. "Yes, yes, that will do, very good, Iris my pet. Very good." He patted the girl on the arm. "You'll bring down the house, yes, you'll be fine, fine."

"Thank you, Jimmy."

The girl touched the flabby cheek, then walked towards the wings. As she did so, she waved to Milanov; it could only be to Milanov, because no one else was in that part of the theatre. Milanov nodded to her, before she disappeared. Then he stood up and went back stage with the others, through a narrow doorway which led from the auditorium. Milanov would probably go and see the girl and they would drive off together.

Corliss got out of his seat and hurried towards the closed door. As he reached it, he heard a faint sound behind him. He half turned, to see who was there.

A man sprang at him!

He saw the pale shape of the man's face, imagined that the lips were drawn back over white teeth. He felt the pain of sheer terror. He saw the man's hand raised, and the distant stage lights glinted on a knife.

Corliss swayed; the knife could not hurt more than his fear.

The knife flashed past him and the lights on the stage went off. Pitch darkness blotted everything out. The only sound was his own harsh breathing mingled with that of his assailant. He struck out and kicked. His fist hit something hard and he heard the man gasp. Then came a sharp twinge of pain on the back of his hand. He kicked again, and drew a grunt. He felt warm blood oozing up out of the cut. His terror grew worse because of the blinding darkness.

He stood quite still, to try to judge where the other was.

He could hear the man breathing, and expected another slash moment by moment. If he shouted, help would come, but how would he explain being here? If he were delayed for long he would lose Milanov. He was getting used to the darkness and could see a little. The pale blur of the face was to his right.

He saw it move.

He jumped forward at the man. He felt the downward sweep of the other's arm but knew that the knife was behind him, carving harmlessly through the air. He shot out his arms and his fingers touched flesh; the man's neck. He gripped, exerting sudden pressure. He heard a gasp, then another sound, behind him; the knife had dropped. He was safe, he could get away. Yet his hands were tight round that thin neck; he squeezed.—*twisted.*

The snap seemed dull.

The man went limp.

Corliss let him go. He fell, heavily, and brushed against Corliss's legs.

Corliss licked his lips and turned away quickly. His hand stung. He ran his left hand through his hair, to tidy it, and stepped nervously through into the foyer. No one was about. A sign said: *"Gentlemen"*. He pushed open the swing door into the cloakroom, and for the first time, looked at his hand. It was bleeding freely; the cut seemed neither long nor deep, but blood had dripped to his trousers and to his coat. His face showed pale in the mirror and there was a smear of blood on his forehead.

He washed his hand under a running tap and scrubbed his forehead with his handkerchief. Then he wound the handkerchief tightly round his wounded hand, straightened his hair, and hurried out.

The blood drips had soaked into his clothes, and had become reddish brown stains.

He didn't look right or left, but went to his car and got in. The Lancia was still parked near. He sat back, fighting first against the temptation to close his eyes, then against another and stronger urge, to get away from here at all costs. The body might be found at any moment. The stains on his clothes, and his own pallor, might have been noticed by dozens of people he had passed.

It seemed as if everyone who went by, stared at him.

Steady; panic wouldn't help.

It was so damnably hard to get the situation in its true perspective. He had killed again, but he was all right, he'd be in no danger. The Z men would look after him, they would understand why it had been necessary.

Would they?

There had been a lot of sarcastic talk about his 'trick' with his fingers.

The stage door opened. The squeaky-voiced man came out with two others and hurried away, waving to every engaged taxi which passed him. Then Milanov appeared with the girl. There was no mistaking the girl, although at closer quarters she looked much more attractive than she had on the stage; that was because she had on only ordinary make-up. She was laughing at something Milanov said; and Corliss felt that he had seen her before. He was sure of it, knew that he ought to know why but his mind wasn't working properly. Probably he'd seen her photograph; that would be it, an actress would often be photographed.

Milanov opened the door of the car for the girl.

She was fair-haired and fresh, reminding Corliss vaguely of Hilda Hansson; it was her type of face and feature rather than any actual likeness. It was shown also in her easy grace of movement. Milanov sat beside her, and they lit cigarettes.

Corliss started his engine.

Milanov couldn't fail to realise that he was being followed. Corliss knew that it was no longer possible to shrug his shoulders and say that didn't matter; for it did. Otherwise, why had that killer sprung at him out of the darkness? Hadn't the man been protecting Milanov? What kind of a secret agent would fail to look behind him, would forget to find out whether he himself was followed?

The Lancia moved off, and Corliss followed. He didn't have to go far, for Milanov drove to a small restaurant, and left the car in a nearby parking place. He hadn't once looked round.

That gave breathing space; the couple would be there for an hour, at least.

Corliss had to do something about his wound. It was still bleeding freely and blood showed through his handkerchief. The obvious place to go was his own service flat, near Victoria Station—he hadn't been there for a week. It was a tiny place, no more than a *pied-à-terre*—exactly what he needed. It would take him ten minutes to go there. Ten minutes to get there, a snack brought up from the restaurant for lunch, ten minutes to get back—he could be here again inside forty minutes, and Milanov was likely to linger over luncheon with Iris.

Iris who?

He hadn't noticed the name outside the theatre; he was crazy, he must learn to notice small things. He still couldn't place the actress yet felt that it should be easy to. He now had ample proof that he was a raw beginner. Never mind that; get tidied up.

He had more difficulty than he expected in driving to the flat, for traffic blocks twice held him up. It took twenty minutes to reach the street. He felt weak and his head was swimming; that was partly from loss of blood, of course, partly from repressed excitement—and fear? Yes, he was still frightened, but also felt a wave almost of exhilaration.

The block of flats was a large, modern, concrete mass, with nothing in its design to please except simplicity. He went up in the lift, glad that no commissionaire was on duty. He opened the door of his own flat quickly and stepped inside.

As he closed the door, he heard a movement.

8

SECOND ATTACK

Corliss stood quite still, his heart thumping. The veins in his injured hand seemed to swell up and down. He felt physically sick. The door closed behind him and the key was still in his hand.

There was no doubt that someone was in one of the three rooms, and no one had any right here.

For seconds which seemed like minutes, Corliss couldn't move. The other man didn't move, either, but must know of the new arrival. He would be waiting and watching—and might be as ruthless and viciously aggressive as the man at the theatre.

Which room was he in?

There were four doors; only that of the bathroom was closed; all the others were ajar, and Corliss knew that he had closed each one when he had left the flat. Seconds dragged by, he could think, but his body wouldn't do anything that he wanted it to do; and he was frightened.

He backed to the door.

If only he had a weapon, a gun—

He would have to get one, it was crazy to be doing work like this without one.

Forget it! He hadn't a gun, just his powerful killer's hands.

Which room was the man in?

Corliss looked round the tiny, rectangular hall. In the hall-stand were two umbrellas and one knobbly oak stick which his father had used for years. He tip-toed to the hall-stand and drew out the stick. It rattled against the handle of one of the umbrellas. Except for his own breathing, there was now no other sound. He held the stick tightly by the ferrule end; his hand hurt, but not enough to weaken his grip.

He moved towards the right hand door.

He reached it, and peered through the crack between the door and the frame. This was the dining-room or living-room. He could see no one there; and the most likely place for a man to hide was immediately behind the door. He pushed it open, gently; nothing happened. As more of the room came into sight, he knew that no one was in here; so the intruder was in one of the other rooms.

He turned quickly.

A man leapt at him; a short, squat man, who had a gun in his right hand, held by the barrel. Corliss struck out at him, but couldn't hold off the onslaught. The gun rose and fell. He felt the blow at his temple, and a knife-like pain went through his head. He swayed, dizzy, beginning to black out—and then felt another blow.

He pitched forward, unconscious.

The man who had attacked Corliss drew back from the unconscious man and pocketed his automatic slowly. He stood and watched Corliss, and a faint smile twisted his lips. He did not look vicious. He was smaller than Chunky Bray, but had the same kind of barrel shaped figure. He was well-dressed and his dark hair was parted in the middle and brushed back from his forehead. He seemed to be listening; soon, he was satisfied, and turned away from Corliss.

Ten minutes later, he stood in a telephone kiosk near Victoria Station, and dialled a Whitehall number. A man answered him with a crisp:

"Yes?"

"Burtt here," said the squat man. "T—T—R—"

"Go ahead," said the man with the crisp voice.

Burtt spoke for three minutes, interrupting himself twice to laugh, and finished: "Yes, he'll be all right. Anything else, Gordon?"

"No, I'll send for you, when there is."

"Right. 'Bye."

Burtt rang off, went out of the box and sunned himself for a few minutes, among the crowd. Then he called a taxi and told the driver to take him to the Carillon Club.

William Loftus, who limped because his left leg was an artificial one, and although he had practised with it for years, he had never really become used to it, left a car in a narrow turning off Whitehall and approached the side of one of the big Ministry buildings. The heavy grew stone was broken, almost unexpectedly, by a small, narrow door. It was a door which many people passed without noticing, little more than a hole in the wall. Loftus went in. A flight of narrow stone steps faced him. He went up, one at a time, frowning; his stump sometimes hurt, and it had chosen this particular time to hurt more than usual.

He went up two flights and came to a landing. There was no apparent reason why he should stop there. The wall facing him was blank and grey. A shiny handrail continued along the wall and up the next flight of stairs. Loftus put a hand on the rail, ran his fingers beneath it and felt a tiny protuberance; he pressed it and stood back.

Almost immediately, part of the wall slid to one side. The handrail parted with the wall, and the gap which appeared was about two feet wide. Loftus went through, squeezing himself sideways without difficulty. The door closed behind him.

A man sitting at one of the three large desks, looked up and said:

"Half a minute, Bill."

Loftus grunted, and went to an easy chair in front of an open fireplace where a small coal fire burned. The room was as familiar to him as his own right hand. He knew every corner, every item of furniture, and the contrast between the end where the other man sat and the fireplace end, had long since ceased to astonish him. It astonished all those who entered this office for the first time, but they were few, for this was the only office of the Department called Z.

The far end was barely furnished; there were the three green metal desks, several filing cabinets, the dictating part of a dictaphone and one or two other oddments; on each desk were several telephones, each of which was fitted with a light as well as a bell-call system. There, the floor was covered with green rubber.

At the other end, the character of the room was completely different. It was like a bachelor's living-room, with two large, old and worn armchairs, a faded but good Persian carpet, a book-case, several oddments, a small radio and a huge corner cupboard. The door of the cupboard was ajar and the handle of a spoon poked out. In this cupboard Gordon Craigie, the chief of Department Z, kept everything he was likely to require from one day's end to the next. Loftus had never seen that cupboard tidy, and the whole of the living end of the room had an untidy appearance in sharp contrast to the neat utility of the other end.

Loftus dropped heavily into the chair.

Craigie finished writing, came over and stretched his arms above his head. He had his back to the fire which burned every day, winter and summer alike, except during heatwaves. The fire was a foible of Craigie's, who was a bachelor. Recently there had been a time when he had seemed likely to marry; Loftus, his closest friend both in and out of the Department, did not know what had made him change his plans.

Craigie had a long face, deeply lined; was grey-haired and had well-shaped, drooping lips and a slightly hooked nose; he was rather like the popular conception of a Red Indian Big Chief. He looked tired; Loftus had never known him look anything else. He was the chief director of anti-espionage in Great Britian. He organised it in his own way, and among his many foibles was the secret entrance to this office.

"Gloomy, Bill?" he said lightly.

"Somewhat."

"Why?"

Loftus grimaced.

"You may think that it's ABC but I'm not with you, Gordon. The ramifications of this Russian business go deep. Russian, Communist, call it what you like. Compared with the anti-Nazi witch hunt which we had to handle before the war, this is outsize. I've been thinking over the simple instructions we had from the Cabinet: *Dig it out, root and branch.*" He laughed. "Cryptic and oh, so easy! We don't know where it begins or where it ends. We don't know friend from enemy. The most unlikely chap gets bitten by the red bug, and when he's bitten, he seems to be affected for keeps. Sorry I'm glum."

"Why not admit the real reason for gloom?"

Loftus said: "All right, all right, we're losing too many good agents. Hilde Hansson—"

"I know," said Craigie. "There was something about Hilde which won us all completely over. Partly, I suppose, because she's one of the few who'd been both in a German and a Russian concentration camp. But we have to take it and we have to find new people."

Loftus grunted.

"Another thing that's obvious is that you're feeling the strain," Craigie said. "There comes a time when you can't be flippant and facetious, when it hits you like the kick of a mule. This is one of them. If we win, it'll be after a long, weary time. It certainly isn't like many of our jobs, with a first-time objective, something we can screw ourselves up to face, finish and then relax for a bit. There's no relaxation coming our way for a long time."

Loftus said: "You're an understanding beggar, Gordon. No one ever gives you half as much credit as you deserve."

"Forget it. I've been working here for over twenty years and most of what comes has come before in one form or another. It's worse, today, because it's at once secret and public. The Kremlin know what we're doing, some part of the witch hunt gets splashed in the newspapers, we never quite know when the thing we're most anxious to keep secret will be on everyone's breakfast table. But it'll work out."

"That is called a platitude."

"Platitudes have their uses. In this particular case, I think we'll get farther more quickly than you expect. We know a lot of their agents, we've some of ours working with them. I know it's cross-doublecross all the time, but it's not so complicated as it seems. And one day we'll remind the Cabinet that if we can dig out the root they needn't worry about the branches. Where do you think the root is?"

"Not a hundred miles from here. Fairly near the Rumanian Embassy."

Craigie said: "At least we're not fooled or shocked by their use of the Embassy and Embassy officials, it's always happened, although not so blatantly as now. This looks bigger, because they've gone outside their Embassy, and have special headquarters. We could raid the place but they're past-masters at covering up and at this stage a raid would probably get us nowhere. But—ever pause to think that there's a curious form of inverted honesty about the way the Communists go about their business?"

"That's one way of looking at it."

Craigie said: "You ought to take a week or two off, Bill. There's no real reason why you shouldn't. Go and sun yourself at Aix or somewhere as gay. It'll blow the cobwebs away."

"Not until we know why Hilde was killed," Loftus said.

"All right—take a week-end at Brighton! I've some news for you, by the way, about young Corliss."

Loftus looked at him sharply. "Oh. Bad?"

"I don't think so. He's run into trouble but he's out of it. Burtt was looking through his flat, for a final check. Nothing was found to give Corliss a black mark, he certainly seems all right. Be a funny thing if his father's son wasn't! But Corliss had been hurt—a cut on the hand. Not serious, but nasty. He'd obviously run to earth, at his flat. Burtt had to make up his mind what to do, pretty quickly. He knocked Corliss out before being seen and recognized—although he says that for safety's sake, he'd better not be given a job with Corliss, who might call him to mind if he sees him again."

Loftus scowled.

"We're doing well! Z man clouts Z man, to show earnest. Talk about cross-doublecross!"

"It was a quick and sound decision," Craigie said. "We'll have an idea how Corliss behaves when he's in trouble. I wonder what he ran into, to get that cut."

"Car crash?" Loftus said, hopefully.

"No. His car's not damaged. He was following Milanov,

who presumably did his daily trip to the Crown Theatre and took Iris Grahame out to luncheon. We'll wait until we get Croliss's report. If he panics, then we can't use him."

"I don't think he'll panic," said Loftus.

Craigie said slowly: "But you're not happy about him, is that it?"

"Yes and no. Judged from the surface, everything's fine. He has what it takes, and—well, you know as much as I do. But there's a curious intentness about him. I can't quite place it. I should say that he has a morbid preoccupation with something or other. It may just be frustration—he talked rather that way. Of course, there's the other, obvious thing—the way he broke that man's neck."

"He learned how to, in the war."

"Oh, I know. There's something more to my fancy, I suppose. I like the cut of his jib and all that, but—well, if I had to sum it up in a few words, I'd say that I think Master Corliss is a killer, and when he's set on a thing, nothing will shake him off."

Craigie said quietly: "Well, if he's already been trained as a killer, it will save us a lot of trouble. You don't have to blink your eyes at the jobs we have to do. Killing does become necessary. That's in Corliss's favour, rather than against him."

"I suppose so," said Loftus. "But I've grumbled enough! Anything else in?"

"Nothing of importance. We've seven more reports giving proof of the existence of strong Communist cells in different places up and down the country—not exactly where you'd expect to find them, either. We're so used to it, that—"

"Where?"

"*Ankloss Limited,* the hosiery people. A small north country cinema circuit, largely among the technicians. A London club of the better kind. A Midlands chain of grocery and provision stores—I needn't go on. The one thing which is consistent in this job is the surprising places where you find these cells."

"And the impossibility of doing anything about them when we know they exist."

"Not our job. We then hand over, and I'm glad someone else has that headache. The day will come when it will be passed to us, of course, then you'll really have something to grumble about. Just for the moment, we're only putting a finger on them. You know, if we have a worry—" Craigie broke off.

"If!"

"A big one, I mean. It's this, Bill. There are times when we get very close to a cell, and it breaks up. It's almost as if they know we're after them *and* know when we're close to a particular cell. Hilde Hansson is a case in point. She was pretty close to a big one centring on Reading. Reading's a centre for the south, a lot of industrial and railway trouble could start there. And—she's killed. Why? The obvious reason is that she might have found out more detailed information about these forced labour camps. They've killed several who could do that. But there are so many people who can help with compiling the records of the camps that it's hard to believe she was important enough from that point of view. But if they knew that she was on to a cell in the Reading district—"

Loftus grunted.

"See what I mean?"

"I see. That makes it much better! Oh, well." Loftus forced a smile, stood up clumsily and went across to the corner cupboard. "I hope you've got some beer, I'm thirsty. There's a thing in our favour, Gordon."

"What is it?"

"The boys are pretty mad about Hilde. Abby, Wilson, Bray, the Errols, Murdoch—all of them are ready to go all out. It's added that little touch of keenness which the job itself was apt to blunt. Don't say that I can't look on the bright side."

Craigie laughed.

Loftus had his beer and went to the largest of the three desks. He sat down, and took some files from an adjacent filing cabinet. Craigie took a meerschaum pipe from a rack in the wall, filled it and watched Loftus. Loftus was going through the lists of the places where the Communist cells had been discovered. Both of them—and they shared the office work here—did that, almost every day. It was an imposing list. It would be of inestimable value to the Russians to know that it existed—worth much more if they could get a copy and know which cell to disperse. At the moment, most of them were working and being watched, but not by the Department; that was Special Branch work.

The Cabinet decided when a cell should be broken up and had to work cautiously; two or three times, a pounce had been made but the men and women caught had mostly been able to 'prove' their innocence. Twice, the Kremlin reactions had been so vitriolic that there were dangers of international incidents. Cross-doublecross, the constant interplay of menace and fear and the enormous issues at stake, made this a task of frightening importance.

One of the telephone bells rang.

Each had a different ringing note; each showed a light when a call had come through on it. Loftus picked up one which had a pink light. The colours were changed from time to time, and each light conveyed a special message; the pink, just now, meant that it was a call from one of the agents working outside; it might be from anyone.

Loftus said: "Yes."

"This is Bray—Y— A—R—"

"Yes, Chunky, what's doing?"

"Odd show," said Chunky Bray, who had used the simple code of spelling his name backwards and thus making sure that it could not be a message from anyone but a full-fledged Department agent. "I was round about the Crown Theatre just now. There was a shindy of some kind. As Milanov is often there, I looked in. They'd found a little chap at the back of the auditorium. Dead. Murdered. His neck was broken."

9

FIRST REPORT

Corliss came round slowly.

He knew that he had been attacked but didn't remember where he had been or what had happened. His head ached, he felt sick and there was a lot of pain in his right hand. Why should that throb? It was daylight, and he lay on something hard: the floor.

Why should his hand—

He remembered, suddenly; everything came back. He kept quite still. Fear, which had been so close to him for hours, was very close now. His assailant might still be here; might have left him for dead while he continued a search of the flat.

There was no sound.

Corliss eased himself to a sitting position, then stood up. He swayed, thrust out his right hand mechanically to save himself from falling, and winced when he banged it against the wall. The handkerchief was soaked with blood, now. He leaned against the wall for several seconds, then went slowly into the bathroom. He felt fairly sure that his assailant had gone.

He ran cold water into the handbasin, took off the handkerchief and plunged his hand in. The water stung, and
damped the cuff of his shirt. The blood spread quickly,
turning the water to a deepening pink. Here and there it had
clotted and looked like little brown dots, turning red. He
sponged them gently, and they moved. The cut was about an
inch and a, half long. It didn't seem deep. It had severed two or
three of the veins on the back of the hand, that was why it had
bled so much. There was still a little but not a great deal of
bleeding. He dabbed at the wound with the sponge, emptied
the basin and sponged his hand with clean water.

Then he put his head under the tap.

Two minutes of icy coldness, and he felt better. He
straightened up and grabbed a towel. Water dripped over his
shoulders and down his neck, soaking his collar; he'd have to
change. In any case, he would have to change because of the
blood on his coat and trousers.

He took some lint and an ointment from the bathroom
cabinet and fixed it over the cut with adhesive plaster. He
could move his hand fairly freely, he wasn't likely to have
much trouble with that now. He washed his face, cleaning
away the last traces of blood. Then he went slowly into the
living-room and sat down.

Well, hadn't he asked for action?

But who had attacked him?

Don't *guess;* they were his strict orders. And don't use the
telephone at his flat for any purpose of His Excellency's; the
Department might have the line tapped. But he couldn't help
worrying about that attack. He wanted to report what he had
achieved, but that would have to wait. He smoked a cigarette
and had a weak whisky and soda; afterwards, he felt so much
better that he was actually hungry. He telephoned the restaurant for an omelette, and then changed. He was still in his

shirt and trousers when the food came up, for dressing was a slow business.

He didn't keep the waiter long.

By the time he had finished eating, it was half past two. He hadn't been unconscious many minutes. He knew that he ought to be at the restaurant, for Milanov, but there would be no sense in going while he felt weak and wouldn't be able to look after himself in any emergency. Loftus wouldn't expect the impossible; there were degrees of foolhardiness, and going out before this would have been asking for trouble.

He was all right, now.

He studied his face in the mirror; yes, he was all right. His eyes were clear and bright, he felt that he could tackle anything. He went out. Never mind who had attacked him or who had been at the flat; his chief job was to prove himself for Loftus's benefit. But he mustn't overdo anything—better to admit a partial failure than to run into trouble through sheer recklessness. He drove slowly. The traffic was so thick that it would have been folly to try to hurry. He turned into the side street near Shaftesbury Avenue—and the first thing he saw was Milanov's Lancia.

He drove past it, smiling with intense satisfaction.

He parked for five minutes at the end of the road, with the driving mirror adjusted so that he could see the entrance to the restaurant. He had just time to smoke half a cigarette when Milanov and the actress came out. It was odd, but he could see the girl's face much more clearly than the man's—she seemed to look down the road and straight into Corliss's eyes. Nonsense! But she reminded him more than ever of Hilde Hansson, and that wasn't all; he knew her. Well, he'd seen her before, somewhere, not just her photograph. Probably on the stage—he was an idiot not to have made sure of her name. He wished she hadn't looked at him, as he was sure she had. He drove the thought out of his mind and started the car. As the Lancia drew level with him, he bent down as if to pick something off the floor and, the moment it had passed, he started in pursuit. This time Milanov drove more swiftly, taking the side streets. Eventually he came out near St. John's Wood and slowed down outside one of the large, Georgian houses which stood in their own grounds.

Corliss drove past.

He thought the actress looked at him; Milanov certainly didn't, Milanov had eyes only for the girl. Corliss turned the next corner, stopped and jumped out and approached the corner on foot. He was fifty yards away from the Lancia and from the couple.

The girl and Milanov were shaking hands.

Milanov left her at the gate, and returned to his car. By the time he passed the end of this street, Corliss was facing in the right direction again, and was able to follow. He allowed two buses to get between him and the Lancia. Milanov drove straight to Grove Court, parked the car and went into what had once been a private house; now there was a notice board with several names on it, fastened to the wall.

Not once had Milanov looked round.

Corliss took his car to the corner opposite from that which he had watched in the morning. This was in the shade. He was cool and able to relax. His hand ached a little and he knew that if he were called on for sudden action, he would not put up much of a show. But he was satisfied with the day's work, he didn't think Loftus would have much to complain about over this.

He had been there for twenty minutes when a man walked up and said: "Having a nice rest?"

Corliss started.

Chunky Bray looked at him, grinning; he had no patch on,

but marks of the patch showed on his cheek and above his eye; there was no mistaking his heavy figure.

"Call it a rest," said Corliss.

"That's what it is. Loftus thinks you've done enough for one day. Will you go to your flat and wait for a message?"

"Oh—good. Milanov's—"

"Gone home to roost. Don't tell me what happened, tell the great man. And—" Bray stopped abruptly.

"Yes?"

"It doesn't matter," said Bray. "Except—Loftus's mood is a bit changeable. Don't be too clever with him, he might snarl at you. He has a lot to carry."

"He could try slimming," said Corliss, and forced a smile, smiling was part of the stock-in-trade of these people. "I'll be good."

Bray grinned, as if well pleased.

Corliss drove off but did not go straight to his flat. He passed by the Crown Theatre. When he saw the crowd gathered outside and the policeman controlling it, and when he also saw police on duty just inside the foyer, he realised that it had been folly to come this way; any of the nearby shopkeepers might have seen his car and might recognise him. He could not move past quickly, the crowd had forced the traffic into one line.

There was a big photograph of the actress outside the theatre; and above it in red letters: *Iris Grahame.* Of course! And it wasn't imagination that he had seen her before, he'd run across her at Cannes. She had been resting. She was one of the stage's up and coming stars, and had worked too hard; three weeks at Cannes had set her up. He had stayed at the same hotel for three days, and they'd met several times. He should have remembered that earlier.

It didn't matter.

No one stopped him.

He reached the flat a little after half past four and this time went slowly and cautiously upstairs. He hesitated before he inserted the key in the lock and when he turned it opened the door carefully. There was no sound. Not until he had looked into every room was he satisfied that the flat was empty. He felt curiously free, almost elated; that was because he had passed within a few yards of the spot where he had killed his assailant and been quite safe. He stopped thinking about generalities, went straight to a small mirror over the mantlepiece and looked at himself.

He was *fine;* he'd never looked better!

It was odd; he'd killed that man and not turned a hair, hadn't thought of anything but the consequences. He'd not even felt the sickening sense of revulsion that he had when he had killed the man at *The Fiddlers' Rest.* It was almost as if he were used to killing—in peace, as well as in war. There was a difference, but—

The front door bell rang.

Loftus?

He didn't open the door at once, but went to it quietly, bent down and peered through the keyhole. Yes, it was Loftus—or anyhow, a big man with a bulging stomach. He stood to one side and opened the door, with a smile of greeting set on his face. It faded, when he saw Loftus's scowl.

Loftus came in, pushing past him.

Corliss closed the door.

"What's the matter with you, Corliss? Gone quite mad?"

Corliss said: "I don't—"

He broke off because of the expression in Loftus's eyes. He realised in that moment that Loftus was a dangerous man, that he could be frightening; he was now. His deep voice had a razor's edge to it.

"If you're going to bleat that you don't understand, you'd better go back to kindergarten. You certainly won't be any help to us. What's got into you? The killing habit?"

Corliss said softly: "Oh, *that.*"

"That's it. Your second victim in three days. The third might get you hanged. We don't give protection to murderers who kill for the love of killing."

He was dangerously near the truth; the words came home to Corliss with a sense of shock: a *love* of killing. It would give him a kick to fling the words back in Loftus's face, but he had to keep on the right side of Loftus.

"I had to do it," he said.

"The same way as you had to kill the man at the pub? He would have been far more useful alive than dead, and—"

"Oh, dry up!" Corliss snapped. He raised his right hand. "He nearly got me first. Rushed at me out of the darkness of the theatre and before I knew what was happening, slashed at me. He wouldn't stop trying. I had to protect myself, and—"

"You didn't have to kill."

"He had the knife. I'd no weapon."

Loftus said: "You're a damned sight too smooth." He stood towering above Corliss, like a figure of doom. In his rugged way, he was both striking to look at and impressive, and again Corliss felt that a man was piercing the façade of his face and voice, and seeing him as he really was. Corliss hoped that he didn't show any sign of nervousness.

"I just had to stop him from using that knife," he said, and there was a pleading note in his voice. "There wasn't any other way, and he struggled. I was scared stiff, and—well, you know what happened. I don't see how I can be blamed, and—what's this talk of murder? Self-defence isn't murder, is it?"

"You'd have a hell of a job to prove it was self-defence," said Loftus. He seemed mollified none the less and limped to a chair and sat on the arm. The chair tipped up a little under his weight, and he managed to steady it. He stuck his leg out in front of him and pushed a hand through his untidy hair. Corliss realised something which hadn't been evident before; Loftus was worried.

There were people who would be very glad to know about that.

"What happened to Milanov?" Loftus asked.

"Bray relieved me. Before that..."

No one could complain about the attention with which Loftus listened to the story. He did not interrupt, except to nod now and again, and he didn't ask for anything to be repeated. He showed no particular interest in the report of Milanov's visits; he would seldom give anything away with that poker face.

Corliss finished: "So I came back here, as I was told. I don't know what you think, but this has been quite a baptism of fire."

"Hmm. Some would call it lucky, others would take a dim view of it. I know a dozen men who would give their right hands to have that kind of action in a day. How do you view it?"

"I can take it," Corliss said. "I wish I knew who had attacked me in the theatre and who was waiting for me here. It's worried me. Why should anyone come here and lie in wait for me?"

Loftus said: "You're being watched. You're known to have talked with Abbott, and from now on, you're in danger. Probably you interrupted a man who was just checking up on you. He didn't mean you any harm or you wouldn't be alive now."

That was true; His Excellency might have ordered another check.

"You'd better give this place up, I'll fix another flat for you,"

Loftus said. "Pack all you need in a couple of cases, and I'll have them collected. I shouldn't stay here another night."

"Okay."

Loftus said, as if with grudging admiration: "I'll say you take it pretty calmly."

"Nothing in this actually scares me," Corliss said impatiently. "Oh, I get scared, but that soon fades. The mystery part of it—"

"There'll be plenty of mystery. Your man of the theatre was probably Milanov's bodyguard. Milanov may know that he is being followed, may have fixed the attack, so that whoever was following him would be warned off. It's deep and involved, but there is an answer to everything and you'll get the answer sooner or later. How's the hand?"

"I can use it. In a couple of days it'll be as good as ever."

"Make sure it is before you start throwing your weight about again," Loftus said. He stood up and looked forbiddingly into Corliss's eyes. "Watch your hands. Don't kill, unless it's essential—as it may be sometimes. Choke a man into unconsciousness, if you must, but that's all. We need to make these people talk."

"It would help if I knew what people they are."

"You'll be told, in time," Loftus said. He dug his right hand into a capacious, bulging pocket and drew out a box which was tied round with string; the box looked too large to have been concealed in the pocket, but Corliss hadn't seen it before. "Here's a present for you. Don't forget—killing's out, whatever the weapon, unless it's a matter of saving your life or preventing the other man from getting away. And in the case of the other man, you'd better be sure that he's an enemy."

"All right. What's this?"

Loftus said: "I shouldn't go to *The Fiddlers' Rest* tonight, either, my boys will come for your cases here and give you your new address, and they'll collect your stuff from the country pub. I'll be seeing you."

Corliss let him out.

When the door closed, he stood looking at it for some seconds; and then his lips began to curve in a smile. He became aware of that suddenly, and knew that it was something quite unfamiliar, almost a reflex action; and it was more sneer than smile. He had fooled Loftus; he could go on fooling Loftus. He'd been blooded into this business now, and there would be no turning back. Nothing to come would be so difficult as that which had passed. He had what it took for this business—and he had a report that he could make to His Excellency which would cause no little satisfaction.

He hated Loftus and all Loftus stood for.

He went back to the living-room. Because he had been away so much, it had an unlived-in look. The chairs and all the furniture were new, there was a lot of tubular steel, the severity of modern furnishing without a great deal of taste; he rented it furnished. The room was large and square, and had a big window overlooking the backs of houses beyond. He took a table knife from the sideboard and cut the string of the parcel which Loftus had given him.

He took the lid off the box.

Inside, were two small automatic pistols with two spare clips of ammunition.

Corliss actually felt his lips curling. The moment he realised it, he stopped; he mustn't let that sneering smile develop into a habit, nothing would give him away more quickly. But wasn't this enough to make a cat laugh? A man he hated had placed these weapons in his hand!

He dropped one gun into his coat pocket, the other into his hip pocket. The ammunition made bulges in his coat. He needed a shoulder holster, it was fairly simple to make one.

But he'd better pack first; absolute obedience to Loftus was a first priority. Loftus must think him both good and reliable; he was already beginning to think that the new recruit was good.

Corliss started to pack.

He had nearly finished when he broke off to light a cigarette, and as he did so, heard footsteps on the landing outside. They were not a man's, being too sharp and light. He waited; the woman might be going to the flat above his. No, the footsteps stopped. He lit the cigarette and stared at the door as the bell rang.

He went forward, slowly.

There might be danger, but he scoffed at it. His assailant at the theatre had made a mistake, but His Excellency wouldn't make any mistakes. Nevertheless, he stood to one side as he opened the door, and his right hand dropped to the gun in his pocket.

It closed round the gun, in utter surprise, not menace.

Iris Grahame stood there.

10

THE UNEXPECTED

The actress stood and looked at Corliss without a smile. He remembered that when he had known her for those few brief days, she had a trick of standing quite still and looking grave, as if she were anxious to make sure exactly what the person with her was like.

He drew back, put enthusiasm into his voice.

"Miss Grahame! What on earth—but come in!"

"Thank you." She walked past him. He noticed that she did not look round the flat, and her face remained grave. He led the way into the bright and shiny living-room. He felt tongue-tied, which wasn't usual with him, and bewildered. This couldn't be coincidence, she must have seen and recognised him.

"Drink?" he invited.

"Thanks."

"Sherry, or gin and something?"

"Sherry, please."

She had a lovely face. He found himself comparing it with the face of Hilary Bennett, who had made such a brief appearance on the stage of his life. That had been hollow, empty; this was full of vitality, had a quiet, pleasing quality, seemed somehow to reflect the mind and attractiveness of the woman herself. Woman? She was young, somewhere in the middle twenties. She was dressed in a black two-piece suit and with a plain cream blouse, without any frills. He went to the cocktail cabinet; it was a relief to have a pretext for looking away from her, the steady gaze from her eyes was disconcerting.

"Do sit down, Miss Grahame."

She went to the window and looked out. When he had poured out her drink and a whisky and soda for himself, he turned and found her staring at him. She had relaxed; there was a faint smile on her lips.

"What have you done to your hand?" she asked.

"Er—I hurt it. Cut it on some glass." He forced a laugh as he handed her the drink: "Here's how!" He was glad to be able to drink his, and drank more than he should at one gulp. He needed that drink.

She might have seen him at the theatre. He couldn't be sure that he had been hidden by the gloom. She hadn't been acting all the time, had had plenty of opportunity to look about her and to see and recognise him. But more likely she had seen him outside.

Why had she come?

"I hope it's not a bad cut," she said.

"Oh, Lord, no! Just a scratch."

"That's good."

Why had she come? He hadn't the nerve to ask her right out, although he knew that he ought to: every moment that he delayed must seem more suspicious to her. Suspicious? He drank more whisky and offered cigarettes.

"I don't smoke much until after the show," she said. "I have to be at the theatre again by half past seven."

Again; did that imply that he already knew she had been there once today?

"Oh, yes. You're in a new play, aren't you?"

She said soberly: "Yes, you must come and see it all through, one of these days."

So she knew.

Corliss felt his fingers itching—quivering, rather; it started at the tips and worked its way up through them, until it affected his hands and his arms. She had been there and knew he had watched her, knew that he could have killed the little man who had attacked him. Had she come here to tell him that? To—blackmail him? Nonsense; there was no need for a woman in her position to blackmail anyone, she was on the top of the world, had a big salary and the whole future in front of her; she wouldn't do that kind of thing.

Why had she come?

"I'd love to," he said. "Several of the notices were good, weren't they?"

"I can't complain. Mr. Corliss, why did you follow me about all the afternoon?"

He finished his drink.

This was another severe test, worse because it was so unexpected; but for the first time he felt a breath of relief; she appeared to think that he had followed *her.* His thoughts raced. It wouldn't be unusual for her to be followed about by admirers. Perhaps that was what she thought had happened. He couldn't be sure. She was looking at him with that faint, almost mocking smile—as if she knew much more than she had said about him and what he had done. The tingling sensation in his fingers faded, he completely forgot it.

He said: "It's a good way of spending spare time."

"Tell me the truth, please."

"Can't you guess?"

"No," she said. "As a matter of fact, I don't think you were interested in me, but in André. You went after him, after he'd left me at my home. Why are you so interested in him?"

Corliss said: "I think you must have made a mistake. I—"

"It was no mistake. You were at the theatre. You followed us to the restaurant and afterwards you followed us to my house. I don't know what happened after that but I saw your car move off behind André's. Why are you interested in André?"

Corliss laughed.

"He's a serious rival!"

"Don't be flippant, please."

Corliss didn't speak. The cooling breath of relief had turned into the hot wind of danger. She had seen him in the theatre; she had doubtless heard of the death of the little man. She would be able to add two and two together as well as the next. Her gaze was so steady and her eyes so clear. She had come because she wanted to know the truth and she was not going to be put off easily. Damn her!

Damn her?

There was some mystery about her, and he couldn't quite give it a name. He had been interested in Hilde Hansson but not in quite the same way as this. She looked so good and desirable, while standing there almost accusingly.

"I'm not being flippant," he said. "I wish you'd forget it, Miss Grahame. It doesn't concern you and it's better for you not to worry about it." The words sounded inane, but were the best he could manage.

"It does concern me."

"I assure you—" he was beginning to sound like 'Uncle' Bill Loftus in his most prosy mood.

"You were interested in André. He is my fiancé. Anything

to do with him, interests me. Why did you follow him? What were you doing? What *work* are you doing?"

The only thing that would serve was a lie; a lie so comprehensive that she would at least have to consider the possibility that it was true.

"You've got it all wrong," he said, and went towards her. Now that he had made up his mind, he could see this through, he'd convince her. He touched her hand and smiled very gently. "You remember that we met at Cannes?"

"Of course. That is how I recognised you."

"I've never forgotten it," Corliss said. "I've seen all your plays several times—I've watched from the circle and sometimes from the gods, so that you shouldn't know. I've read every paragraph in the newspapers about you. I've kept telling myself that I was a fool, and yet—well, I couldn't help it." His voice was low-pitched, he managed to put a vibrant edge to it. "Lately, it's been worse. Oh, I'll be honest—that's probably because I've had very little to do. I've fooled around with this girl and that, but—I always had to turn back to you. I knew you were engaged. I wanted to see this man Milanov, find out how far—things had gone. It was silly of me to come to the theatre this morning, but I couldn't keep away. I slipped out as soon as you'd left the stage. I had an idea Milanov would spend the rest of the day with you, and—well, call me crazy if you like, but I was overjoyed when he came away."

Corliss laughed, softly. The pressure of his fingers on hers had tightened as he had talked. He knew that he was convincing; he almost convinced himself. Then, quite suddenly, the next impulse came to him. He pulled her close, put his arm round her, and kissed her, fiercely.

She didn't draw back.

He kept his lips pressed tightly against hers. He felt the softness of her body, imagined that he could hear the beating of her heart. She didn't respond but didn't move. When at last he drew back, he was breathless; and she caught her breath. Her lipstick was smeared, her hat pushed a little to one side. She looked younger and even more attractive; enticing.

"You see," he said.

She still didn't move and didn't speak until she had her breath back. Then she picked up her drink and sipped it—her eyes twinkling.

"You make a good liar," she said.

"Iris!"

"Oh, please, don't pretend." Her voice was quite calm, she wasn't at all put out by what had happened. "You've lied very nicely, I liked it. But it's not true. If I were to ask you the titles of the plays I've been in, you just wouldn't know. And you couldn't have known that André and I were engaged because it didn't happen until last night, and he hasn't said a word to anyone. Nor have I. We're waiting until we know what's going to happen to this show, before we announce it."

Corliss said: "That kind of thing—"

"That kind of thing does *not* get spread about by accident. If you were in the play business you might have suspicions that something was happening, but you couldn't be sure. And anyhow, no one at all has been told the truth. This hasn't taken us very far, has it?"

Corliss didn't speak.

She smiled easily. "I'm sorry if I've made you feel a fool; I didn't mean to. I'm so anxious to know why you're interested in André." Beneath her laughter there was genuine anxiety.

Corliss shrugged.

"He has some old friends," Iris said, "and I've wondered what work he does. He never talks about his work, just laughs when I ask him about it. You know what his work is, don't you?"

"Look here—"

Iris said: "I suppose it was a waste of time coming. I hoped you'd tell me. I thought I knew you pretty well, although we only met for a few days. We exchanged addresses—remember. I was wrong about knowing you, and I'm sorry. But—"

She broke off, neither smiling nor laughing now, all the gravity was back, and behind it, fear. Corliss had a feeling that what she was going to say next really mattered to her. He didn't help her. He was wondering how he would get out of this, whether she guessed, or half guessed, what he was doing for Loftus. This was a thing which needed long experience— he had to decide whether to give her a further inkling of the truth, or just to let her go and guess what she liked. They would be wild guesses.

She said: "It's quite important to me, Mr. Corliss. Do you know anything *against* André?"

"No."

She flashed: "Is that true? Or a lie?"

"Now look here—"

"I'm afraid it's a lie," she said quietly. "I suppose I can't blame you, it was really outrageous of me to come, but I felt that I had to. You heard what happened at the theatre, didn't you?"

"The rehearsals?" He knew what she meant but might convince her that he didn't.

"No, no!" She shrugged off rehearsals. "So you don't know." She opened her handbag. Inside was a folded copy of *The Evening News*. She handed it to him, without a word, and as he glanced down, finished her drink. He read the headlines, about the dead man at the theatre, and the words *'Foul Play Say Police'*. There wasn't much more than a simple report of the finding of the body and the fact that the man's neck was broken. There was one significant sentence:

"The police are anxious for help in identifying the dead man, who is believed to be a Russian or a Pole."

"You see what I mean," Iris Grahame said.

Corliss forced a laugh.

"Well no. I haven't bought a paper, hadn't seen this. It's a strange business, but—"

"The man was found soon after we left the theatre," said Iris. "I'm probably crazy to tell you this, but the police know, anyhow, they're bound to find out everything they can about everyone who was in the theatre this morning. André could have killed him."

"What?"

"Well, he could," she said quietly, and for the first time she deliberately evaded his eyes. He felt a sudden lifting of his spirits; her idea might be fantastic, but it drew all suspicion away from him. "He was in the auditorium—"

"Well, so was I!"

"Yes, I suppose you could have killed the man," she said, so casually that it took his breath away. "But I'm not going to blind myself to any of the possibilities. You see, André knew this man, who accosted him in the street two days ago. They quarrelled. It—oh, never mind, they quarrelled, the man threatened, and André hit him. There was quite a scene, but luckily no one recognised me, and we managed to get away quickly. The man followed André about several times, of late. Now, you've started following André. Why?"

11

ADVICE

Corliss turned away from the girl, took her glass and went back to the cocktail cabinet. It was a little after half past six. He took his time, filling the glasses. He knew that she was looking at him intently. That last outburst had been almost incredibly naïve; a girl rather than a mature woman had spoken. She was worried and frightened, and obviously had reason to be. That didn't greatly matter, at this stage; what mattered was that she must feel sure that he had nothing to do with the killing.

He went nearer to her.

"Have another sherry," he said. "Look here, I'm not in a position to tell you much, Miss Grahame, my hands are tied, as it were. But I'm doing special work. One of my jobs is to watch André Milanov. I wish I could be more explicit, but I can't. I may be able to get permission to tell you, later on, but just now—nothing doing."

"I see," she said slowly.

"I'm really sorry. Mind you, I've no reason in the world to suspect that Milanov killed that man."

"Haven't you?" She wasn't convinced.

"No. I would say that he was back stage pretty soon, but—well, I slipped out immediately and just don't know. I don't even know why I'm ordered to watch Milanov—I'm told only what is considered good for me to know. I'm not being very helpful, am I?"

"Helpful enough," she said. "Oh, I won't ask any more questions, I can see that you can't answer. I know what I wanted to find out, now."

"There's no point in jumping to conclusions."

She smiled; and the smile seemed to hurt her.

"No, I suppose not. I don't know whether to say I'm sorry I came or not. On the whole, I think I'm glad. Mr. Corliss—"

Corliss took her hand gently.

"I know the Riviera spells what they call magic, but we were Charles and Iris then."

"Yes. Will you tell me more about André as soon as you can? You'll have to get special permission, I suppose, but—I must know."

"The moment I can tell you more, I will."

"Thank you," she said, quite simply. She put the second drink down, untasted. "I must go, I shall be late at the theatre. Thank you for being so friendly—and for lying so well." The laughter which followed that had a hollow ring, he knew that she was badly shaken.

"Look here, can we meet again? Lunch tomorrow, or—"

"Let me know when you've more news," she said.

She went to the door. He waited until she reached it, then stepped after her. He put his hands on her shoulders and looked frankly into her eyes; and she was good to look at.

"What do you suspect?" he demanded.

"It doesn't matter."

"It could matter a lot. You became engaged to the man last

night, but you must have had suspicions of something, before that. You knew about this chap who threatened Milanov. What do you suspect?"

She didn't try to free herself, as she said:

"I hardly know."

"You must know something."

"Oh, I'm crazy! Please—"

"Look here," said Corliss, and drew her nearer. Exerting pressure with his right hand hurt him, but he didn't flinch. "I put on an act just now—or it seemed to be an act. It's true that I haven't dogged your footsteps as much as I said I had, but I've never forgotten those few days in Cannes." The lie came out so easily, he almost believed it himself. "And you are a very lovely woman. I want to help, do you understand? I want to help—and I can't if you're not quite frank with me."

She said: "When you can tell me more, I'll talk more freely to you. I shouldn't have come, but—"

There was a ring at the front door bell. It cut sharply across her words, startling them both. Corliss glanced towards the door, across the tiny hall. He didn't want an interruption, but there was nothing else for it; any temptation she might have had to speak freely must have faded when that bell sounded.

He drew his hands away.

The caller rang again, twice.

"I'm sorry," said Corliss. "Look here, I must see you again tonight. Will you come here? I'll be able to tell you more, then, and—"

The caller put a finger on the bell and kept it there. Sounding inside the hall the bell was very loud and Corliss couldn't make her hear unless he raised his voice.

"Oh, damn! Telephone me." He remembered, suddenly, that he wouldn't be here. The caller was probably Loftus's man, who had come for his cases. "No, I may be out, I'll call you at the theatre. If that beggar doesn't stop ringing, I'll break his neck!"

He felt a sudden surge of anger; rage. It was so strong and tempestuous that it even surprised him. He checked himself and forced a smile—and wondered if she had seen the glint in his eye. Just for a moment, he had experienced a murderous impulse against the man who had interrupted them.

"Call me," she said.

"Right!" He went forward. The bell stopped ringing. He opened the door, prepared to shout at the caller, but the words died on his lips.

"Good evening," said André Milanov.

The Russian stepped into the hall before Corliss could stop him. Corliss heard Iris gasp and saw her back away, astounded. Milanov went to her, took her right hand and raised it to his lips. He pressed it, then let it fall gently. Next, he slipped his arm in hers, and turned to smile at Corliss.

He was a handsome beggar; much more handsome than his photograph had suggested. That was because of his expression and his colouring; he had a dark tan over a rather sallow complexion, and had bright, light brown eyes which gleamed, at that moment, with real merriment. Milanov had a quality of enjoying himself and a relish for life, and it revealed itself, then.

He squeezed Iris's arm, and said.

"So, you are old friends!"

"We met—" began Corliss.

"Please! It is right that my lovely Iris should have hand-some young men as her admirers, what is more fitting?" The extravagance of the words and the phrasing seemed to be natural to him. "We will not have explanations, they are such a bore. But my sweet, you will be late for the theatre. I would not like that, and I am sure that Jimmy, he would tear his hair, those few poor strands of grey hair, in worry."

"Yes, I must go." Iris was pale. Frightened?

"Your car is downstairs," said Milanov. "I will come down with you, unless Mr. Corliss—"

Corliss said: "I'm just going out. We'll all—"

"Oh, please!" The man's face seemed to be made of India-rubber, he twisted it now in an expression of desolation. "I am so anxious that we should talk, Mr. Corliss, it is obvious that we have many things in common. But now! I will set the minds of the two of you at rest. Of course, I knew that I was followed this morning, I knew that Iris observed that, and guessed that she would be worried. So, I had two reasons for being interested in the man who followed me. It was not so difficult to find out where he came, and—I come for a talk. After the show, we will all have supper together, please, and we shall discuss any problems. Now, Iris!"

He hustled her towards the door.

Corliss did nothing to stop them from leaving.

He closed the door behind them and turned back into the living-room. He had never known his heart thump so hard. This development was worse, in its way, than the attack in the theatre; it would be more difficult to deal with. Milanov would return, and—

The telephone bell rang sharply.

He hurried across the room and snatched off the receiver. "Yes?"

"This is Wilson," said a man in a voice which Corliss recognised on the instant—Reginald Wilson, the exquisite's. "Stall Milanov along. Get all you can out of him. Don't follow him when he leaves, we'll look after that. All clear?"

"Yes."

"Luck, old boy!"

116

Wilson rang off. Corliss stood for a moment with the receiver in his hand. The call had said so much more than Wilson's actual words. He felt as if Loftus and the Z men could see through brick walls. It was easy to explain, of course; Milanov had been followed and seen to come here, and Wilson had telephoned Loftus for instructions. That was obvious, but—was there something else? Were the Z men watching the flat all the time?"

They may not have known that Iris Grahame had come here; they would know that she had been, because they would see her getting into the car.

There was hardly time to breathe.

His second whisky and soda was barely touched. He put the glass to his lips. Then he drew it away, sharply; if he tossed whisky down his throat in every emergency, he would come to depend on the damned stuff. He carried the glass back to the cabinet.

Wilson hadn't given him a chance to speak, to ask advice.

He heard footsteps outside, and recalled that he had not heard Milanov's on the first visit. Had Milanov approached stealthily, or had he and Iris been too absorbed in what they were saying to notice anything that had happened outside?

He opened the door before Milanov pressed the bell.

The Russian stepped in, smiling, looking cherubic. He watched Corliss close the door, then clapped him on the back and went with him into the living-room, as if they were old cronies.

"But Corliss! You work miracles!"

Corliss said: "I don't know what—"

"Oh, my friend, you do know what I'm talking about," said Milanov, grinning as if he were delighted. "I come from a mutual friend of ours, of course, we work together." He took a card from his pocket—it looked like an ordinary visiting card.

He went across to the electric fire, switched on, and as the elements warmed up, held the card in front of the pale red bars.

Corliss joined him.

Milanov held the card out, and Corliss saw the hammer and sickle, with the two marks which had been on the metal symbol which His Excellency had shown him.

"So, we are friends together," said Milanov. "And to prove it, please, I will be grateful for a drink! You do not, of course, keep vodka." He was laughing silently.

"No."

"Schnapps?"

"No."

"Then it will have to be whisky," said Milanov. "How drinking habits change from nation to nation. Please! No soda. You only spoil it. Thank you, my friend!" He tossed the drink down. "Tell me, does Iris think that I killed the man in the theatre?"

Corliss moved away from the cabinet and the Russian, and stood looking at him, frowning, hostile. Milanov's smile grew set. The card was still in his hand, and the marks of the hammer and sickle were beginning to fade. He did not look at it, only at Corliss.

Was there any reason to doubt the truth about him?

Could he be taken at his face value?"

Was this an elaborate trick?

Corliss's mind raced as he returned the man's stare. The look of vivacity which had made Milanov seem handsome had vanished; he seemed to be menacing without words.

Corliss took out his cigarettes, he must gain time to think. Supposing this were part of the test which Loftus had set for him. How would it work? Give him a man to follow who was not against but *with* the Department; make him think that he was with an enemy; and then send Milanov along, to make sure. It would be—or it could be—deadly dangerous to make any admission to Milanov now.

Yet Milanov had that code sign.

Milanov said: "You do not believe me, my friend." The words were whispered.

Corliss said: "I don't know what that sign means—except the obvious one. If you're a Red—"

"My friend! Please! His Excellency—"

"I don't know what the hell you're talking about," Corliss said harshly. "His Excellency who? Who are you? What do you want?"

Milanov stood very still. The silence in the room was almost painful. Corliss's thoughts twisted and turned, he was both hunter and hunted. In playing safe, was he actually making trouble for himself?

"I think perhaps you will change your mind," said Milanov. "I will tell you how much I know. Today, you have followed me. Department Z is interested in me, I have known that for some time. I am also informed that you will work within the Department, for His Excellency. You know who that means. Now, Iris is alarmed. Why? Because a man who followed me before and with whom I have had trouble, was killed in the theatre. She knows that I was followed by you. She comes to find out why. How you satisfied her I am not sure. Without making trouble, I hope. I am here, on the excuse which is so obvious—because she has been here—with instructions for you."

Corliss said roughly: "Oh, are you?"

"Yes. You are instructed to give me a complete report on how far you have succeeded."

"You've made one hell of a mistake," Corliss said. "I don't

know anyone called His Excellency. I do know that card means Communism, and I hate commies."

"I see," said Milanov, softly. "So you do not believe me."

"That's it. I know you were at the theatre when the little man died. The police—"

He moved to the telephone.

Milanov dropped his right hand to his pocket. There was no obvious bulge there, the coat was cunningly cut; but Corliss felt quite sure that he carried a gun. Would he go this far if he were acting as a kind of *agent provocateur* for Department Z? It wasn't likely.

"You will not call the police."

He did not show his gun. He was no longer good looking; the expression in his eyes was ugly.

Corliss dialled a number, slowly.

Milanov walked across the room, watching his finger, he must have known that Corliss was not calling Whitehall 1212. His expression did not change, his hand did not move from his pocket but was bunched up inside. Was he holding a gun? Corliss felt sweat breaking out on his forehead. This was a desperate risk; he had been ordered not to call 'their' number from his flat. But would Loftus have the line tapped if he intended to move him?

The usual long *brrr-brrr* sound followed.

He could hear Milanov's breathing.

A man said: "Yes," in the same crisp voice which had answered him when he had last called this number.

He said: "Have I a visitor?"

"Yes."

"With instructions?"

"Yes."

Corliss didn't reply, but replaced the receiver. He ran his hand across his forehead; it came away wet. He turned and faced Milanov, who had taken his hand from his pocket and was smiling with relief. He hadn't enjoyed that interlude, either. He had shown Corliss something else; that he was weak and found decisions hard to make.

Corliss said: "This is too dangerous for me to take chances."

"I agree with you fully, my friend," said Milanov warmly. "I congratulate you on the way in which you have done this work. But now—you are satisfied?"

"Yes. I think it's crazy for you to have to come here, but I suppose you know what you're doing."

"That is right! We always know what we are doing," said Milanov. "Now! It is clear that you are working for Loftus. That is so?"

"Yes."

"Wonderful! We have one other working with them, but he is not very close to them, he is not active, as it would appear that you are active. I am to congratulate you, and you are to tell me everything—you understand, everything."

"You can start. Who was the man killed in the theatre?"

Milanov waved his hands. "It was unfortunate, that affair. He was, of course, one of us. He followed me, to find out whether I was followed. Iris discovered that, she was worried, so I arranged a quarrel with him in the street. He continued to watch over me, and discovered your interest. He was not aware of what you are doing, and he was far too enthusiastic. He tried to act when he should only have reported. He is one worker less, and he was clever in his way, but—"

Corliss went across to the cabinet and picked up his drink, tossed the whisky down and dropped the glass back on the flap of the cabinet, roughly. He didn't speak, but glared at Milanov; and the other man looked uneasy. It was good to be able to make him feel uneasy.

"What is worrying you?" Milanov demanded. "There will be casualties. They are inevitable. A life here, a life there—they do not greatly matter."

Corliss said slowly, harshly: "If you think I'm worrying about him, you're mistaken. I'm worrying about myself and the job I'm supposed to be doing. That fool could have killed me. He came pretty close to it. I thought His Excellency had this well organised. That doesn't seem like it."

"It was unfortunate—"

"Unfortunate! It was suicidal! Why do you think I've been told to get in with the Z men? So that some fool you forget to instruct can cut my throat."

"Corliss—"

"*Did* you forget to tell him?"

"I did not expect—"

Corliss said: "Somehow I don't think His Excellency would be very pleased, Milanov. I shouldn't make many more mistakes like that."

It was good to see the man lick his lips and avert his eyes, as if he were terrified; it was good to make a man cringe. Corliss felt a sense of power, and liked it. He laughed suddenly, went across to a chair and sat down.

"I'd better make it simple and hope that you won't forget to report this at once. Loftus has accepted me. The trick with the Bennett woman was successful. I am on trial. My first job is to watch you and to report your movements. After the theatre incident, I was relieved from that. I got hurt." He raised his hand but made no further reference to the little man. "I was also attacked by a man I found in the flat—perhaps you sent him."

"No, no!"

"I'd like to know who did," Corliss growled. "Listen. I'm being moved from here today. I have no useful information, except that Loftus sometimes meets at the *Hell's Bells* club, and sometimes at 31 Brigham Square. I am to move to another apartment, I don't yet know where. I am not to return to *The Fiddlers' Rest*."

Milanov said eagerly: "It is *very* good. Wonderful!"

"Tell me what I've told you."

Milanov shrugged his shoulders deprecatingly, but obeyed. He had every detail perfect; obviously had a mind trained to memorise words. He was still subdued, nothing like the man he had been when he had entered the flat.

"That's all right," Corliss said casually. "Now there's one other thing. Loftus and the Z men are good—really good. I'm watched. They won't give me a job that matters until I'm much deeper in their organisation than I am yet. I'm still on trial. While you were downstairs with Iris, I was telephoned and told to learn all I could from you."

"So."

"That's it. Don't make many mistakes, Milanov, because they'll pounce as soon as you do."

"Yes, they are clever," Milanov said.

"Now! Why did you come tonight? What made you think it was safe?"

"My friend! The opportunity was obvious. I had only to be jealous about Iris Grahame, isn't that so?"

"I'm not sure. I think it was asking for trouble. I'll tell Loftus that you came in a flaming temper because I'd followed you and you wanted to know why. Also that you threatened. They are already on to you, so that won't do any harm. To keep myself clear, I've got to damn you."

"Yes. I understand." Milanov was humble; *humble.*

"I hope you do. And I hope His Excellency gives you a different job, I don't want to have to watch you as well as the Z men. Why are you engaged to Iris Grahame?"

"That is my own affair," Milanov said sharply.

"Is it?" Corliss sneered. He knew that his lip was curling, he knew what he looked like, but it didn't matter with Milanov, who was already cowed. "I'm not sure. There isn't room for young love in this work."

"It is not simply that I am attracted by her," Milanov said carefully. "You will learn, soon, that we are winning over many well-known public figures. When the time comes, we shall want them to declare themselves. The fact of stage and screen and sports idols speaking for the Cause will have a great effect on the public. I am to find out if she will join us."

"Will she?"

"It is possible," Milanov said.

Corliss shook his head slowly, and the other tried to avert his eyes but could not; Corliss felt the influence which he was exerting over the man, and it went to his head like wine.

"No, it isn't possible, Milanov. She wouldn't touch the Cause, she's blind to the truth and loyal to the old standards. You ought to know that by now. You're wasting your time with her. Worse, you're wasting *our* time. I should report that she is a hopeless case, if I were you, and stop dancing attendance on her. Break that engagement."

Milanov said: "I shall report. The other is my affair."

"Ours," Corliss said.

Milanov did not answer.

Twenty minutes after Milanov had left, Wilson and another man whom Corliss did not know, came to tell him his new address and to collect his cases. He told Wilson that Milanov had spotted him and called here, using the pretext that he had followed Iris Grahame. Wilson seemed satisfied. Corliss left the flat just after eight o'clock, and went to his club for dinner, leaving his car at a nearby garage for servicing. He walked from the club towards his new flat, which he knew only as an address: 81 Hyburn Mansions, W.1; it was central enough. As he mingled with the crowd, he felt a strange sense of power—power over *them*. Sometimes, he felt a tingling sensation in his fingers—twice it came when he saw a small man, who could have been mistaken for the man in the theatre. Then, he felt his lips twisting in that sneering smile, and had to check himself. He walked slowly along Piccadilly. He kept picturing the change in Milanov's manner; that was when his sense of power had first made itself felt.

He was *good.*

He was twenty times better than Milanov. 'They' were fools to rely on the Russian. He itched to make a report, damning the man. He did not want to waste time on Milanov, and did not want Milanov to spend time with Iris Grahame.

But she wasn't a hopeless case; not by a long way. Milanov would never win her over, but he—

Taken by a sudden impulse, he hailed a taxi and went to the Crown Theatre. The play was well into the second act, but he had expected that. There were only two back stalls available, one on a gangway. He sat and watched the play, untroubled by the fact that because he had not seen the first act he couldn't pick up the story; again he felt the fascination of the playing. Iris was superb.

The audience thought so.

The curtain fell on the second act, before the triangle scene. Corliss sat in his seat, and there were a dozen empty seats about him, during the interval. He waited impatiently for the curtain to rise.

Iris wasn't on in the opening scene, the two men were— husband and lover. He wasn't really interested in them, only in Iris. He lit a cigarette, and an usherette came and reminded him that there was no smoking. He felt irritated as he put it out.

Then, out of the gloom, a man came and stood beside him, and pressed something into his hand. It was of metal. He felt sudden tension as he fingered it. The shape was of a hammer and sickle; there were two tiny flaws in the smooth edge.

The man whispered: "You will report on Milanov, quickly, please. Telephone the number you know."

12

PUNISHMENT

The eyes in the portrait above the solitary man at the desk were as vivid as ever, but Milanov did not look at them. He looked only at His Excellency, who sat reading a typewritten document. He must have seen Milanov come in, but had not looked up and showed no sign that he knew he was not alone.

Milanov stood motionless.

His Excellency put the paper aside, and picked up another. He still did not look up, but began to read aloud. He kept his voice at a low, monotonous level. He read a report, which summarised what Corliss had already telephoned, and summarised, too, the time which Milanov had spent with Iris Grahame. The detail in the report was exhaustive; there seemed nothing which was not known. There was no change in that flat voice as he read of the attack on Corliss in the theatre.

His Excellency finished, and looked up; his eyes were as compelling as those in the portrait. Milanov shivered.

"That is not good," His Excellency said.

"Excellency, I can assure you—"

"You will return to Moscow," His Excellency said.

"Excellency!"

"And is it not a privilege for you to return to Moscow? Is it something against which you should protest?"

"No—no, Excellency."

"I'm glad you do not think so. You will go now to your home, pack sufficient clothes for one night, nothing more, and you will then be instructed where to report for the journey, which will be by air."

"Yes, Excellency."

"There is one thing to remember," His Excellency said. "There are some advantages in England. You have been here too long, you have lived too softly. You might think that it would pay you to give away some information which would assure your freedom in England. It would not, Milanov."

"Nothing so treacherous would enter my mind, Excellency!"

"It is to be hoped not. You will be watched. You have committed many crimes. You would receive no mercy from the English, if they were to know of them. They would be told. You will be sensible, Milanov, and pack your clothes and report, as instructed."

"Yes, Excellency."

His Excellency nodded.

Milanov walked through the narrow room, and the door opened, without a sound. A dark figure stood outside, and the door closed behind him. He went along a narrow passage and up a short flight of stairs and found himself in another building, accompanied all the time by the man who had stood outside the door. He was shown out by a back way, and in fact left a private house near the building in which he had been interviewed.

His car was outside.

He sat at the wheel; and his fingers were cold, he kept shivering. He knew that he was being watched. He started off, and another car followed him. He drove straight to Grove Court and pulled up outside his own house. When he approached it, the front door was opened; 'his' staff was not really his; they watched him closely and reported regularly, or His Excellency could not have known what he did know.

The three lower floors were offices.

Milanov went up in the lift, accompanied by 'his' servant, to the fourth floor. An open suitcase, a lightweight of the type used for air travel, was lying open on the bed. 'His' servant stood in the doorway and watched him, without offering to help.

Milanov felt hot and cold in turns.

His face was ashen grey and his cheeks and forehead were greasy with sweat. His hands and fingers were damp, too, although it was not really warm in the room. He started to pack. Whenever he stopped the man at the door coughed, as if to spur him on. He would be accompanied to the point of embarkation, not left alone for a moment until he reached Moscow.

Then?

He lit a cigarette. His fingers trembled. He would be given no chance to betray 'them', they knew the danger and were making quite sure of that.

He drew back from his case. The man coughed. Milanov did not look at him, but moved towards the dressing-table. It was a small one, in front of a large window. The window was closed.

Milanov *ran* towards it.

"Stop!" The word came softly from behind him, he could hear the menace in the man's voice. He ignored it, reached the window and flung it up. The 'servant' was bounding after him as he climbed out of the window—and jumped.

The man in the room heard the heavy thud below.

Loftus was on duty, alone, in the office of Department Z, when the telephone showing the pink light rang. He took it off quickly:

"Yes."

"It's Burtt here—T—T—R—"

"Fire away."

"Quite a turn of events," said Burtt, almost indifferently. "I followed Milanov. He went to their suspected headquarters, was there for an hour, left by the back way and drove straight back to his home. Fifteen minutes later he jumped out of the top window and broke his neck. Broke a lot of other things, too. I saw it—he dived, head first. No doubt, he meant to do away with himself."

Loftus snapped: "Yes?"

"I nobbled a copper, and we didn't lose any time getting in. There was no one else at home, although one man was there during the time, I saw him at the window. He must have cleared out the back way. There was nothing in Milanov's pockets except one of the cards with the hammer and sickle sign which shows up when the secret ink is warmed. I've started to look through the flat, but need some help. I haven't found anything yet, and doubt if I shall."

"Keep trying. I'll send someone else."

"Thanks."

"Anything more?" asked Loftus.

Burtt said: "Nothing in the way of facts, Bill, but our new recruit seems to be blazing a trail, doesn't he?"

Corliss's new flat was smaller than the old one, and less modern. It was comfortably furnished, and gave an impression of having been lived in recently. Corliss liked it. Also, he liked the sight of a carved oak court cupboard, of Jacobean period and black with centuries of use; it was well stocked with wines and spirits. There were two telephones, one in the only bedroom, which had twin beds. He sauntered about the flat. The bathroom wasn't exactly modern but was clean and had a shower. The kitchenette had been modernised, the larder was full; yes, someone had lived here quite recently.

The living-room, the largest one in the flat, had no sofa, but five or six armchairs and several stools and pouffes. It was shabby but comfortable—and he wondered if this place was used for meetings. But it wouldn't be the headquarters of the Department; he still had to find that.

There was no hurry; whatever anyone said to him, he wouldn't let himself be hurried. Not that he need worry; 'they' were good even if Milanov was a fool. There was no doubt about the cause of Milanov's trouble; he had fallen in love with Iris Grahame and had tried to do his job while pressing his suit. The old-fashioned phrase made Corliss grin.

He decided not to telephone Iris.

He was glad that he had reported up to date. The encounter in the theatre had been perfect, it was almost certain that no one had noticed it. The man hadn't been there more than a moment. Even if Loftus had had him watched there, nothing had been betrayed. The first objective would be to convince Loftus that he did not need watching all the time. The need to cover both flanks and rear was trying, but—

He hadn't done so badly; he was *good*.

This job was cut out for him.

He hoped 'they' didn't use many men like Milanov. If they continued to use Milanov, he would begin to doubt whether they were as thorough and clever as he had been led to believe. He felt a little uneasy, but tried to shrug the thought away; he would find out the truth eventually.

At half past eleven, the telephone bell rang.

He took off the receiver.

"Don't go out," said Loftus. "I'm coming to see you."

Loftus loomed as large and bulky as ever, and kept a poker face. Corliss felt uneasy; he wished he could be sure of what was passing through the ungainly man's mind. Loftus accepted a glass of beer and lowered himself into one of the large armchairs—so large that it almost seemed as if it had been put here for him.

"Well, how's it going, young Corliss?"

"All right, I hope."

"Keeping a firm control on those hands of yours?"

"I don't need telling twice. Anyhow, that theatre job was unavoidable. I had the wind up twice this evening."

"Why?"

"Iris Grahame's arrival shook me. Wilson's told you about that, I suppose?"

"Yes. You didn't make a very good job of shadowing Milanov, did you?"

"I take it that if you'd wanted someone who wouldn't be noticed, you'd have used someone with more experience," Corliss said impatiently. "I'm not omnipotent, and there are limits to the jobs I can do at this stage."

Loftus actually smiled.

"I'm glad you realise that," he said dryly. "Take it easy. You say the girl was anxious to find out why you were interested in Milanov, and there was this story of the little man who quarrelled with Milanov in the street. Could be."

"It's what she told me!"

"I'm not calling either of you a liar," Loftus said calmly. "And when Milanov came, he was nervous."

"I'll say he was!"

"He had cause to be. He's working on the other side. Also he—"

"One day I suppose I'll know who the other side is," Corliss said, with what he judged to be the proper mixture of friendliness and exasperation. "There are limits to how much I can see in the dark."

"You've a mind, haven't you? Use it. Anyhow, Milanov committed suicide, an hour or so ago."

Corliss said slowly: "*Did* he, then?"

He felt a surge of jubilation but schooled himself to show only surprise; though he wasn't surprised. In his heart, he'd known it to be inevitable. If it were really a case of suicide, Milanov had been driven to it, and he'd helped to drive him there. *Power.* He already knew about the ruthlessness 'they' showed; here was further convincing proof of their thoroughness.

"You don't need any more telling that this is a dangerous job, do you?"

Corliss laughed. "I'd taken that for granted. There's something I didn't tell Wilson," he said abruptly. "I wasn't sure whether I should, and saved it up for you. I don't think it's of first importance, but Iris Grahame thought Milanov had killed my chap in the theatre. At least, that was her reason for coming to see me, if she can be believed."

"Didn't you believe her?"

"I'm not sure," said Corliss. "Milanov thought she was worth a lot of trouble, and that may mean that she's worth some attention from us. Just an idea, I'll make you a present of it."

"Thanks."

"And I'll have to tell her something. She was already halfway to thinking Milanov was a spy and I an agent. She's no fool. I stalled, but it wasn't easy. Is it all right for me to say I'm a Special Branch man?"

Loftus surprised him by answering after only a moment's pause:

"Yes. And I've another job for you."

"That's fine, keep me busy."

Loftus said: "I want a thorough search made of Iris Grahame's house. I want to find out whether this was a case of true love or conspiracy or spy spying on spy. I want you to get one thing clear, young Corliss. There is a notion running around that we have only one enemy—Russia or the Cominform or the *Communist International*. It's a nonsense notion. There are dangers from other sources. When you read in the newspapers that Fascism isn't dead, that's precisely true. Nation hasn't ceased spying upon nation, even those with whom they've sworn friendship. Quite the most able espionage man the Branch was ever had to deal with was an American working for America. Get that clear, will you."

Corliss said slowly: "Yes. The lesson's gone home."

"Keep the door closed on it," said Loftus.

He left soon afterwards, giving no further instructions. He did not refer to espionage again, but he had made it clear what they were doing—tonight was the first time he had actually admitted that. He'd widened the issues considerably; wonderful! If he or anyone else thought that the other people were worth a minute's time, the better for His Excellency! Loftus called them members of a 'branch', too, had not yet admitted that they were Z men. There was a coolness in Loftus's manner towards him which Corliss wished weren't there, but the man seemed prepared to trust him, where he did not trust Iris Grahame.

He, Corliss, had plenty of excuse for paying Iris a lot of attention, much more than Milanov. Suicide? It didn't matter how the man had died, he had been a careless, incompetent agent. And—he was out! There was plenty of room for good men at the top.

It was bright and sunny. The weather made a difference to one's outlook; so did a good night's sleep.

Corliss hadn't opened his eyes until just after eight o'clock. Then he had found newspapers tucked in the letter box and had read them while making and drinking tea. There was a small paragraph about a Russian named Milanov who had leapt from a fourth floor window in the West End and killed himself; the newspapers didn't say much. There was more about the murder of the man in the auditorium of the Crown Theatre. Iris got a big splash of publicity, was prominently pictured and featured, was quoted as saying: *"I am quite sure it did not happen while we were rehearsing."* He did not think it likely that there would be any spare seats at the Crown for some time to come; this publicity was a gift from the gods to the management and the company.

At nine, Corliss went out, fetched his car from the garage and drove by a roundabout route to St. John's Wood. He was quite sure that he wasn't followed. He drove past Iris Grahame's house three times, to make sure; no one took any notice of him. It was possible that the house was already being watched from one of the gardens or houses opposite, but not really likely; it hardly seemed worth the trouble to put a man on now. Loftus had shown a greater degree of trust in him than before; he was probably suitable impressed.

Corliss turned the car off the wide road and into the drive of the house. It was surrounded by a high brick wall, cemented at the top. House, walls and garden seemed old but the garden was neat and obviously someone here liked gardening. Beds of daffodils and tulips, the tulips not yet blooming, of wall-flowers and other plants, made the square patch at the front

135

look attractive; so did the large square lawn, which had just received its first spring cutting. The house was newly painted, the brass letter-box and knocker shone.

He pulled up outside a square, pillared porch. He did not think he had been noticed from the house itself, but waited for a few minutes to see whether anything happened. Nothing did. The household might be late in getting up, as Iris probably hadn't returned from the theatre until after midnight. There were no papers in the letter-box; and there were two damp rings where milk bottles had stood not long ago. Someone was up and about, then.

He got out and rang the bell, giving three sharp bursts. A maid answered almost immediately; a middle-aged, timid-looking woman. But she didn't open the door wide, and only just showed herself in her blue overall. She did not wait for him to speak.

"She's not up!" There was a waspish note in her voice.

Corliss said: "You don't know who I've come to see, yet, it might be you, Lizzie."

"Don't you Lizzie me! Miss Grahame isn't up yet. It's disgraceful, you people worrying her at this hour of the morning. She won't see you later, either, none of you!"

The maid pushed the door to. Corliss moved his foot and stopped it from closing.

"I'm not a report," he said. "Tell Miss Grahame that Mr. Charles Corliss has called, will you?"

"Mr. Corliss!" the maid's voice, expression and manner changed as if he had waved a wand. "Oh, she'll see *you*! Come in, come in, she'll see you."

It was going to be easy; he was halfway to success already.

He stepped inside and the door closed on him.

13
SEARCH

I ris came hurrying down the stairs. She wore an apple green house-coat, high at the neck, with wide shoulders and flared sleeves. Her hair was untidy and fell to her shoulders; it was the colour of ripe corn. Her eyes were wide with distress, and as he hurried towards her, she gripped his hands tightly.

"Have you heard?"

"That's why I'm here."

"It's unbelievable!"

"It's happened," said Corliss gently, "and you aren't going to improve the situation by worrying about it. Where can we talk?"

"In here." Iris led the way into a homely room, with books in open shelves on two walls, a corner fireplace, a bowl of daffodils and, by an easy chair without arms, a work-basket, open as she had left it when she had last been working. On a table was a sewing-machine, with a polished wooden cover. It was hard to associate that with Iris Grahame, yet this was obviously her room. There were several water colours on the walls and, on an upright piano, three photographs; one was of André Milanov.

"The newspapers are upstairs," she said, and sounded breathless. "Shall I fetch them? Annie didn't know. She just brought the papers in with the tea, as usual. I telephoned you, but there was no answer."

"I've moved."

"Moved! Do you mean—"

"I don't mean anything, except that you'll have to call me at a different number," said Corliss. "You're worrying too much, my sweet, and it's been a hell of a shock. It would have been for anyone, and after the strain you had yesterday, it hit so much harder."

"Yes," she said. She looked at the photograph; it had been taken when Milanov's bubbling personality was evident, and had caught him in his most attractive mood. "I just can't believe it, Charles. Yesterday he was so gay, even last night—"

"Did you see him after the show?"

"No. It didn't worry me, he said he might not be able to make it last night. It was this damned work of his!"

"Now take it easy." He put an arm gently round her shoulders, but she wasn't crying or anywhere near crying. "People have all kinds of queer jobs to do. Some of them get hurt while doing them."

She turned her head and faced him, with those great eyes so grave and her expression so intent.

"Charles—was he a spy?"

"My dear—"

"I suppose you'll never tell me the truth," said Iris. "You're not allowed to. You were watching him because he was suspected of spying, wasn't he? He was a Russian. He told me that he was a white Russian, that he hated the *Politburo* and everything to do with it, but probably he was working for them. Tell me, Charles."

Corliss said slowly: "Yes, Iris, that's right."

"And you—"

"You can look at it two ways," Corliss said. "Either that I chased him to his death, and he preferred suicide to being caught. Or else that I drove him to kill himself, which was better for him than the disgrace of a trial and perhaps execution." He took his arm away and moved slowly towards the piano and stared into Milanov's face; he wanted to laugh at the picture, to mock the man who was dead, but his features were composed and his voice pitched very low. "I've permission to tell you a little, my dear. I've a job to do. It's called Special Branch work. I've been at it some time. There was reason to suspect that André worked for another power. I didn't and don't know which power it was—it might not have been Russia. He knew that I suspected him. Last night, he really came to try to find out how much I knew about him."

"And—you knew so much?" It was difficult to hear her words but she didn't look away from him. He studied the photograph; somehow, it wasn't easy to meet her eye.

"Enough, apparently."

"I see," said Iris. "It was just one of those things. It's strange, you know. I—loved him. I *did* love him. When he was with me and we were laughing and gay, there was no one more wonderful in the world, and yet—I was always uneasy. I wouldn't have come to you last night if that weren't true. I could never feel happy about it when I was away from him. I never found the courage to ask him bluntly—"

"It's as well you didn't," said Corliss, and turned and looked at her.

"What do you mean?"

"The man who died in the theatre yesterday knew a little,

and—you knew a little. Or you guessed. It makes no difference. Spying's a damnable game. There aren't any rules. It comes so often to the issue—his life or yours. That's another of those things, Iris. I wish it weren't so. But I'm glad you didn't ask him that question."

She said very slowly and as if wonderingly: "He wouldn't have killed me."

"Forget it! I shouldn't have said that." He forced a laugh and linked his arm through hers. "It's an odd situation. No matter how you try to look at it, you'll always come back to the conclusion that I hounded him to his death. I'd rather anything had happened than this, because—I'd hoped. I could have beaten him, had he been alive, but dead—"

"Don't, Charles."

"Oh, I'm being a brute! And it's time we talked seriously. You know there's one inevitable consequence of this, don't you?"

She looked at him with gravity clear in her eyes. That way, she was superbly beautiful. She stood quite still, without speaking, but the question was there all the same: "What consequence?"

"You'll be involved," Corliss said.

The question changed to "How?" but she kept silent, standing like a statue in alabaster.

"You are known to have been friendly with André, and in spite of what you said last night, your engagement must have been rumoured. You were splashed in all the newspapers this morning because you happened to be at the theatre when the little man was killed. So was André. People will link up the two affairs. They'll assume that André killed the man and then killed himself to avoid trial. It's going to smear you with a lot of mud, Iris. I'm terribly sorry, but it's obviously true. You know that, don't you?"

She said: "Yes," as if it hurt her to speak.

"And you'll have to decide how to tackle it. It isn't any use putting the bar up against reporters. You might succeed while you're at home but you can't dodge them at the theatre. Yours is one of the names that makes news. If you don't make a statement, words will probably be put in your mouth or reported at second hand."

"What do you suggest that I should do?"

"Be quite frank. Admit you were engaged to André. You hadn't quarrelled, and you can't understand what happened. That's quite simple and your own press agent would agree that it's the right thing to do."

"And after that?"

"You've got to try to get André out of your system. It won't be easy, but it can be done."

"That isn't what you've really got in mind," said Iris quietly.

"It is. But I've a strong recommendation to make—I sound like a chairman of directors, don't I? That you get André out of your system by finding out all you can about him, and by telling me of everything and anything he said that might throw light on what he was doing. We don't know what he was doing, we only suspected that it wasn't so good."

"There's nothing I can say to help."

"You'll find that there is. Odd words he used, odd phrases, places he visited—all that kind of thing will be useful. We shall have to find out who his friends were, where he spent his time when he wasn't with you—all that and much more. Checking on the past of a man who's dead isn't easy, and you can help. It's important that you should."

"Who *are* you, Charles?"

"I've told you—I'm a member of the Special Branch."

"I see," she said slowly. "I suppose you're right. I'll do what I can to help, but I don't think it will be much good. There's something else, isn't there?"

Corliss said: "Never mind it! There's plenty of time, and—"

"Let's get it all over."

He put his arm round her shoulders again.

"All right, Iris, you're probably wise. André was working for another power. His employers may suspect that he talked too freely to you. They may be afraid that you'll be able to give something away. In spite of what I said earlier, it's pretty obvious that they drove him to suicide, possible that they might try to harm you. I'm sorry, but it has to be said sooner or later."

She showed no reaction at all to that.

It puzzled him. He'd known that he was likely to frighten her, and it would have frightened most women. She took it too calmly, and that disappointed him. It was as if she had resisted the power that he had over her.

"I suppose you're right," she conceded. "What do you suggest I do about it? It's all nonsense, of course, I don't know anything of his work, but—"

"You'll have to be very careful where you go and what you do—and be especially cautious with strangers. I shall recommend that you're watched by—let's say a friend of mine. One or two of my friends, in fact, will always keep an eye on you, until the period of emergency is over. Isn't that wise?"

"I suppose so."

"Give me an itinerary of your probable movements for today and the rest of the week, let me know if there are going to be any changes. Tell me what you can about your maid, who else lives here, when the house is likely to be empty. That's important—the house must be watched when no one is at home. Otherwise you might come in one day to find an unexpected visitor."

She shivered; that was better!

"It's like a nightmare."

"It *is* a nightmare but it'll soon be over if you'll do what I say."

"All right," said Iris. "Is there anything more?"

"It ought to be enough if you'll do all this," said Corliss.

She nodded, as if she fully understood.

She lived alone in the house, with the maid. There was a gardener who worked three days a week—this was not one of his days on duty. The maid always had her half-days when Iris was due at a matinée, and there was one this afternoon.

Corliss went back to his new flat. No one waited for him, there were no messages, and no one called. He had luncheon on his own, sent up from the restaurant. He spent an hour going over the situation in his mind and came to one inescapable conclusion: complete success could not come until he had won Loftus's confidence, and he had failed to do that yet, partly because there hadn't been time, partly because he hadn't brought off a big coup. If he were able to report a completed search at Iris Grahame's house that night, it would probably make all the difference in his relationship with Loftus.

It wasn't quite so simple as that.

He must make the search in such a way that none knew, at first, who was responsible. He must prove to Loftus how good he was. Gradually, he evolved a plan by which he could probably succeed.

Corliss left the flat soon after lunch, drove in his sports car to his bank, drew out a hundred pounds in cash, and then drove to St. James's Square, where he parked the car, then he went on by foot to Piccadilly Underground Station. He did not know for certain whether he was followed. He went down the subway and stood near the fruit store, watching those who came after him. He saw no one he knew; he wasn't likely to recognise any man whom Loftus had detailed to see that he did his job properly.

He booked a ticket to Edgware, went down to the trains and took the first that came along. At the next station he jumped up, hurried through the subways to a train going in the other direction, travelled past four stations, then changed to another line. Half an hour after leaving Piccadilly, he stood at the exit from the tube at Waterloo. He saw no one whom he had seen before that day; he felt sure that he was no longer being followed.

He hurried out into Lambeth Road, tried two garages and found a third which hired out 'drive-yourself' cars. He paid a fifty pound deposit, and drove off in a newish Austin. He wished it had more power, but it would do for driving about London. He went to the East End, and at an old second-hand shop, in Mile End Road, bought a suit of rough clothes, which fitted him fairly well. At another second-hand shop, he bought an old theatrical make-up kit and a suitcase. He drove to Liverpool Street, walked slowly through the smoky, noisy station and, still satisfied that he hadn't been followed, went to a cloak-room.

There was a small mirror in the dressing-room. He changed quickly into the old suit, and made up a little. He didn't overdo it, but went to a lot of trouble to fit a small moustache and to darken the skin beneath his eyes. When he left with his own clothes in the case, no one was likely to recognise him without a close scrutiny. He drove immediately to St. John's Wood and reached Iris's house just after three-thirty. When he drew up outside the front door, he took out the small roll of adhesive tape and stuck a strip round each finger and thumb, to make sure he would leave no fingerprints.

He knocked, and rang the bell; there was no answer, the house was empty all right. He walked round to the back. This was overlooked by houses some distance off, but two large plane trees hid him if he kept at a certain spot. He was at the kitchen window.

The window was shut but the catch wasn't fastened. He owed a lot to his war-time training, including a knowledge of the quickest way to force a window. Within five minutes of his arrival, he was inside the house, with the window closed again. He walked quickly through all the rooms, to get the hang of the place. It was a large house, much larger than Iris Grahame really needed; that didn't matter. He glanced through the rooms on the attic floor; they were crowded with old furniture and used as store-rooms; he wasn't likely to find anything of interest there. The bedrooms on the next floor down all seemed to be unused. The first floor was more hopeful.

He found Iris's bedroom.

There was something in its lofty spaciousness and in the quiet colour scheme of pale blue and grey which was characteristic of the actress. On the dressing-table was a photograph of Milanov. Corliss gave the smiling face a mock salute, then began to search the dressing-table, cautiously, careful to replace everything where he had found it. He became absorbed in the task; it was fascinating. He knew that Loftus suspected the actress of working with Milanov; knew exactly what kind of thing to look for.

What should he do, if he found evidence that she was on His Excellency's staff?

He laughed the absurd thought off; there wasn't a ghost of a chance of that. He found oddments of jewellery, none of great value; a wardrobe crammed with clothes, all of good quality, all with style.

In the bottom of the wardrobe he found a locked drawer.

He used a thin screw-driver to force the lock. Unavoidably he left traces of what he had done, but they wouldn't be noticed unless there were a close examination.

Inside, were letters, all were from Milanov. There was nothing else.

He read three, which he picked out at random. It was exactly right. Milanov had written much as he had talked. There was nothing here to implicate Iris; these were glowing, rather cloying, love letters. As he read, he felt his lips curling back in the sneer which was now familiar; he let it stay.

Ought he to read more letters?

He chose another two, at random; they were little different from the others; sick-making stuff. Why on earth a woman like Iris Grahame had been impressed by the man and had become engaged to him, almost defied understanding; there was no accounting for taste. Silly thought! He put the letters away and locked the drawer; he'd made more marks on it than he had expected, she *might* realise what had happened.

Was there really any point in concealing the fact that someone had been here?

He couldn't make up his mind. It would give Iris a shock if she knew that there had been burglars, she would probably lean on him more than ever. It wouldn't take five minutes to make it obvious that the place had been ransacked. But he hadn't finished yet, there must be a safe. He didn't find it in the bedroom or in any of the rooms on this floor. He went downstairs. Would she have a safe downstairs? It was usual to keep it above ground level.

He went into the morning room, where she had talked to him. Everything looking exactly the same, except that the work-basket was closed. He moved some of the books aside, then went through them all to make sure that no papers were lodged behind them. He found none; but behind one of the bookshelves, he found the safe.

It was built into the wall.

He stood back, frowning. First he had been given the task of following Milanov, and blamed because he'd been noticed although he'd no special training for the job. Now, he had to try to do another for which he'd had no real training; Loftus would hardly expect him to open the safe.

But that was exactly what Loftus wanted, to find out how resourceful he was. He must impress the man favourably.

He found that the shelves were easily movable, and took them away. The door of the safe, which was about a foot square, was painted the same colour as the wall-paper, so that it couldn't be easily noticed. It looked impregnable to a man without proper tools or the knowledge to use them. He stood back. If he had a key—

Had Iris taken the keys with her?

He'd found none upstairs.

He left the safe and searched the rest of the room. He was beginning to think that it was a waste of time, he would find nothing here. He felt acutely depressed and irritable. Soon, the only thing he hadn't searched was the work-basket. He opened it and looked at a mass of cotton reels, mending silks, buttons, buckles—all the paraphernalia a woman needed. He took each thing out of its little section—and beneath some loose darning wool were five keys.

Keys.

He snatched them up and swung round to the safe. As he did so, something moved at the window, but he noticed nothing. He tried three keys; they were too large. The fourth seemed the right size. He inserted it; yes, it fitted. He felt almost sick with excitement as he twisted, and the lock moved. He heard it click back. He drew away, leaving the key in the lock, and then slowly opened the door.

It gave him no trouble.

There were two partitions in the small safe. He took out several jewel boxes, a cash-box and some legal looking documents which were tied with red tape. He laid them all aside. There was a small cardboard box left in the safe. He took it out, and pulled the lid off.

Before it came off, he heard a movement behind him. It was the first sound he had heard since coming in here.

He crouched there, absolutely still, and his right hand moved towards his pocket.

Had it really happened? Or had it been his imagination?

He heard no other sound.

He touched the gun. He would have to move, once he had taken it out, because his right hand pocket was away from the door and away from whoever was there—if anyone was. It was all he could do to pretend that he had noticed nothing. Slowly, he stood up and looked out of the window, with the box in his left hand.

He heard another movement, soft, stealthy, as if someone were creeping towards him.

The gun was halfway out of his pocket, now.

He thought he heard someone else, breathing softly.

He snatched the gun out, and swung round—and as he did so, a big, burly man smashed at his head with a broom. It struck him on the side of the head and sent him lurching against the wall, but he didn't lose his grip on the gun.

The man smashed at him again.

Corliss fired twice at his stomach.

14
HIDE THE BODY

The two reports from the gun seemed deafening. The man stood with the broom drooping in his hand, an expression of pain and astonishment on his big face. The astonishment was greatest. He looked ludicrous, and didn't even cry out. The broom dropped. The man swayed, and his hands moved towards his stomach. The bullets had gone high, blood stained the khaki shirt where the coat and waistcoat gaped open.

The thick lips parted.

"You—" the man croaked.

Then he crumpled up and fell.

Corliss didn't move. The roar of the shots was still in his ears.

The man had fallen on his side. Blood dripped from the wound towards the carpet but actually fell on to the skirt of his coat, which saved the floor. There was no sound from outside, nothing to suggest that the shots had been heard.

Corliss moved forward, slowly.

He turned the man over, so that the blood didn't drip or

run on to the coat or on to the floor. He buttoned the coat round the thick waist. Then he went to the window and looked out on the narrow stretch of garden which ran up to the high wall dividing it from the next garden.

Nothing stirred.

The other's eyes were half closed and his mouth was slack. Corliss felt his pulse, but that was a superfluous gesture, it wasn't beating.

Who was the man?

Another thief? One of His Excellency's agents? One of Loftus's men, who'd followed him, after all? Corliss felt a sick sense of dread but none of horror, that he had killed again. Dread merged into anger against the man who had complicated this situation. On impulse, he turned and kicked the heavy body in the ribs; it quivered a little.

"Fool!" Corliss spoke to himself, of himself. He had started to sweat, felt warm and clammy all over. Then he came to the obvious conclusion: the body mustn't be found. If Loftus knew that he had killed again, he would probably wipe him off the list of agents. *The body mustn't be found.* How could he get rid of it, how—

His gaze fell on the telephone.

He went to it quickly and, almost without thinking, dialled 'their' number. This time the call was answered quickly, and the speaker was a different man from the man with the crisp, impersonal 'yes'.

"Who is that?"

Corliss said: "This is urgent."

"Who is it?"

"Corliss." He whispered the name which stuck in his throat.

"What do you need?"

Was it safe to talk? Safe or not, he had to.

"I have to remove—" he looked down at the flabby face of the dead man, and added with a gulp: "A large parcel."

"Parcel?"

"Like—Milanov."

"Oh." There was only a slight pause. "Have you a car?"

"Yes. An Austin 16."

"Put the parcel inside and drive immediately to Barnes Common. Do you know where that is?"

"Yes."

"Park near the railway bridge and stand on the path, with your right hand in your pocket. Do you understand?"

"Yes."

"That is all," said the man.

Corliss dropped the receiver back. He was shaking all over, with relief. The relief suddenly turned to giggling laughter. He couldn't help himself, it was so funny—he could get away with anything, all he needed to do was to dial a number and it was like a magician saying *hey presto!* Put the 'parcel' in the back of the car and drive to Barnes Common; that was all he had to do. It would be easy! The car was close to the front door. He could carry that man—he'd have to; the thing to remember was not to allow blood to drip anywhere on the carpet.

Who was the man?

In a way, he wasn't unlike Loftus; a smaller edition of Loftus, with a big, brown, straggly moustache. His hands and nails were engrained with dirt, his clothes were rough—he looked like an outdoor worker of some kind. Loftus certainly wouldn't use this type. His Excellency might, and yet that didn't seem to be the explanation. His Excellency would have the sense to leave Iris to him, for the time being.

He laughed again, shrilly, and checked himself.

He bent down and felt inside the man's breast pocket, drew forth an old brown wallet and shook out the contents. There were two letters and a blue registration card, and all named the man: *Thomas Gray.*

"Poor old Tom," Corliss said aloud. He looked inside the cardboard box. There were some cameos, an old watch and other oddments probably of sentimental value. He put the box back in the safe, locked the door, bundled the books back into the shelves and the keys back into the work-basket. It would be wiser to hide his traces now that events had taken this turn.

He hurried to the front door. Knowing the man's name didn't help much, he would have to worry about the problem of identity later, or let someone else worry about it. The car was immediately opposite the porch. He opened the back door and pushed it wide. There was no rug; he would need a rug, to cover the body. He hurried through the house to the kitchen, remembering that he'd seen a rug spread over a chair. He was about to snatch it off when he changed his mind; that would be missed immediately the maid returned. He turned away—

Supposing it was missed?

He hurried upstairs and took a blanket out of a cupboard on the landing, took it into the morning-room and spread it over Thomas Gray. Then he bent down and put one arm beneath the dead man's knees, another under his shoulders. He lifted. The dead weight was almost too much for him to carry, and he staggered. He gritted his teeth and straightened up. Once he was standing upright, it was easier. He had the man in his arms, so that he was facing the ceiling; there was no danger of blood dripping. He went as quickly as he could through the hall. No one could see him from the gate, the only danger was from nearby houses. He didn't look round, but eased the body into the car, on the floor in front of the back seats.

Nothing but the blanket showed.

He closed the front door, and then for the first time, looked about him. He saw no one at the nearby windows. He got into the car and drove off.

As he turned out of the gates, a policeman approached from the right. Corliss saw him, and his heart seemed to turn a somersault. He gritted his teeth, to prevent himself from crying out. The constable gave him only a casual glance, but a policeman's casual glance can take in a lot; that one would take in most of the details of the car.

The front wheels wobbled.

Keep steady!

He caught a glimpse of the constable in the driving mirror, and the man wasn't looking round.

A large car was parked near Barnes Common Bridge when Corliss reached there. He stood on the pavement, with his right hand in his pocket. A man approached from the other car.

He was as English as Corliss.

"What's it all about."

"I'm to watch Iris Grahame, for Z. I was told to search her house. The man interrupted me—it was one or the other of us."

"Who is he?"

"You'll see his name in his pocket. I don't know anything about him."

"Find anything at the house?"

"No. Ask the boss to lay off that actress until I've finished the job I've been given, will you?"

"Right. Take the other car and leave it at Hatt's Garage in Kensington. You needn't say anything, just park it outside. Doing all right?"

"Yes."

"You'll make the grade," the other said.

Corliss laughed, told him where to return the Austin, and took the suitcase, and drove off. He changed back into his own clothes and removed the greasepaint before collecting his car from St. James's Square.

Corliss went into his flat, just after six o'clock, feeling relaxed and tired. He dropped into the easy chair which Loftus had used, and closed his eyes. He didn't see visions and his mind was slack and dull. He hoped nothing would turn up to be done tonight. He hoped he wouldn't have to worry about the corpse. Taking a dispassionate view of himself, he knew that the attack with the broom had given him a severe shock, and it would take him a few hours to get over it.

He'd probably hear from Loftus, but wasn't likely to hear from Iris until much later; she didn't go home after a matinée performance. On her afternoons off, the maid didn't get home until late evening, there was no likelihood that anything would be discovered at St. John's Wood until ten or eleven o'clock, if then. He was still sitting there when he heard a sound outside; soft footsteps. He sat up and stared at the door; surely Loftus wasn't here already. He heard a scratching sound, as if someone were trying to get in.

He stood up.

A snap told him that the letter-box had closed sharply. He went into the hall. A single letter lay in the basket beneath the letter-box. It was in a plain envelope. He tore it open, and read: *Hell's Bells,* 10.30. He read it twice, although there was no need to, then burned it; Loftus would like to think that he had done that. He was beginning to hate Loftus more than anyone else; more than the vague, nebulous thing which he had suddenly crystallised as his country. Loftus seemed to typify everything he disliked, everything against which he had sworn vengeance. Probably it wouldn't be long before he was instructed to do something about Loftus.

He stood absolutely still. Why *wait* for instructions? He could kill Loftus, could make it appear as an accident, and no one would complain. A great deal of the Department's work turned on Loftus, that was already evident.

But there might be a bigger job waiting for him, he mustn't act on impulse. He had done so too often already; and the impulse was always the same: to kill.

A dead Loftus wouldn't be much good to Department Z.

He could put it up to His Excellency: kill Loftus, and probably they would do more damage to the Department than by any other single act. But Loftus wasn't the only leader, there must be someone else. If *all* the big men of the Department could be wiped out, he would have earned his keep. Yes, he would put this suggestion up to His Excellency! Later.

He had four hours to spare. He'd bath, change, have some dinner and stroll along to the *Hell's Bells* club. Was it significant that they'd used those premises twice; were they really the headquarters of the Z men?

Loftus was certainly one of their leaders.

If he killed Loftus—

Corliss heard music coming from the upper floor of the night club as he entered the front door, but it was early, the revels had not really started. He wasn't asked for a membership card but was taken straight upstairs. Three couples, hugging each other, were 'dancing' on the tiny floor and a few others were sitting round the tables, watched blankly by the buxom nudes with cloven hooves. Corliss went up to the top floor; Abbott sat outside the door, like a steward.

"Hallo, Charles!"

"Hallo."

"The great man's in there."

"Is he?" 'Great man!' Big fool was more like it.

"Go straight in," said Abbott, with a grin.

Abbott and the other man seemed unimportant, Loftus was the man who mattered. He sat in a large armchair, leg stretched out as usual, a pipe between his lips and a mug of beer at his side. Anyone less like a Secret Service chief it would be hard to imagine. He nodded, without smiling; that poker face had the familiar effect on Corliss; he didn't like it, wished he could guess what Loftus really thought.

"Hallo, young Corliss."

"Busy?" Corliss asked dryly.

"What, after hours? Don't forget the union." Loftus waved to a chair. He seemed good-tempered. "What have you been doing with yourself this afternoon?"

"Obeying orders."

"Find anything at the house?"

"How did you know I'd been there?"

"You've just said so, haven't you?" Loftus smiled. "Don't jump at me as if I were treading on a pet corn every time I speak, old chap. Did you find anything?"

"Nothing at all, except a bundle of love letters from Milanov."

"Read them?"

"Yes, and felt like a heel as I read. But there was nothing in them except the lush stuff you'd expect from Milanov."

Loftus said slowly: "I hope not. They could have been in code, you know."

Corliss sat down heavily; it was a simple fact that he hadn't thought of that. He felt Loftus's steady gaze, read a faint smile in his eyes. The man was mocking him, gloating over a failure which had seemed a complete success; his fingers began to itch.

"They probably weren't," Loftus said.

"It didn't occur to me."

"Honesty's a big point. It ought to have occurred to you and it will in future. How did you get in there?"

Corliss went into some detail. Loftus nodded, as if approvingly; the patronising oaf! He sat there like a modern Buddha and as if he were the very fount of all wisdom. He had a fat neck; he was too fat everywhere. But strong fingers could embed themselves in that fat neck and reach a vital point, it was almost as easy to snap the neck of a fat man as a thin one, and Loftus wouldn't be expecting an attack. It would be easy. He could get away, and Abbott—

Idiot! Abbott and everyone would know who had done it.

Loftus said: "Did you do much damage?"

"Not a lot. I hadn't any tools but was lucky with the safe, I found the key in her work-basket. I put everything shipshape before I left, but made some marks on the lock of the drawer where she kept her love letters."

"Hmm. Have a drink?"

"Thanks." Corliss got up and helped himself; the barrel of beer was behind Loftus—they seemed to carry that around with them, as part of the trappings.

"You did a good job," Loftus said ponderously. "I've been having you tailed, and you shook our man off. He was one of the best men we have. What was the idea?"

"To show you what I could do." Corliss laughed. "I wasn't sure that I was being followed but it seemed a safe bet. Glad you're pleased."

"Oh, we can use you," said Loftus. "But I'm not sure that you've found out all there is to know about Iris Grahame. There is some funny business in theatrical circles. They have their share of Commies and we're anxious to find the leaders. Where the Commies are concerned, the leader is always the person you least suspect. Tired of keeping an eye on the lady?"

"I'd take a lot of tiring of that!"

"I can't say I blame you."

"And I think she'll turn to me if she's in a jam," Corliss said. "It's a queer thing. She lives alone in that great barn of a house, and it could hold a whole family."

"Exactly," said Loftus dryly. "Why should she keep a big place like that going? Why does she occasionally have a kind of house party, ostensibly for theatrical folk, usually the *same* theatrical folk?"

"Does she, by George!"

"Yes, the next time she throws a party, I want you to be there."

"I will be."

Loftus actually laughed.

"You've the nerve for the game, anyhow," he said. "Have any trouble at the house?"

"No—it was empty, I'd made sure of that. It's always empty on the afternoons and evenings of matinée days, according to Iris."

"That's worth knowing," said Loftus. "Well, don't overdo anything with her, but keep in touch. If you can make her a close friend, all the better. You might even show one or two indications that your political sympathies veer pretty strongly towards the left, that way you'll find out if she's interested in politics. Don't say too much, just give her the opportunity to invite you to join her racket, if she's in one. They love to get at Special Branch men."

"All right." Corliss could have laughed in his face.

Loftus was barking up the wrong tree, anyhow; Iris wasn't in any racket. It was almost incredible that the big man thought that possible, in view of what he knew about Iris's visitors; but left Loftus go on making a fool of himself. That would be fine.

The telephone bell rang.

Loftus turned, to answer it, and so couldn't see Corliss. As he stretched out, the back of his neck was presented to Corliss, who felt his hands rising and the fingers crooking. He forced them down to his sides; he mustn't play the fool here, but—

"Yes, Gordon?" said Loftus.

There was a pause.

"Well, I don't see that it makes much difference," Loftus said. "I've just heard from Corliss—he found nothing at the Grahame house ... Yes, I've told him to carry on." So 'Gordon' was a man who worked with Loftus, who was talking to him as an equal; leader was talking to leader.

There was a long pause; then: "Yes, I should think so ... Probably it's time you did ... Yes, I'll bring him round."

Corliss buried his face in his beer tankard.

Loftus put down the receiver, and when Corliss lowered the tankard, he said: "We're going to pay a call, old chap. You're going to be given the once over by the big shot. Ready?"

15

INNER SANCTUM

Corliss had often passed that narrow door, but had he been asked, would not have remembered that one was there. He walked by Loftus's side, through the doorway and up the stairs. A feeling of intense excitement gripped him; he hoped he would be free of it before he was face to face with the 'big shot'. He looked about him, seeing the blank walls of the narrow staircase. Then he saw Loftus stop and put his hand beneath the handrail. Corliss noticed the exact spot.

The door in the wall slid open.

Corliss's excitement was so great that his heart seemed to beat as noisily as distant thunder.

They stepped inside, Corliss first.

Everything was new to him; and the room, with its contrasting ends, made a vivid impression on his mind. So did the man who sat in an armchair by the fire; everyone always seemed to be sitting in armchairs.

The man looked at him steadily.

The sharp features, the hatchet face, the drooping lips, the tired eyes—all of those things registered on Corliss's mind. He felt both disappointment and elation; it seemed unbelievable that this man was really the chief of Department Z, and this its inner sanctum. But could he reach any other conclusion?

"This is Gordon Craigie," Loftus said.

"How—how are you?" Corliss made himself meet the man's eyes. He couldn't prevent the slight stammer.

"Hallo, Corliss. Pull up a chair." Craigie waved vaguely, and took a meerschaum from the rack at his side; there were several others in it. He began to fill the pipe. "Loftus has been telling me that you haven't lost much time in getting your job done."

"Well, I've tried."

"Yes. He also tells me that he's made it pretty clear that there's a lot of danger in this affair."

"I know."

"And you want to go on with it?"

Corliss said slowly: "Yes."

"Aren't you sure?" There was no haste in Craigie's words, it was a simple but probing inquiry.

"Yes, I'm sure." Corliss hesitated again. "But I'd like to know more of what it's about. I gather that all my references are satisfactory." He forced a smile; that was a touch of flippancy which he felt the others would like. "I know it's not possible to trust anyone too much, but—" he broke off.

"In this job, everyone is trusted with just as much as they have to know in order to do their part, and nothing more," said Craigie. "You're part of a kind of jig-saw puzzle."

He was as prosy as Loftus!

"Yes, I can see that."

"You came in by accident because of the murder of Hilde Hansson. It's one of those things that sometimes happen. Hilde was doing several jobs. One, was finding out how far Communist activities have spread in the theatrical world. It was through her that we first discovered that Milanov was a Communist."

Corliss said: "I'd guessed that was about his number. And you think Iris Grahame might be mixed up in it?"

"We want to make sure."

"Well, I'll do what I can."

"I believe you will," Craigie said, and smiled dryly. "I particularly wanted to see you, because—" he paused, Corliss felt that something of importance was coming, was on edge to receive it; and yet when it came, it took him completely by surprise. "I knew your father," Craigie said.

"What?"

"He was often in here," said Craigie.

Corliss sat absolutely still; but his fingers twitched, he couldn't stop them. He forced himself to stare at Craigie and he tried to keep all expression out of his eyes. Neither of these men could ever understand the surge of fury which rushed over him then; how it affected him physically, made him feel sick, made him go hot and cold.

Craigie went on: "He was one of the most courageous men who has ever worked for us."

"For—*you?*"

"He was in Intelligence as you know," Craigie said. "Part of the time he was attached to this branch—let's call it Z. His last job started from here. It was a highly dangerous and extraordinarily difficult one."

"I—see." Corliss's voice trembled, he couldn't prevent that.

"He succeeded," Craigie said. "He managed to get information about the Chancellery out of Berlin before the Russians got there. But although he sent it out, he was caught. You've been told about that."

"Yes."

Craigie said: "He was caught by the Russians."

It was a foul lie! A deliberate lie, used to work up his feelings against the Russians. He knew that. He was sure of it. Craigie could sit there looking almost harmless, and lie—and Loftus could look on, nodding. The swine.

"I've told you that for two reasons," Craigie said. "The first, to explain why we've used you so quickly, and why we think that you can give us the services we need. The second, to give you an additional reason for pulling this off. In spite of what Loftus told you about espionage being carried out by all countries, our chief concern at the moment is with Russia. You can say Communism or what you like, but there's no need to mince words.

"They're much stronger in England than a lot of people realise.

"One of their biggest cells, or groups of cells, is undoubtedly in the theatrical world and its environs, but there are plenty of others. Milanov was more than on the fringe. He failed his employers badly—chiefly due to you I think—and they drove him to suicide. Can you guess why?"

"I'd rather know, than guess."

Loftus nodded and smiled.

Craigie said: "He killed himself because he knew that he would have to suffer for his failure, because he was afraid of being sent back to Russia, afraid of the punishment he'd receive. They're good at punishment. Hilde was our most likely contact with this particular group. It has great possibilities for doing harm. It's not only in the West End, but throughout the provinces. A theatre is a good place for people to meet casually, without being noticed. There are all kinds of hangers-on, at rehearsals, when the stage is being set—I needn't go into detail. I doubt if the number of people in the cells is large, one or two in each place would be sufficient. We think that they are dangerous because they have so many contacts. We want to find out how dangerous. If they discover what you're doing, and they probably will, they won't have any mercy. And if you get caught, there won't be much we can do to help you."

Corliss nodded.

"Iris Grahame may be the wrong lead, but you may be able to get at it through her. Ready to try?"

"Yes."

Craigie took his meerschaum from his lips.

"Good. I don't think you'll be sorry. In general, you'll work on your own. You may have to get an urgent message through to me or Loftus. If you do, telephone Whitehall 10011. There will always be someone here."

Corliss repeated: "One double-o double-one."

"When you call, you will give your name first and you will then spell it backwards. That will make sure that we know you're genuine. It's a simple code but it's always been effective. Do you understand?"

"Yes." The word almost choked Corliss.

"Good. Now, we're not going to give you help for a start. You will no longer be followed. If you need help, you know what to do, but don't send for it unless it's of vital importance. Is that clear?"

"Yes."

"All right," said Craigie. He stood up—so did the others. Craigie held out his hand; Corliss took it. Craigie's hand was small but his grip firm and cool. "Good luck, Corliss. If you pull it off, it'll be a big job."

"I'll do what I can."

Craigie nodded. Loftus turned to the wall where the door had appeared. Craigie leaned forward and pressed a knob which was hidden in the carving of the mantelpiece, and the door slid open.

Two minutes later, Loftus and Corliss stood on the pavement in that narrow street and near the narrow door. A cool wind blew; Corliss found it welcome.

Loftus put his hand on Corliss's shoulder.

"Luck, young Corliss!"

"Thanks."

"Off you go."

Corliss strode to the corner. He looked round at Loftus, who made a big, vague figure in the semi-darkness. He felt his lips curling in a sneer which Loftus could not see, so he let it stay. Then he turned out of sight. He hailed a taxi, and it wasn't until he dropped back in the corner that he let himself go.

He had everything—*everything.*

He made sure that he was not followed. Then he went to the telephone kiosks at Leicester Square station and dialled 'their' number. He said: "I must see *him.* At once."

"Where are you?"

"At Leicester Square."

"You will stay outside the station opposite the theatre on the corner, and a Daimler car will come for you."

Nothing had changed in the long room; it still seemed narrower at one end than the other. The eyes in the portrait remained vivid, and in spite of the news which was bubbling up inside him Corliss felt the influence of those eyes and looked at them, not at His Excellency. Yet His Excellency was staring at Corliss, not pretending that he wasn't there. He had his pale, plump hands flat on the desk.

"Sit down," he said.

"Thanks." Corliss dropped into a chair. He didn't smile; he had worked out his approach, and knew that it would not be wise to throw his weight about too much; he could let the facts do that for him.

165

"You have urgent news?"

"Yes. Two hours ago I was with Gordon Craigie and William Loftus, in the headquarters of Department Z. I know how to approach that office. I know how to get in. I know how to telephone a message to them."

He stopped, and the room was hushed. Slowly, the pale face of the man at the desk broke into a smile. He stood up, came round the desk and took Corliss's hand. He didn't speak, but patted him on the shoulder, lightly—oddly like Loftus had a habit of doing.

"That is *most* satisfactory. Craigie is the leader, yes, we have known that for some time. Is there more?"

"They think Iris Grahame is one of—us."

His Excellency said softly: "What mistakes they can make! Yes?"

"I'm to find out whether it's true. They think—" Corliss talked at some length and found it surprisingly easy to be dispassionate; but His Excellency surely guessed at his feeling of exultation. He finished, and took out his cigarette case. He had been told that he must never smoke in this room, but the cigarette was alight before he realised it. He took it from his lips, quickly.

"You may smoke," said His Excellency softly.

"Er—thanks."

"There is more?"

Corliss said: "It isn't my job to make suggestions."

"I am asking you to do that."

"Thanks." Corliss felt almost as if he were with an equal, the sense of inferiority was quite gone. "Loftus and Craigie appear to handle this Department between them. Take them away, and you will do a lot of damage."

"Yes."

"And the Department's records must all be in that office.

They'd be worth finding and examining, wouldn't they?" He almost laughed at the thought.

"That is so," said His Excellency.

"I can get in any time I like. If we fixed a time, we could raid the place. A van could be drawn up outside, and—"

"No, no," said His Excellency softly, "that would not do, but the raid—yes, we can arrange that? We shall arrange for men with cameras, we can photograph all the documents, that will be simple, there will be less risk of the arrangements failing. If we took many packages away it would perhaps be more noticeable. Don't you think so?"

Corliss gulped. "Yes. When—"

"We will prepare as quickly as we can," said His Excellency. "You will be told when to go there, and once it starts, you will have to be quick. Is there any time when the office is empty?"

"No."

"Then—"

"I'll telephone them first and tell them I must go along," said Corliss. "Or better still, just go to the office. They won't expect trouble. There aren't likely to be many there, two or three at the most. It will be easy."

"Yes," said His Excellency. "Do not make the mistake of thinking that it is too easy, be very careful. You will do nothing for us until you have the signal to proceed with this."

"Right."

"Is there anything else you wish to know?"

Corliss said: "No, I think it's all set. I'm on my own, now, they're not watching me."

"They have been very careful," said His Excellency. "Your flat, the first one, was searched three times, very closely. So was your room at the inn in the country. Your identity helped you to be accepted so quickly, of course, but—it is well done.

We shall continue to be careful, you will telephone as usual in an emergency."

"Yes."

His Excellency shook hands again.

Corliss went out of the far door and along the narrow passage and up the short flight of steps; they seemed to be made of air, not concrete. There was a greater deference in the manner of the men who accompanied him and met him. He reached the back part of the house near by. The lights were switched off as he went out. A small car was waiting outside and a man said:

"Use it and leave it where you wish."

"Thanks."

It was dark here; the only light was a hundred yards away, for this was a short street, and it was very late. But as Corliss approached the car, another turned into the street, and headlights suddenly flashed on. He had no time to dodge, the beam caught him and made him close his eyes quickly because of the glare.

As he opened them, the lights were being switched off; but he caught a glimpse of a man standing in the porch of a house opposite—a man who was obviously watching.

It was *Abbott*.

Then the light went off as the car stopped farther along the street. Abbott was invisible, but there was sufficient light for Corliss to see him if he moved away from the porch.

Had Abbott seen him?

Could he have failed to?

16

SAFETY MEASURE

There was a man behind Corliss; the man who had told him to use the car.

Corliss whispered: "I was seen."

The other man said: "We should have been told a man was watching," in an agitated whisper.

"Go to the other end of the street," Corliss ordered. "If he runs, stop him. Stop him somehow."

"Yes." The man moved off silently, walking along the pavement opposite the porch where Corliss had seen Abbott. Corliss got into the car and pulled the self-starter. He switched on the headlights, then switched them off again, eased off the brakes and drove slowly towards the end of the street, using only his sidelights.

Abbott did not move.

Corliss passed the porch, then stopped the car but left the engine running. He got out. He could not hear the man walking towards the end of the street, he heard only the hum of distant traffic. He turned and walked softly towards the porch, and saw a man peering out, just catching sight of his head before it was jerked out of sight.

Did Abbott know who he was?

There was a chance that recognition had been avoided.

He turned round abruptly, went back to the car and drove off. He stopped round the corner. The man he had sent along was waiting there, near a telephone kiosk which showed up, red and near-white, in the light of a distant street lamp. This street was also short, a cul-de-sac with its entrance from a little-used main road. The car pointed towards that road.

"Is there a light in the telephone kiosk?" Corliss whispered.

"It has been removed."

"Can you drive?"

"Of course."

"Take the car, rev the engine up to make plenty of noise and wait for me round the corner."

"Yes, sir."

It seemed an age before the engine roared and the car snorted towards the main road. Gradually, the sound faded. Corliss stepped off the pavement into the porch of a house near the telephone kiosk. He flattened himself against the side, and peered towards the corner. Despite the darkness he could make out the pale rectangle of the street name-plate; he would be able to see anyone who came round here. He would see them, too, if he went to the other side of the road; he wasn't likely to do that, because of the dead end.

He heard nothing.

Suddenly, a dark shape appeared at the corner. It was a man—Abbott—peering round. Abbott was cautious. He made sure that the car had gone before stepping forward more boldly. He headed for the telephone kiosk, quickly, making no noise.

He and Corliss were equi-distant from the kiosk when

Corliss moved. He had taken four paces before Abbott, already with a hand stretched out to touch the door, saw him. Abbott swung round. As he leapt, Corliss saw his right hand move towards his pocket. Abbott had no time to get his gun out, and with one hand in his pocket, was at a disadvantage. Corliss hit him savagely on the side of the chin. Abbott staggered away. Corliss followed, grasping for his neck. He felt it beneath his fingers.

Abbott brought up his knee and caught him a sickening blow in the groin.

Corliss gasped with the pain.

Abbott struck at his face, caught him a glancing blow and then brought his right hand into play and gripped Corliss's wrist. The pressure of his fingers was powerful, and it hurt. Abbott pulled, to get his neck free, and Corliss's grip was weak, because pain still went in waves through his stomach. If Abbott escaped—

He kicked at the Z man's legs, felt a sharp impact and heard Abbott's hissing intake of breath. Abbott's hands dropped from his, but as the small man fell, Corliss lost his grip on his throat. Abbott started to shout. Corliss kicked him in the face, and the cry was stifled. Corliss dropped on to his knees, bending double to ease the pain and groping desperately for Abbott's neck. He felt the warmth of blood, where the kick had broken the skin. Abbott squirmed, but couldn't get free.

Corliss gripped his neck tightly; a thin, scraggy neck, which would snap—

No!

He mustn't break Abbott's neck, that was a trademark of one man only, Loftus would know at once who it had been. He stopped. Abbott tried to butt at him with his head but only just touched his chin. Corliss took his hands away from the neck, and felt a feeling almost of regret—he wanted to kill Abbott in that one way.

He had to kill, somehow.

He gripped Abbott's head and smashed it against the pavement; three times. After the third, Abbott stopped moving.

Corliss spoke to the man who had driven the little car away and was standing by its side.

"I've killed him. He's in the third porch from the corner. Get him away. Wash the pavement, make sure there are no signs of a struggle there. Understand?"

"Yes, sir."

"Report what happened. Say that I was recognised by a Z man, it was unavoidable."

"Yes, sir."

"Where shall I leave the car?"

"The corner of Moon Street."

Corliss got into the car. His hand was quite steady on the wheel, he felt a little cold, that was all. He drove to within a hundred yards of his new flat, and left the car in a street near by and walked the rest of the way. No one followed him, he didn't see a soul. He went up in the lift. The first thing he did was to examine himself in a full-length mirror; his clothes were dusty but there was no sign of blood on them, although his hands were smeared with it. He washed them, thoroughly, then realised that there would be bloodstains on the steering wheel of the little car.

He went into the bathroom, wetted a sponge and hurried out. He washed the steering wheel but didn't wait for it to dry before driving to Moon Street. He was sure that he wasn't being watched, yet all the time it felt as if eyes were prying towards him from the darkness. Once he was back, he began to shiver; it was from reaction and his own folly; he had done everything else properly, and nearly damned himself with that one careless act.

Forget it.

Abbott couldn't betray him now.

The house he'd come from was suspected by the Z men, then, but he could not have been recognised when going there, he hadn't shown himself. There was no real danger that he had been seen and reported; well, little danger. Surely if he had been seen, Loftus or one of the others would be here now. He looked at the telephone, half expecting it to ring. Nothing happened. He undressed and got into bed, but didn't put out the light; for some reason which he couldn't understand he didn't like the idea of darkness.

He stared at the plain, white ceiling.

How long had the Z men known about that house? Was it possible that he had been seen on his first visit? No, he needn't harass himself with that, he had gone in a closed car; and he knew he hadn't been seen going there tonight. The death of Abbott spelt the end of danger from that direction. But if the house were to be watched in future, then the Z men had some idea why it was being used. Craigie and Loftus hadn't told him everything.

He knew that he couldn't keep up this pressure for long; no one could. But His Excellency would realise that and make plans quickly.

They couldn't be too quick for him.

He went to sleep, with the light still on.

A bell was ringing.

It was the telephone, of course, between his bed and the other in that unfamiliar room. It was daylight, but there was no sun this morning, and spots of rain showed on the window glass. The bell kept ringing. Corliss lay there, wide awake. The caller could be Loftus. He might have been betrayed, he could easily have fooled himself the night before. Hazy thoughts suddenly took on sharp and menacing outlines.

But would Loftus telephone him?

He stretched out his hand, and the ringing stopped.

"Hallo."

There was no answer.

"Hallo, are you there?"

No one spoke.

He banged down the receiver and sat up slowly. Perhaps the caller had just wanted to make sure that he was at home; or had grown impatient and rung off. He ought not to have wasted time; he might live to regret delayed decisions.

He went to the kitchen and made some tea. All the time he was on edge in case the bell rang again, but there was no sound; the block of flats was quiet. He looked at his watch; it was half past eight. Not early, not late. He took the newspapers from the letter-box automatically, and not until he was in the kitchen with them did he realise that the Department looked after everything, even made sure that he had his morning papers.

He laughed; it was a relief to hear the sound.

He drank tea and looked through the three papers. There was no report of a man's body found anywhere in London— there wasn't time for Abbott's to have been discovered, but Thomas Gray's might have been. Oh, he needn't worry; 'they' would make sure that no one found either of the bodies. He was beginning to have absolute trust in the great forces behind His Excellency; and unless he were badly mistaken, they were beginning to trust him absolutely. Who was His Excellency? Someone of great power in Russia? It wasn't likely, the big men stayed at home.

He shaved while his bath water was running, and got into the bath—and the front door bell rang.

Loftus?

It rang again. It would be pointless not to answer it. He shouted: "Half a mo'!" and climbed out of the bath, dabbed himself with a towel and put on a dressing-gown; it clung to him, damp and unpleasant. He tied the sash as he reached the front door.

He opened it.

Iris Grahame said: "Charles, I had to see you."

She was going to pieces.

It was remarkable and unexpected but he was sure he was right. Her eyes were filled with dread, there was no other word for the expression in them. She pushed past him agitatedly. She had on a hat which looked askew and he could see that her hair wasn't properly done; he actually saw a metal curler, poking near her right ear. She had dressed hurriedly, and her make-up was perfunctory.

"What is it, Iris?"

"My house was burgled yesterday morning."

He said: "Well, that's better than if one of you had been hurt. Sorry if I'm breathless, you dragged me out of the bath."

She didn't smile and didn't apologise.

"I think someone has been hurt," she said hoarsely.

"Oh?" He was at the door of the living-room, and so she didn't see his face stiffen. He waved to her. "Wait here while I get some tea, it's made—"

"I don't want any tea. Charles, I didn't find out until this morning. Annie realised it first. She'd arranged to meet Tom at the house yesterday afternoon—"

"Tom? Who's Tom?"

"The gardener. He's been walking out with Annie for years! He has a key to the house. I didn't know they were meeting there yesterday. When Annie arrived, he wasn't there. He didn't turn up at all."

Poor old Tom! And poor old Iris! She spoke quickly and was undoubtedly frightened; Corliss rejoiced simply because of that, she hadn't felt fear quickly enough. Or rather, she'd hidden her fear; now that things were moving fast she couldn't keep up the pretence. As his thoughts ran on, he watched her with outward sympathy and concern.

"It wouldn't be the first time a gay young lad has failed a lively young thing—"

"Charles, please don't joke. Tom isn't at his lodgings. He left to come to see Annie, but didn't arrive—or there's no sign that he arrived, except that the back door was open. He always used a back door key. Annie left after me, to do some shopping, and she's sure that she locked the back door."

"I see," said Corliss. He'd not thought of that. "Is anything missing?"

She hesitated.

"No, but—"

"I've a feeling that you're letting this play on your nerves too much," Corliss said reassuringly. "Sit down, let me get that tea—"

"I don't want any tea!" She flared up at him, came forward and gripped his arm. "Annie was worried stiff last night, but I told her not to worry. Then this morning, I—I discovered that we'd had a burglar."

"Sure of that?"

"Yes. I—I keep some papers in the wardrobe drawer. There were scratches on it, I saw that it had been forced. So I went downstairs. The books had been taken out of the bookshelves and put back in the wrong order. My safe is behind them and it had been opened. Nothing was missing, but—"

"Did they force the safe open?"

"No, they used a key. Charles, this is true, I'm not imagining it. The things in the safe were all there but in different places—I always leave them in a certain position, I'm quite sure of that. An old box of keepsakes was at the front, I always leave it at the back."

The mistakes he'd made!

Corliss said slowly: "It looks as if you're right."

"I know I'm right. The thing that frightens me is that Tom might have arrived and discovered the thief, and been hurt. You warned me that these people were dangerous, didn't you? And Tom hasn't turned up this morning, usually he's at the house at eight o'clock sharp. I telephoned you, but—"

"You'd gone off the line when I answered."

"Shall I go to the police?"

Corliss said easily and reassuringly: "You've come to the police, don't worry about that. The question is, how much ought to be done openly? There's no proof that Tom called, is there?"

"Except that door."

"You'd hardly call that proof, would you? Annie may have been absent-minded. She might even have left the door open for him, and be chary of telling you—they get like that, you know." Lies rolled off his tongue easily, with hardly a second thought. "I'll report it, but I think that my chiefs will think it better to say nothing."

"Annie—"

"Surely you can deal with Annie," said Corliss. "She seems pretty fond of you."

"I'm not sure that she'll be satisfied to leave this to me," said Iris. She fought for her self control, was actually poking her fingers into her hair; she touched the curler and pushed it out of sight. "She may do, but what can I tell her?"

Corliss walked away, frowning, rubbing his chin. He was chilly, because he hadn't dried himself properly. He concentrated, looking out of the window, until suddenly he snapped his fingers and said:

"Got it! If Annie thinks you're in danger—"

"She does. Charles, she isn't a fool."

"Fine! If she's convinced that by talking too much about this she might make difficulties for you, she'll keep quiet for a day or two. Tell her I will see that the mystery is reported and that the police will make inquiries. Look here, will it help if I come and talk to her myself?"

"I think it will," said Iris.

"You go back. I'll be there in an hour, perhaps less. And— don't worry, my dear."

"Don't worry!"

"I'm making sure that you're looked after," Corliss said, and drew her to him. She held herself rigid but relaxed when he pressed his lips gently against her forehead. "I won't fail you, Iris, there's too much at stake for that. All the future." She didn't speak.

He went back and had his bath, breakfasted leisurely in the restaurant downstairs and, driving his own car, went to St. John's Wood. By then it was nearly two hours since Iris had left him, he hadn't hurried. He had half expected to have a message from Loftus, and was anxious not to miss one.

It wouldn't hurt Iris to wait. His sense of power over her was stronger; it was so obvious that she relied a great deal on him; he was filling the gap Milanov had left.

She opened the door, and spoke quickly but quietly:

"I've been talking to her. I think it will be all right."

"I know it will be," Corliss said.

He excelled himself when talking to a bright-eyed Annie who was nearly tearful. Yes, it was possible that her Tom had interrupted someone at the house and that he had been hurt. He had already put inquiries in hand—to the uniformed police

178

and to the hospitals. If there were any news, she would be told at once. If there were none, then she needn't worry too much, it would mean that Tom was alive. It was even possible that Tom had followed someone from the house, and well, one just couldn't tell. There were many cases of loss of memory, it affected the most unlikely people. At worst, Tom was being kept out of the way for a day or two. All the resources of the police would be put into the search for him, but—she mustn't talk. If she did, the story would get into the newspapers. They were bad enough already with their reports about the theatre murder. Miss Grahame was having far too much unpleasant publicity, and if anything else were added, it might do her untold harm.

That argument finally convinced Annie that he was right.

Iris said: "You've a way with women, haven't you?"

"You don't call Annie—"

"Annie's all right," said Iris, with a tired smile. "Don't keep her waiting if the news is bad, will you?"

"No."

"What do you think they wanted?"

"To find out if Milanov had left anything incriminating here."

"He seldom came here! They can't be that crazy."

"They're not crazy, they're just crafty and careful," Corliss said. He took her hands. "I don't think you've anything to worry about now. There's been no report that you've been followed. They're probably quite satisfied after searching the house. It's a pretty big place for you, isn't it?"

"I suppose it is. I was born here."

She had changed since coming to the flat, and her hair was loose and falling to her shoulders; she looked at her best that way; desirable. Her colouring was lovely, and there wasn't a flaw in her complexion. "I've thought of turning it into flats, but I think I'll keep it as it is for the time being. There used to be more of the family living here, and I often have friends and quite big parties."

"Parties?"

"Why so surprised?"

"I thought of you as a home bird."

"Aren't I? You know my family has been on the stage for generations, don't you? There's a kind of history in this house, Charles, and—well, in the old days the parties were almost fabulous. Everyone who was anybody always came. When I was young, I can remember the place being crammed, you've never heard such a noise! It's become a kind of tradition that I should carry on. Silly, isn't it?"

"Delightful," said Corliss.

There was Loftus's wanted explanation; he read a Communist plot into a sentimental habit! One great difficulty was to keep a grave face when wanting to laugh.

"When's the next party?" he asked.

"On Friday. Tomorrow."

"As soon as that!"

"Yes. I don't know whether I ought to cancel it. What do you think?"

"It's the very last thing you ought to do," said Corliss. "Go on as you've always done. Isn't that in the tradition of the theatre, too?"

She laughed, but he thought that the laughter hurt her. He saw her glance towards Milanov's photograph; she hadn't taken it down yet. She was not prepared to try to wipe out all memory of him because of what she now knew. In her way, she was a simpleton; oh, beautiful and with a mind of a kind, but so naïve in other ways. He could do practically what he liked with her.

"Busy today?" he asked.

"There's a matinée."

"They work you like a horse, don't they? Come and lunch with me."

"I don't think I'd better leave Annie, she'll only brood. I shall take her to the theatre with me for the next few shows, she'll feel happier that way. Thanks, Charles, for everything."

"It's nothing." He squeezed her hands. "Nothing to what I'd like to be able to do."

It would make a pleasant little interlude, to break down her resistance. If he pulled her to him and kissed her now, she would be offended, but—tonight? Tomorrow? She was in a highly emotional state and had shown how wretchedly senti-mental she could be. She hadn't fully recovered from the shock of André's death, and odd things could happen on an emotional rebound. He needed something to do, while he was waiting for instructions from His Excellency; he'd get edgy unless he had something on which to concentrate. Why not the conquest of a beautiful woman?

"I'll come and see you between the shows," he said.

"Do that, dar—"

She broke off abruptly, checking the endearment just in time. Was he making a fool of himself? 'Darling' was nothing among her friends, and yet—she wouldn't use endearments lightly.

She watched him drive off.

He drove out of London along the Great West Road and let the sports car go all out. With the speed he gained a sense of exhilaration; he loved speed. Why? Because there was a measure of danger in it. He'd been blind for a long time but wasn't now; he wanted to live dangerously, and was beginning to do it properly. 'They' had known what they were doing when they'd enlisted him! He pressed harder on the accelera-tor; the speedometer needle passed the hundred and then quivered wildly. He swerved to pass a lorry; the thing seemed to be standing still.

Speed; give him speed!

He drove at a breakneck speed on the country roads, and couldn't do a thing wrong. He was in complete control of the powerful little engine; he had *power.* He had the power of life and death over people; over Loftus and Craigie above all people. Craigie wasn't personally important to him, Loftus was; he hoped he would be able to kill Loftus with his bare hands. That would be real revenge.

The drive refreshed and exhilarated him.

He was back in London before the matinée finished, took Iris out to tea, and for the sake of it, saw the show through during the evening. It wasn't really much of a play, a kind of made-to-measure domestic tragi-comedy, but the acting, Iris's especially, gave it something which the audience couldn't resist. He still felt the attraction, particularly during the scene which had been rehearsed just before a little man had sprung at him—and been killed.

He drove home ahead of Iris and Annie, went through the house from top to bottom, to reassure them, and said good night. He could have kissed her passionately and she would not have resisted; he sensed that, but decided not to. Tomorrow? Remarkable things might happen tomorrow.

17
ORDERS

There was nothing in the newspapers about Abbott, Tom or anyone connected with the affair, except Iris and the first man who had been murdered, and they had been relegated to an inside page. There was nothing new. There were no messages. It was an ordinary kind of morning, but for the different flat, almost exactly the kind of morning he had spent a hundred times. They had helped to drive him to distraction, and had made him brood. He wasn't distracted any longer.

He telephoned Iris but didn't keep her on the telephone for long.

He went out for a brisk walk. He was accustomed, now, to glancing round when at corners and at shops, to see whether he recognised anyone behind him. He saw no one, there was a complete feeling of freedom. But before he had finished, he felt the first nag of impatience; he didn't want to wait long. If 'they' were too cautious, they might miss the boat. He could go into Department Z's office any moment he liked, just walk up those stairs, press the button in the hand-rail, and *hey presto!* he would be inside. Or he could telephone and announce himself, then spell his name backwards. Of all the childish tricks!

He'd forgotten to report that, last night; not really surprising, but—he shouldn't have forgotten. Forgetfulness and carelessness were twin and unforgivable sins. He felt himself go hot and cold. He remembered how nearly he had left blood-stained finger prints on the wheel of the car last night; and that he had made so many trivial mistakes at Iris's house. She'd known that the safe had been found immediately she had looked at the bookshelves. He could call himself lucky, but luck wasn't likely to last for ever. He must be more careful. He couldn't afford not to—

"Look out!"

A man shouted in his ear, someone clutched at his arm. A car horn hooted. He saw a car near him, only a yard away. He was at the kerb, stepping off.

"Didn't you see the lights change?" the man asked.

"Eh? Oh, no. No, I didn't. Thanks."

"Better keep your eyes open."

"Yes, I will. Thanks."

He had been telling himself that he mustn't be careless, and nearly walked into a car. It wouldn't do. It wasn't like him, either. Until he'd remembered that reverse spelling of names as a code, he'd felt on top of the world. Now, he wasn't so good; he felt dizzy.

He turned into the first café he reached and sat down. It wasn't crowded. The waitress came up and he growled: "Coffee." He wanted a drink, not coffee, but the bars weren't open yet; this damned country! He sat upright, his hands gripping the edge of the table. It was a cheap café, there were no table-cloths; normally he wouldn't have been seen in such a place, but—he'd had to sit down. He heard a movement by his side and glanced round.

"Are you all right, sir?" It was the waitress, a drab with the coffee in her hand, some of it spilled in the saucer. He couldn't bear coffee and tea spilt in saucers.

"Don't I look all right?" he growled.

"I—sorry, sir. Very good, sir."

She hurried off, and gathered with several other waitresses near the big tea and coffee urns, and a counter stacked with yellow buns and thick sandwiches. All of the girls looked at him; and they were whispering. He was calling attention to himself, and it wouldn't do, if he lost his nerve here he might do elsewhere.

Better be *careful;* drink the coffee, pay for it, and go out when they weren't able to pay him much attention. A sudden rush of customers helped him to do that. He left a shilling for the coffee, and hurried off.

It was better in the fresh air. He soon felt all right again. Odd thing, that sudden forgetfulness and the dizzy spell. This life was a strain, but he revelled in it. The trouble now was that he hadn't anything to *do.* Last night he'd thought about breaking down Iris's resistance; what had he really meant? Simply that he wanted her. If it weren't for that old sow, Annie, it would be easier. Pity Annie hadn't been with her Tom that day, then both of them—

Steady!

He needed a drink.

He had a neat whisky at his flat—a generous drink; he would not allow himself a second, but drank this one slowly. The effect soon made itself felt. Within ten minutes, he was able to laugh at himself. He hadn't had enough sleep, he hadn't been used to living at this pace lately; he was just tired. That explained his forgetfulness. If something big didn't break soon, he'd call 'them' and say that there mustn't be any further delay.

Where should he lunch?

He telephoned Iris.

"Charles, I'd love to, but I can't—don't forget it's the party night."

"Oh, yes." He'd *forgotten*. "I'll be seeing you there—if that's all right.

"Of course."

"Look after yourself." He rang off.

He would have to lunch on his own, then; and he had to let Loftus know about that party, Loftus *would* be pleased! He went to the telephone and held his hand above the dial, then took the plunge. W-H-I-I-O-O-I-I. It was impossible to say why he felt greater excitement than when he had telephoned 'them'. The *brrr-brrr* was exactly the same sound, he wouldn't be surprised to hear that familiar 'Yes'.

"Hallo, there." No one could mistake Loftus's deep voice.

"It's Corliss—Double SILROC—Corliss."

"Fire away," said Loftus. He didn't question the wisdom of the call but seemed to take it for granted, another little indication that he really accepted the new member.

"Our girl-friend is throwing a party at her house tonight. I'm going along."

"Thanks. Anything else?"

"Not that I'd call urgent."

"Keep your eyes wide open and your hand near your pocket," Loftus said, "there are indications that our boy-friends are being active."

"Aren't they always?"

"They have their dull periods," Loftus said. "This show is working up to a kind of climax."

"It'll pass," said Corliss. "Good-bye."

"Good hunting."

Corliss let the receiver fall slowly, then clapped his hands together; it made a startlingly loud sound. He laughed, a deep laugh of satisfaction. Loftus saw a climax looming ahead but hadn't any idea what kind of climax it would be. Loftus was worried; he wouldn't have said all that if he weren't. Abbott hadn't reported for duty, of course; it was even possible that Abbott's body had been found. If so—

No, 'they' would make sure nothing like that happened. Abbott and Tom would just disappear, no one would know what had happened to them. He clapped his hands together again, and was in high good humour when he went out. He decided to lunch at *Cherry's*. He might get a message from the waiter who had breathed so confidentially down his neck.

Loftus limped up the stairs of the house in Brigham Square, pocketing his keys as he did so. When he reached the first floor landing, a door opened and Reggie Wilson came out. Wilson was faultlessly dressed, as bright and polished as a new pin; but his usual amiable expression was missing.

"Any news?"

"Not a sign or a sound," said Loftus.

"It's damned odd."

"It's more than odd, it's fatal," Loftus said, and pushed past him, to a chair. He sat on the arm. "Abby would have sent word through if he'd had half a chance. Where's Chunky?"

"Having a belated shave. He overslept."

On the words, Chunky Bray came in, shaved out with lather still on his cheeks, his ears and nose. He scrubbed his face with a towel. His dressing-gown gaped open, showing a massive chest.

"News?"

"No. I want both of you to go along to Feltham Street. There must be some indication of what happened somewhere near. The likely thing is that Abby was spotted and shanghaied, but he wouldn't have been taken completely by surprise."

"I'll be ready in two jiffs," said Bray, and hurried out, the tail of his dressing-gown flying.

"Who's been along there so so far?" asked Wilson.

"A couple of the boys you don't know."

"Corliss?"

"No, he's on a different job."

"That young man seems born to trouble," said Wilson, smoothing down his already smooth hair. "Could he be a Jonah? They do exist, you know. I don't want to go in for omens and all that kind of thing, but—"

"I know what you mean. We'll watch him." Loftus lit a cigarette, a thing he seldom did, sure proof that his nerves weren't so good. "I don't want you at Iris Grahame's party tonight, after all. Corliss will be there, and I'll have someone else whom he doesn't know around. You can have a night off."

"No, thanks."

"Meaning?"

"Non-stop, until we find Abby," said Wilson.

Loftus shrugged. "If you can pick up a line on him, follow in. In fact both you and Chunky can call it your job until I have to put you on to something else. By the way, Beresford is coming back from Reading today. The show there has closed up, we haven't made any progress since Hilde was killed. It wasn't a dead end, but they know we were on to them and put up the shutters."

"What about Hilde's pal, the man in brown?"

"Vanished."

Wilson said soberly: "You know, these people are good, Bill. Too good for my liking."

"They've had a long time to prepare," Loftus said. "We weren't allowed to do much about them in the early days.

We're up against something more widespread and deeper than we've ever tackled before, and the worst of it is that we don't know which of our own people might be bitten by the bug."

"You mean—"

"Oh, not the boys. Just the British. We'll see it through after a fashion. If we can break this particular rising, we'll have made some progress."

"Rising," murmured Wilson.

"Outbreak, sortie, call it what you like. They're after something special or they wouldn't be taking the risks they are taking. By the way, you'll see several other of our men near Feltham Street, just keeping an eye on the place. After Abbott's spot of bother, the other side may close up there. They must know we've been watching them for some time. You concentrate on finding something about Abby."

"Right," said Wilson.

"Ready!" called Bray.

They went by car to the Bayswater Road side of Kensington Gardens, parked it in a side street, and walked briskly to Feltham Place. This was a little cul-de-sac off Feltham Street where Abbott had been attacked. There was a woman in the telephone kiosk, talking nineteen to the dozen. Wilson and Bray sauntered past her, and crossed the end of the street where the suspect house was situated. The house itself was at the far end, Feltham Street was also a cul-de-sac. They saw no one about; the Z men on duty there were making sure that they wouldn't readily be seen. The Department had the use of a front room in one of the houses near by, and the suspect house had been under surveillance for nearly a month.

"If we raided that place we might get somewhere," Bray said.

"Bill Loftus will have a go at it as soon as he thinks it's time," said Wilson.

"Ever known him as jumpy as he is over this?"

"No. It's enough to make anyone jumpy."

Bray said: "Yes, I know, but I've a feeling that it's more than the job itself. Bill has a notion that something really big is going to break. There's a suspicious lull on the international front, especially in Europe. Think anything is in the wind?"

"We'll know, when there is." They turned at the end of Feltham Place and walked towards the telephone kiosk. The woman left it and hurried to a house across the road. A door slammed. "See that?" Wilson asked. "You can pick it out from here—look."

He pointed.

Near the kiosk was a light patch on the pavement. As they drew near it, the light changed and it became less obvious—it would be seen easily at a distance but was less noticeable at close quarters. When they stood immediately in front of it, they could see that the pavement had been washed down, and one spot scrubbed. In the gutter there was a little heap of dirt, dark with damp; it was where the pavement had been swept and the heap made tidy.

Wilson poked the heap with the ferrule of his walking-stick. He turned over sodden dirt, a few scraps of paper and other oddments; among the oddments was a stub of pencil. Wilson picked it up.

Bray said sharply: "Abby's."

"He always carried one, yes, but it doesn't tell us anything." Wilson poked among the dirt but found nothing else. "Better have this stuff collected and see what the Yard can make of it. A job for Miller, first." He turned to the kiosk and put in a call to Scotland Yard, then asked for Superintendent Miller. Ten minutes later a police car came up and the pile of dirt was taken away in a metal container.

Loftus and Craigie were in the Whitehall Office when the

telephone bell rang. This time, a yellow light glowed; which meant that it was a call on the private line to Scotland Yard.

"Hallo, there?" Loftus said.

"This is Miller," said a man with a deep, penetrating voice. "About that stuff from Feltham Street."

"Yes?"

"Some blood and hairs—short hairs, which could be Abbott's, they're the right colour. I don't know about texture. But there was some damage done to a man's head just there last night, we found matted human hairs, undoubtedly the blood came from a scalp wound. The pavement had been washed down with soap and water."

"I see," said Loftus heavily. "Anything else?"

"No, there's no report of a body having been found to correspond with Abbott's. A man's body was found in the Thames, near Kingston this morning, with the face mutilated and the fingers amputated—obviously to prevent identification. He'd been shot through the stomach twice. It certainly wasn't Abbott—more a man of your size. Does anyone answering that description interest you?"

"I can't say it does, offhand. Any bullets in the body?"

"No, they'd been removed. They didn't mean us to find out who'd killed him or who he was. We'll identify him sooner or later, but I'll make a special of it if you think it's one of your men or connected with your job."

"Make it special, anyhow," said Loftus, "we might get a line during the day. Thanks, Dusty."

"You're welcome," said Superintendent Miller.

Loftus put down the telephone and lit another cigarette. Craigie noticed that; and noticed, also, that Loftus's forefinger and thumb were slightly stained with nicotine; Loftus certainly wasn't happy.

"Abby's had it, Gordon." Loftus said why he thought so.

"I'm not surprised, but—it seems pretty crazy. Think it's time we raided that house?"

"Do you?"

"I'd wait a bit."

"I think so," said Craigie. "When we raid, we want to make sure that we get results, if we fluff it there's bound to be trouble. You know the thin ice we're on."

Loftus said: "When that ice cracks, it's going to make a hell of a row."

Corliss was not served by the same waiter at *Cherry's*, although he was given the same table and treated with greater deference than he'd been used to receiving there. He wished he weren't alone. It would have been more entertaining if Iris had been with him. There wouldn't be much chance of getting on his own with Iris that night; there was sure to be a seething mob, at the party.

There *could* be fun there, too.

He might make a phoney report to Loftus; say, report a conversation which didn't in fact take place, from which it could be inferred that there was a conspiracy at the St. John's Wood house. It didn't greatly matter what the conversation was about in detail, all he needed was to 'confirm' Loftus's suspicion that Iris Grahame was mixed up in the business. The stronger the wrong scent seemed, the faster Loftus would follow it. He might take good men off other work and concentrate them on Iris and her party friends. Yes, not a bad idea, it wouldn't be necessary to ask permission to do it, no one need know that it had been done so far as His Excellency was concerned. It would be perfectly safe.

He'd make a bigger fool of Loftus, and would give Iris something to think about.

"Yes," he said aloud, "that's not at all bad. I might make up the conversation before I go alone! I wonder if there'll be a man with a beard present, Loftus will leap at a man with a beard." He grinned to himself. Then he saw a man at another table looking at him, and he realised that his lips were curling. The man looked away, quickly. Corliss straightened his lips. He must prevent that from becoming a mannerism. He already sensed that it didn't look so good, and the glance from the man near by confirmed it; the man had seemed to be fascinated.

He called for his bill.

The waiter he had seen the other day came up with it, leaned forward to take the money, a five pound note, and whispered:

"There will be a note with your change, sir."

"Oh. Thanks."

"I hope everything was satisfactory, sir."

"Perfect!"

As he waited for his change, he felt his fingers quivering; that little quiver was becoming familiar, he rather liked it. The sense of exhilaration was back, too; he was going to get his orders, and there wasn't much doubt what those orders would be: to raid the inner sanctum of the Department.

When the change came, he thrust it into his pocket without looking at it, and went out. He had to fight to retain outward composure. He didn't look for the small slip of paper among the notes until he was at the wheel of his car. There was a pencilled message:

Go tonight at one-thirty. The others will follow five minutes later.

18
PARTY NIGHT

A man in a reddy brown suit said: "What a mob! Have a drink?"

"Thanks," said Corliss.

"Shattering, isn't it?" The man pushed a glass into Corliss's hand. "You've got to hand it to her, old boy, you must have to. Proper old trouper, that's Iris."

"Oh, yes."

"And tonight—felt sure she would cancel it tonight. We all knew what she thought about André. Made a mistake, of course, I always thought that she was making a mistake. The Russians! Or was he a Pole? But you've got to hand it to her. Just look at her!"

He did more than look; he pushed his way towards Iris, while Corliss stood by the door and watched both her and the surging mass round her. All sizes and types were at the party. Most were well dressed and some extravagantly. She stood out among them, with clear-eyed, simple loveliness. Her gown was of apple green, her favourite colour, and had long sleeves. The cunning cut showed all the lovely lines of her figure. She seemed to be enjoying herself, happy because the others were. It was a façade, of course, she was badly worried. It would be interesting to see that façade crumple.

The big drawing-room was so full that there was hardly room for another couple of people. At one end, a long bar was crowded. Two of the guests, acting as volunteer bartenders, were serving drinks as fast as they could. A dozen familiar faces were among the hundred nonentities, people with big names in the theatrical world. There were *three* men with beards.

It was nearly midnight.

Corliss kept looking at his watch. Time wouldn't go fast enough. He wasn't sure that it had been wise to come here, after all, but better here than sitting moping at his flat and waiting. Impatience was hardly the word for his surging desire for action. He remembered feeling like this at the beginning of a sprint, waiting for the starter's pistol. *Bang!* And off he'd go. He always had been good at short distances, just as he was good at this job.

A big, florid-faced man in evening dress was pawing Iris. She didn't much like it, and shrugged his hand away. In the corner, a man with a shiny bald head was playing a confused medley on the grand piano. By the wall, a man was standing and declaiming Shakespeare; only an occasional sentence reached Corliss above the general hum of talk.

The *fools.* The pleasure-seeking, pleasure-loving *fools.* If they only knew what was going to happen in an hour's time, they'd laugh on the other side of their faces. It would be nothing less than the complete defeat of British counter-espionage and everything it stood for. All the records would be copied, there would be no way of saving the day.

It would be *easy.*

"I haven't seen you before, darling, have I?" a girl came up and asked. She wasn't tipsy, just happy. She had a black off-the-shoulder evening gown; a plump, shapely little piece. She took his arm and hugged it tightly to her side. "Be a pet, get me a drink. Gin. *Anything* with gin in it."

"Come and help me get it."

"Love to, darling."

Corliss forced his way through the crowd, with the girl holding tightly on to him. She used a good perfume, and wasn't as young as she had seemed at first. Her lips were full and glistened red, her nose snub. She kept giggling, and 'darlinged' every other man she passed.

He had to go near Iris to reach the bar.

"Hallo, Charles," she called.

"Hallo! See you later."

She nodded; he fancied that she was trying to give him a message, but he had no chance to speak to her again before she was swallowed up in the crowd. The girl was pulling playfully at his arm, now.

"Say, who's getting this drink?"

"*We* are."

"Oh, you are a one, darling!" They got their drinks and she dragged him towards a corner. "Isn't Iris a duck? After all that's happened, she's kept the party going. I'm so glad, I'd have been furious if she'd cancelled it."

"Why?"

"It's my first, darling, I don't know how I managed to get invited. Oo, look! There's John Lester!" She pointed to a handsome fair man who had just entered. "Now, wouldn't *he* be just right for Iris? They do say he's keen on her, you know, but she—"

Lester didn't look real; he was like a figure in technicolour.

He went straight to Iris. "I'm sorry I'm late, my dear, I just couldn't get away before."

"It's lovely to see you, John."

Did she mean it, or was it just a platitude? The man took her hand and raised it to his lips; she seemed to like that. It might explain why she had fallen for Milanov—she had liked his foreign exuberance, his extravagant courtesies. But when she was in trouble she didn't go to John Lester, she came to Charles Corliss. He could tell that she wished she were alone with him now.

It was a quarter past twelve. Corliss meant to leave at a quarter to one, and to wait near the turning off Whitehall. That was no more than five minutes' walk away from the Department Z office, and he would be sure that he wasn't late for his appointment. The party would probably still be going on, then.

"Darling, take some notice of me!" the girl pouted up into his face. "You're so preoccupied, and we haven't so very long left."

"Why not?"

"Everyone always leaves at half past twelve, didn't you know. Say, who *are* you? It's a kind of unwritten law. Weren't you going to get me a drink?" Her glass was empty.

"I won't be long," said Corliss.

He forced his way through the crowd, and didn't go back to the girl. She wouldn't have much chance of getting near him without his noticing her. If the party were to break up at half past twelve, he would have fifteen minutes with Iris; he wanted that, it would add perfection to the evening.

Time dragged. Now and again his heart thumped so hard against his ribs that he felt suffocated, but he mustn't have too much to drink. He would be all right, once he had started on the raid. Probably he would be better outside, in the cool, but—he had to see Iris alone for a few minutes. He kept dodging the pretty girl, who was obviously searching for him.

The pianist stopped, the Shakespearean finished with a final lordly gesture, there was suddenly a mob of people about Iris, saying good night. Many of them kissed her lightly, she looked gay and happy. It was almost a miracle; for at twenty-five minutes to one, only he and Iris were left in the room.

It was a shambles.

He said: "Work to do in the morning!"

"Thank heavens it's over," Iris said. She spoke as if to a life-long friend. "Were you bored to distraction?"

"Great Scot, no!"

"I was glad you were here."

"Thanks. Is it always a mob like that?"

"Usually. The worst of it tonight was seeing strangers. There are always a few gatecrashers. I felt myself growing cold whenever I saw a stranger."

"One or two were not unknown to me," Corliss said. "We're looking after you."

"I know." She gripped his hand, the lie pleased her. "Any news of Tom?"

"Not a word."

"Annie's been dreadful all the afternoon, but she cheered up tonight," said Iris. "Have another word with her tomorrow, won't you?"

"Gladly."

Iris poked her fingers through her hair. "It's so hot in here. I ought to be tired, but I'm not."

"You look—superb."

She actually laughed. "Charles, that's just an echo of what you've been hearing everyone else say, they love paying me compliments on these nights." She went to the window, pulled aside the curtains, and then opened the window and leaned out. "Oh, what a relief, *fresh* air."

"It's nippy outside."

"It's like champagne. I—Charles!" Her eyes glowed suddenly.

"Yes?"

"Take me for a drive! Not long, just half an hour, it will do me a world of good. I didn't think I could stand it tonight, it was hotter than ever, and André—I'll get my wrap."

She hurried towards the door.

"Iris!"

She stopped and looked round at him.

It was a quarter to one, precisely; he hadn't time to take her out and then get to Whitehall. Suddenly he hated her; she'd spoiled their tête-à-tête, she'd not be in a mood for one here.

"What is it, Charles?"

"Er—I'm sorry. But you mustn't go out tonight, it would be folly."

She didn't speak, but the glow faded from her eyes.

"Sorry," he muttered. "I didn't intend to say anything, but—you'll be better off in the house. It'll be well guarded, no one can get in. Don't ask me to say anything more, I've said more than I should already."

"I see," she said. All the gaiety had gone, fear was back in her eyes. "Thank you, Charles." She closed the door, and shivered. "I'd almost forgotten for a moment. What beasts we can be, I'd almost *forgotten.*"

"We all forget."

"There are times when I hate myself," she said. Her face, still shadowed by fear, was close to his. He could see every feature in its perfection. "Charles, I don't think I can stay in this place much longer. I ought to move. You said so earlier. Something's missing, it's hollow."

"You'll get over that feeling," he said. "Don't forget that as soon as you've got André out of your system, you'll be all right. Now! I must go—you *look* tired, you must get to bed."

"I suppose I am tired," she said.

She followed him into the hall, and found his hat. Someone had left a pair of gloves behind and a silk scarf was on the floor. He picked it up and dropped it over a chair.

"Sleep well."

He took her hands, pulled her gently to him, he wanted to kiss her violently; wanted her. He felt that this could easily be a moment of triumph, she was frightened, lost and lonely, and she had broken down after maintaining that poise for so long. If he suggested that he should stay—

He kissed her lightly on the forehead.

"See you tomorrow."

He banged the front door. His car was parked out in the street, there had been no room in the drive when he had arrived. He walked rapidly. Damn her; why had she waited so long? Why had she let him feel that he was needed tonight, of all nights? Why had she made him hesitate, even for a moment, because he had been torn between two desires? He laughed; and yet there was an edge of uneasiness in his laughter. There was something about Iris Grahame which he couldn't understand, her effect on him was—dangerous? Almost dangerous; there would be no room for romance in the job he was going to do. But there might be time for quick conquest.

His car looked forlorn, parked at the side of the pavement. He reached it and opened the door.

"Why, *hallo!*" said a girl.

She had been slumped down in the seat next to the wheel, and he hadn't seen her. Now, she sat up. A street lamp lit up her face and gave it a hard, glittering brightness; it was the girl who had cornered him and sent him for drinks.

Corliss gripped the handle of the door so tightly that it hurt.

"Take me home, precious," cooed the girl. "I thought I'd wait for you, wasn't it clever of me? I arrived just after you, I recognised the car. I—"

"Get out," said Corliss in a high pitched voice.

"But, darling!"

"*Get out.*"

"Sweetheart, you don't know what you're saying. It's a long way home, I can't *walk.* I thought you'd *love* to have company for a bit. Wouldn't you? I took to you the moment I saw you."

"Get—*out.*"

His fingers and arms were quivering. She sat there looking up at him, her neck curved; it would be so easy to grip it and squeeze, and he wanted to. She didn't know how near death she was. His hand left the door, his fingers actually brushed her neck, and she didn't realise what he was doing.

"*That's* better. I—*dar*—"

He squeezed. The word came to a choking end. Her body stiffened. Her great eyes, lit up by the street lamp, were somehow like the eyes in the portrait; but they were startled, *frightened.* He didn't particularly want to frighten her, just to get her out of the way. He could drive—

He snatched his hands away.

He felt a wave of dizziness coming over him, and grabbed the side of the car. He knew that she was staring at him, but he couldn't move and couldn't speak. The girl edged away. The dizziness became worse, there was a kind of black shadow over his mind. He kept on his feet by sheer willpower.

The dizziness faded.

The girl said: "What's the matter with you?"

"Er—sorry. Not well. Shell shock." He said the first thing that came into his head. "I'll be all right. Get in the back. I'll drop you somewhere. Must get home as soon as I can."

She clambered over the front seat and dropped down.

"Thanks," she said. "Anywhere I can get a cab will do. Marble Arch."

"Yes, all right, Marble Arch." He sat at the wheel. His hands were cold, and started the engine mechanically. The wheels wobbled as he drove off. He sensed that the girl, now completely sober, was sitting rigidly on the edge of her seat; he wondered idly what she was thinking. He drove too fast, and a policeman shouted to him; fool, as if speed mattered at this time of night. Corliss slowed down, nevertheless.

He drew up by the side of the *Cumberland Hotel.*

"Thanks," said the girl. "Good night."

She jumped out and half ran towards Oxford Street, and she didn't once look behind. Corliss laughed. A porter, at the door, said: "Want a garage, sir?"

"No—no, thanks."

He drove off, more cautiously. He was better now, there would be nothing more to worry about. First Iris, then that little fool, had nearly snapped his self-control. It was much more of a strain than he had expected. But wouldn't anyone have felt like that after being baulked on such a night?

It was five past one.

He drove slowly through Hyde Park, then down Constitution Hill, and wondered where he should leave the car. On the Embankment? That would be convenient but was too near Scotland Yard. There was no point in asking for trouble, and he might have to get away in a hurry. He left the car in Petty France, at a wide spot, then walked briskly towards Parliament Square. It was a clear night and the stars were bright; the tall spire of Big Ben and the graceful lines of the Houses of Parliament showed clearly against the sky. The huge clock face glowed yellow and clear. It was twenty minutes past one, there was no hurry, he was in good time. A few cars and taxis were about and several people were walking, mostly couples.

He saw three policemen on duty outside the House, but there was none in Whitehall.

He felt buoyant.

It was probably as well that he had let off steam with the girl; he had worked the nervous excitement out of his system and would be absolutely cool and confident from now on. Better go over the plan again—he'd done that a dozen times since luncheon. Now!

Enter by the side door, go upstairs, run his fingers beneath the handle rail; press. Almost immediately the man inside— Loftus?—would press a button and the door would open. He would step through. He'd be quite calm but intent. He would apologise for coming without warning, explaining that he had something urgent to report, and he hadn't wanted to telephone but didn't want to delay. Loftus—it *must* be Loftus!—would say:

"Well, what's it all about?"

"Have a look at *this*," Corliss would answer, and he'd put his hand to his pocket and draw out his gun. He would be out of Loftus's reach—please the fates, it would be Loftus and not Craigie, there wouldn't be half the fun if it were Craigie—and there would just be time to see horror spring into the big man's eyes.

That would be a superb moment; a moment to remember and relish all his life.

Loftus would jump at him, of course, but wouldn't have any chance, being unable to move quickly with that artificial leg of his. By then the door would be closed; it was probably a soundproof room. He would shoot Loftus in the stomach, twice. Three times? He would wait until the big man fell, and then he would spend ten seconds, just ten seconds, telling him what was going to happen. Then—it was a pity but he must not waste too much time—he would shoot Loftus between the eyes. By then, His Excellency's other man would be outside. He would find the way to open the door-in-the-wall from inside, that wouldn't be difficult. The others would come in, with their special cameras. He didn't know how long it would take but the camera would probably be the cine-type, 'they' would know that the job had to be done quickly.

He reached the end of the street.

He felt quite calm and buoyant, now.

He reached the narrow door. It was a dark oblong against the grey facing of the building. He stretched out his hand for the handle—and then a thought crashed into his mind which made him snatch his hand away, filled him with an awful burden of terror.

This door might be locked.

19

THE RAID

He'd *forgotten* to make sure about that door!

He felt sick. A car passed the end of the road and he could hear a man walking along Whitehall. It might be one of the Z men, coming to report. He looked round, wild with terror. There was no cover in sight, he couldn't hide.

Big Ben struck one deep note; the half-hour. 'They' would be near at hand.

He saw a dark outline farther along the street, away from Whitehall; the squat dark shape of a car. He crossed the road quickly and went towards the car. Two men passed the end of the road; they weren't coming here, he must get a grip on himself. He hadn't even tried that door.

He went back.

The door opened at a touch.

He slipped inside and closed the door behind him. A dim blue light glowed from the first landing. He leaned against the door, with his heart thumping, then forced himself to go on. *He must steady himself.* He reached the first landing and hesitated, then he took out the whisky flask, unscrewed the cap and took a long swig; he started to cough, and checked it as best he could. Some whisky spilt over and splashed on his shoe.

He felt better; much better.

He reached the second landing. The light was brighter here. This was the landing on which Loftus had stood; that was the handrail. He was suddenly filled with doubts; was it going to be as easy as he had expected? Was there a trick Loftus knew and he didn't?

He ran his fingers beneath the handrail, slowly, careful not to exert too much pressure. He felt *nothing*. He drew back. Icy sweat stood out on his forehead. He tried again, pressing gently, and this time he felt a slight ridge. He took out his torch, went down on one knee and shone the light on to the underside of the rail. He saw a tiny circular mark. Nothing actually protruded there, no one could press that button by accident.

He switched off the torch, stood up, felt for the ridge again, placed his forefinger on it, and pushed.

Nothing happened.

He pressed harder; it was like pressing against the solid rail. The mark might only be a knot in the wood. Had he gone crazy? Was he at the wrong landing?

He felt as if he were suffocating. Five minutes must have passed now, the others would be up at any time. He pressed again, with the tip of his nail—and something moved! He pressed harder, and discovered the trick. There was a tiny slot round the circle, which he'd seen; you had to press into that, not the button itself; of course, that made it virtually impossible to give the warning signal by accident.

He pressed again.

He stood back, with his right hand at his pocket. An age

seemed to pass, and nothing happened. He had been fooled; damn Loftus, damn Craigie, they had fooled him, he—

The door in the wall began to open.

He snatched his hand away from his pocket; he mustn't have it there when he first went in, it might look suspicious. He gulped, and set his teeth, but could do nothing about the pulsing beat of his heart.

Loftus—it *must* be Loftus.

The door was open at its widest. He stepped through.

Neither Loftus nor Craigie was in the room, but a big man whom he had seen before—even before he had realised what was going to happen during this week. This was the six foot fellow of the sky-blue roadster, the man who had nearly run him down outside *The Fiddlers' Rest*.

The door closed behind Corliss.

The big man was sitting at one of the desks, looking towards him and smiling. Corliss was so worked up that he read something sinister into that smile; it was as if the man were wary already.

"Hallo, Corliss. What's doing?"

"I—had to report in a hurry."

"Well, you wouldn't come here to pass the time of day, would you?" The man stood up. He had his right hand inside his pocket, the thumb resting lightly on the outside. Had he a gun? Did he suspect?

Corliss said: "It's damnably urgent. I've found this."

He put his hand to his pocket. The other was staring at him, there *was* something sinister in the way he looked, he was suspicious. Corliss didn't speak, didn't draw his hand out, but fired three times through his pocket.

The man fell back against the desk. His mouth gaped, his eyes were wide with astonishment; he looked absurdly as Tom had when Tom had fallen. His hands were in sight, now; he hadn't a gun. He clutched the edge of the desk, then made a great effort and tried to grab a telephone.

Corliss shot him through the forehead.

Corliss did not look at the dead man again, but crossed to the fireplace and felt up and down the carving. Finding the button gave little trouble. The door seemed to open, as he pressed. Three men stepped in, glanced at the body, then at Corliss. He had seen one of them before; it was the chauffeur who had first taken him to the house near the Embassy. They didn't speak. The door closed behind them. Two of them carried a heavy looking box; they put it on a desk and took out a camera; he was right, it was a cine-camera, glistening and new. They pulled open the drawers of the filing cabinets and with a methodical thoroughness which seemed appallingly slow to Corliss, they opened file after file.

They needed more than one camera, this would take hours. Corliss moved forward as the chauffeur took a second camera from the box. The chauffeur turned to the desks. The drawers were all locked, but he forced them expertly with tools he took from his coat pocket. More files were taken out.

"Just move these," the chauffeur said, and gave Corliss two rubber gloves. "These will save finger prints."

Corliss saw what the others were doing; one man was using the camera, the other was turning over paper after paper. It was fast but not fast enough. He forced himself to keep steady, and to do what he was asked. His mouth was dry, how he needed a drink!

He kept looking towards the door.

Where was Loftus? Where was Craigie? Would they return at any moment? The gap between success and failure was so narrow, and this slowness began to infuriate him. He had suggested clearing all the stuff out; wouldn't it have been much quicker than this? Quicker, yes, but more dangerous—

they'd need several suitcases to get the contents of the drawers away. But he hadn't realised that it would take so long.

The chauffeur stopped working.

"We will send what we have finished," he said in careful English. "You will take the films, Mr. Corliss, and outside you will find another man, who will drive you to a meeting place with His Excellency."

Corliss said: "There isn't much time—"

"We shall do what we can. If we are caught—" the man shrugged. "Much will be accomplished." He took the reel from his camera and sealed it. One of the others brought a second reel. Corliss pushed them into his pocket, and went to press the button. The chauffeur watched him, and as the door opened, he said:

"Another will come in."

There was a thick-set man on the landing, who waited for Corliss to leave, then entered before the door closed behind him. A second man stood at the head of the stairs; he had an automatic in his right hand. He didn't speak. A third guard stood just inside the hallway and opened the door for Corliss. Cold wind struck at Corliss's hot face as he stepped into the street.

A man crossed the road.

"Quickly."

They turned right, and right again, towards the river. A car was drawn up at the kerb. The door opened as Corliss approached.

"Quickly!"

Corliss stepped in.

There was only the chauffeur in the car, and he drove off immediately. Corliss sat back, and wiped his forehead. He felt shivery and needed a drink more than he'd ever done in his life. He put his hand to his flask, but drew it away again; it wouldn't do to be reeking of whisky when he met His Excellency. How long would the drive take? How long would the men at the office stay there? Would they get away with their reels as easily as he had escaped with his? They pressed against his side—secrets from the inner sanctum of Department Z.

The car moved swiftly through the empty streets. He had not noticed which way they were going. Now, he looked out of the window, and saw that they were driving through one of the parks. No other car followed them—

Didn't it?

He turned and screwed his neck round to look out of the rear window. He fancied that he could see a car coming behind them. That suffocating feeling rose up in him again. He tried to speak but the words wouldn't come, he only made a faint noise in his throat, and the driver didn't hear.

There *was* a car behind them.

They reached Hyde Park Corner, turned towards the Park, then went left again, towards Knightsbridge. The car swung off the main road and took several more turnings before it stopped. Corliss, his eyes glued to the rear window, watched for the following car.

It turned the corner.

"We're here," said the driver.

Corliss said in a taut voice: "We were followed, that car—"

"Yes, we were guarded," said the driver.

Corliss gulped; he was in no mood for laughing, but changes of mood could come quickly, and one came then. For the first time since he had approached that door in Whitehall, he felt a wave of elation and buoyancy. He'd pulled it off, whatever happened now, they had those secrets! He stepped from the car to a tall, narrow house in a terrace. The front door was open. As he went in, a man in dark clothes bowed and said: "This way, please." He followed the man up a flight of carpeted stairs, and into a room on the right.

It was a small room, furnished as a study. His Excellency stood in front of the fireplace, where a coal fire burned. A woman, middle-aged, faded with grey hair and tired eyes, sat in one of the easy chairs, smoking. Above the mantelpiece was a picture of the rugged faced man—but these eyes were ordinary eyes, there was nothing vivid about them.

His Excellency said: "You have the reels?"

"Two of them." Corliss handed them over. "The others—"

"We shall get the others," said His Excellency. He was dressed in a loose-fitting lounge suit, his narrow features were relaxed, his eyes were glowing. He was human with excitement. "We shall get them all, Corliss, and—we are delighted with you. Delighted."

Corliss said: "Loftus and Craigie weren't there."

"But naturally, Corliss. Come!" His Excellency laid a hand on his shoulder and led him across the room to a cocktail cabinet. The woman didn't move but watched Corliss all the time. "We did not leave everything to you, my friend. You will drink—whisky?"

"Please."

"No, we did not leave everything to you," said the woman. Her voice was low-pitched and musical, obviously native English. "You must not make the mistake now or at any time of thinking that you will be permitted to do *everything* yourself. Listen, Corliss." He turned to look at her, with the whisky in his hand. "That doorway, of course, is always watched by the police and by the Z men. Tonight, we arranged for the watchers to be removed. Once each hour, a man makes a patrol, to see that all is well. Our own agents replaced those who had been removed, and satisfied him, and he will not return again until all is finished."

Corliss exclaimed: "That's wonderful!"

"It was, of course, wise that Craigie and Loftus should not be at the office. So, arrangements were made for an emergency to happen, which took them both away, and they left another agent to look after the office. This emergency took place in the Midlands. There is no chance of them returning for some hours."

Corliss gave a bark of a laugh, and sipped his whisky. He didn't need it so badly now.

"Also, we wish you to continue with the Department," the woman said flatly. "So—it is necessary for there to be conclusive proof that you did not force your way into the office tonight. Evidence that you have been elsewhere has been provided, you will be given a written summary, so that you can learn it off by heart and know exactly what to say."

Corliss began to laugh again, and this time he couldn't stop himself. He didn't try to speak. The whisky lapped over the edge of the glass and on to his fingers, but still he couldn't stop.

Then he felt dizziness coming over him.

He was standing near His Excellency, and knew he would fall unless he sat down quickly. He moved back, leaned against the cabinet and tried to keep his eyes in focus; but the woman's face seemed to be going round and round.

She kept speaking; he did not know what she said.

The dizziness passed.

"So, there is no need for you to be alarmed," she said. "You understand?

"I—"

"I will repeat the last instructions," the woman said patiently. "You will return to your flat and go to bed. If you should be asked why you were in so late, you will find the answer in the sheet of instructions, which you will read in the car. You will be taken from here to Marble Arch, where you will find your own car—it has been moved from where you left it."

"I see," said Corliss. He finished his drink. "It's perfect!"

"You will do much more good work," said His Excellency gently. "Very much more, Corliss. It is important that we quickly learn the effect of this raid upon Loftus and Craigie. You understand that?"

"Yes, of course."

"Good, very good." His Excellency pressed a bell in the wall behind him, and after a pause, a man came in. "Alexis, these are to be developed, quickly, and one print and the film sent off, by air, before morning."

"Yes, Excellency."

"Now, Corliss! Another drink?"

"No, thanks."

"Then you will go," said His Excellency, "and remember that you have earned *his* gratitude."

He glanced at the portrait above the mantelpiece. Corliss looked up. The eyes weren't vivid; it was a pity, it spoiled the savour, somehow. He smiled mechanically and went towards the door.

His Excellency had covered everything.

Corliss sat in the car with the blinds drawn and the light on, reading the summary of 'his movements' since he had left St. John's Woods. 'They' knew that he had dropped the girl at Marble Arch, and there was a note: 'The porter at the hotel will have recognised you'. From there, he had 'driven out of London on one of his night jaunts'. He would be able to give particulars of three places where, for one reason or another, he had stopped and where his car would be recognised. In each case, one of 'them' would be prepared to swear that he had seen the car and recognised him. It was so simple, as well as in keeping with his usual habits.

He wanted to laugh wildly.

His own car was parked behind the *Cumberland Hotel* and ten minutes after he had taken the wheel, he was at his flat. He went up the stairs, quickly, memorising everything that was in the sheet of instructions; the first thing he must do was to burn that; he had everything off by heart, now.

He opened the door and hurried inside. The door slammed behind him.

Then he saw the light on in the living-room.

He stopped. His right hand dived towards his pocket, and tucked the paper away. That lost precious moments, and before he drew out his gun, a man called:

"I surrender!"

It was—*Wilson*, the exquisite.

20

COMPANY FOR THE NIGHT

H allo, old chap," said Wilson brightly. "I'm not a ghost. Solid as ever. Out a bit late, aren't you?"

The remark seemed casual.

Corliss recovered his poise and took his hand away from his pocket; the paper was in there, with the gun. Wilson was in a pale blue silk dressing-gown, decorated with lions; he looked as exquisite as ever, and his fine eyes were bright.

"You've company for the night," he said. "Sorry if you're disappointed about the purposes of the other bed!"

"Er—don't be an ass."

"That's almost impossible," said Wilson. "I have the reputation of being an insufferable ass. But I have other qualities which come in useful. Didn't you go to Iris's party?"

"Yes. It was like a Turkish bath. Afterwards, I went for a drive."

"Odd habit of yours, that," said Wilson, and turned into the living-room; that remark also sounded casual. "Not a bad notion, as a matter of fact. Heard anything?"

"About what?"

"Some kind of shindy in the Midlands," Wilson said. "Loftus went tearing off there—something to do with an atomic pile, I believe. Hark at me! One day I shall remember not to talk. Well, what about a drink?"

"I think I'll have some coffee."

"Please yourself, old chap, I want a nip of something a bit stronger."

"I'll go and make the coffee," Corliss said.

He hurried out, and found his fingers clenching by his sides; the tingling had started. His head felt as if it were swelling like a balloon, too; was he going to have a dizzy spell? He didn't go straight into the kitchen but to the bathroom. He shut the door, tore the instruction sheet into several pieces, dropped them into the bowl and pulled the plug. He felt better when that was done. He took it easily, went into the kitchen and put on a coffee percolator; it wouldn't take long to heat up. He lit a cigarette. He hadn't panicked, but he'd never felt so bad as when he'd seen that light.

Wilson, of all people!

His lips curled.

The dizzy spell faded before it really developed, but he had time to tell himself that he really needed a rest. He ought to have a few days in the country; why not at the *Fiddlers'*? And a few days ago he had been complaining bitterly because there was so little for him to do! He laughed, quite naturally. The coffee began to bubble. He took it in, with two cups and saucers and some biscuits. Wilson was drinking gin; he sat in one of the easy chairs, with a book open on his knees, a pipe between his lips; he wasn't, somehow, a man you would expect to smoke a pipe.

"That didn't take long."

"No."

"I suppose we ought to tuck ourselves in and go bye-byes,"

216

said Wilson brightly. "We might get a sudden call to go to the ends of the earth—you haven't been with us long enough to know what happens when there's a real emergency, have you? I've known Loftus was worried about something lately, of course—you can always tell, with the great man."

'They' had made one mistake; Loftus ought to be dead by now. He'd have to go, and he, Corliss, would have the job as executioner, 'they'd' have to allow him that privilege. He wouldn't mind getting rid of Wilson, too; he was beginning to hate the man's bright chatter and silly phraseology; in its way, it was as bad as André's. But Wilson was garrulous and accepted Corliss without any reservations; he would be as good an informant as any of the Z men. Let him live! Corliss had so wanted to be alone tonight, had expected—

He must show an intelligent interest in what Wilson said:

"You think Loftus has been expecting this Midlands business?"

"Could be. I've just known that there's something on his mind. We're having a tough spell, you know. I—but you probably haven't heard."

"Remember, I'm just a new chum."

Wilson said: "Once you're in the game as deep as this, you rate as an old stager. One of the quickest—not *the* quickest—promotion jobs I've ever seen. Yours, I mean—you have what Loftus calls all the necessary qualifications." Wilson spoke lightly, but he was frowning and there was a different expression in his eyes; it made him seem older and, for the first time, gave an inkling of the strength in the man. "You haven't heard about Abby, of course."

"What about Abby?"

"He's had it."

"Oh," said Corliss. He sipped his coffee; and inwardly fumed. How on earth had 'they' slipped up in such a way as to let the Department know what had happened to Abbott? They shouldn't be able to do more than guess, at this juncture. "That's bad. I'm—"

"Yes, I know. He and I have strung along a lot, during the past ten years. No doubt he's had it, though. And no doubt that we'll get those who gave it to him, either."

Corliss said: "It's a hell of a game. I always knew it was. My father—"

"Forget it," said Wilson. "My trouble is that I talk too much. That's really because there are so many times when it's almost fatal to say a word. Well! I'm going to turn in."

"I won't be long."

Wilson closed his book and went to the door. Corliss thought he'd gone, but the man looked back. He spoke in a shrill tone of alarm and managed to put alarm into Corliss, who stared at him steadily, gripping the arm of his chair with his free hand.

"I say, Corliss!"

"Well?"

"Be honest. You don't snore, do you?"

Corliss felt like hurling the cup at his head.

"No. You can sleep in peace."

"Thanks be for that," said Wilson fervently. "Nighty-night."

"Good night."

The door closed. Corliss put his cup down and sat quite still. He was alone at last, but Wilson had completely spoilt the savour of his hour. He felt flat and wary—and angry. The maudlin fool! To talk like that about snoring, as if he were terrified of a bad night's rest. What on earth had got into Loftus that he used men of such calibre?

Corliss remembered Wilson's expression when he had talked about Abbott. That had shown a different side to the man. He could be sure that any of the Z men had some qualities and that Loftus wouldn't pick many failures.

He began to smile.

It was half an hour before he went to bed. Wilson seemed to be fast asleep. His head was bent forward, and the nape of his neck showed, like an invitation. Corliss undressed and got into bed. Forget Wilson; remember that he himself was still under orders to work with the Department, and if he could stay after this there would be no limit to the damage he could do. If he were sensible, he would realise that Wilson would be looking for a confidant; why not be that man? Out of his experience with the Department, Wilson would be able to tell him a great deal. It would be worth putting up with the man's babbling talk.

He went to sleep.

It was like seeing the same shot of a film, over again. He woke up with a ringing sound in his ears; it had happened like this before. The harsh, discordant note was loud in his ear. Why the devil wouldn't it stop, who—

It was the telephone.

And Wilson was in the flat.

Corliss sat up in bed. The bell was still ringing. He shot out his hand for the instrument and it stopped ringing before he had touched it, just as it had the previous morning. There was no telling who this might be, and—

He put the receiver to his ear.

"Who—"

"Well, I'll try," Wilson was saying; so this was an extension. Wilson was up and at the main instrument. "He's a bit heavy-headed this morning, sleeping like a log. Who shall I say it is?"

"Miss Grahame."

"Right-ho. You may have to hang on for a bit."

Corliss heard the clatter of the other instrument being put

down. He replaced his own, quickly, and dropped back on to the pillows. Wilson poked his head round the door; he looked like a tailor's dummy, and his mouth was shaped into a large O.

"I say, Corliss."

"Eh? What?" Corliss let his eyes flicker open. "I—didn't I hear the 'phone?"

"That's it. A certain young lady would like to speak to you. Iris Grahame."

"Oh. Thanks."

"Pleasure. Wake yourself properly, I've warned her that she may have to wait." Wilson winked and disappeared. Corliss grabbed the telephone, and steeled himself to speak calmly; he was agitated, because Wilson *might* listen in at the other instrument. If Iris said anything about Tom—

"Hallo, my dear!"

"I'm sorry to wake you, Charles, but—"

"That's perfectly all right. I ought to have been up hours ago. I'm coming straight over to see you, as soon as I've had a cup of coffee."

"Don't be long, because—"

"I know what it's like," said Corliss hastily. Was he doing what was needed? Was he fooling Wilson, if the man were listening? He climbed off the bed as he spoke. "I shouldn't worry too much, Iris, you need not."

He peered through the crack between the door and frame, but couldn't see Wilson. Then he heard a tap running; so Wilson was in the kitchen or bathroom.

"Sorry," Corliss said gently and softly. "Another man was with me, but he's gone. I didn't want anyone to overhear me."

"I see. You will come?"

"Why?"

"Annie is more agitated than ever this morning, I don't think I can keep her quiet much longer. A policeman called."

"About—what?"

"Tom. Apparently his landlady reported that he was missing, and the police came round to inquire whether we'd heard from him. Annie seems to think that if they knew about it from you, they wouldn't have troubled. I know she's foolish, but—"

"You're half as foolish yourself." Corliss laughed. "I wish you'd called because you wanted to see me. One day—"

"I should be lost without you," Iris said. "Quite lost."

"That's good to hear," said Corliss. His lip was curling. "I'll get along as soon as I can."

Wilson, fully dressed, had a towel tied round his waist and was cooking eggs and bacon. He brandished a fork.

"Smells good, old boy, doesn't it? Two eggs or three?"

"Glutton. One—"

"Not when you've friends who live in the country, and friends like mine," said Wilson. "Call it two. Take a quick tub, and eat in your dressing-gown. Nothing shocks me. I say, you're not one of the strong and silent type first thing in the morning, are you? I've known men who wanted to strangle me for burbling before ten o'clock."

"I just don't listen," said Corliss.

Wilson chuckled; it would be simple to make him a friend. How much should he tell the other man? Did Wilson know of the mission he was serving for Loftus with the actress? The wise thing would be to assume that he didn't; Loftus would probably be more impressed if he were told that he'd said nothing about the call.

Wilson wasn't all talk; he was a good cook.

It was sunny again; the brightest morning of the week and quite warm. The air was fresh. There were traces of dampness in the gutters, so it had been raining. Corliss walked briskly to his garage, and was surprised that he could feel so free. That was partly due to Wilson; it had been a good thing, after all, that he'd had company. He could imagine that by now he would have been worked up and tense, peering round corners, in case someone came for him. Instead, Wilson's complete trust had reassured him. In the clear light of morning, it was evident that he was secure.

He could deal a savage blow at the country's security, and next morning walk past policemen without turning a hair—without being in danger and without feeling nervous! He felt very much better than he had the previous day, because the raid was in the past. It wasn't to be wondered at that he had been jittery the previous day; the marvel was that he had kept his nerve so well. It hadn't let him down at any crucial moment. Quite the worst moment had been standing by the side of the car, and seeing the fluffy-haired girl sitting there. He'd come within an ace of breaking her neck.

There was only one serious snag.

He had a complete answer to any questions they might ask about the previous night. He'd simply give that faked itinerary. They would make inquiries if they felt suspicious and find the witnesses to prove that he had not been in the centre of London. The snag was Tom; it was always the unexpected that caused the trouble. If he'd been warned that Tom was going to be at the house, that would never have happened, he would have timed his visit better. That was really Iris's fault, she had led him up the garden.

She would be lost without him, would she?

He laughed.

Everything was normal. He drove to Parliament Square and then along Whitehall. There was no unusual assembly of police near the narrow door, nothing to suggest what had happened. Of course, there would be nothing about the raid in the newspapers, the whole business would be hushed up. But it would shake the Government's confidence in its Intelligence service pretty badly. He had to be careful now, to be sure that he didn't make a slip. He had to prove himself exceptionally 'good with women'; with Annie. He could be dispassionate this morning, and face this simple fact: if Tom were reported missing too soon, it would probably be associated with what had happened at the house. Loftus would guess the truth, and Loftus wouldn't have much faith in a man who would fail to report a thing like that. It went deeper, too; Loftus would want to know how he had managed to hide Tom's body. It was simply a fact that he must keep Annie quiet, at all cost.

How?

A dead Annie?

"Steady," he said aloud. That wouldn't do; a dead Annie would also need a dead Iris, because if there were a further tragedy, Iris would probably realise the truth; she could hardly fail to. The real weakness of his position was centred in that house, and while either woman remained alive—

Well, face the fact; they could damn him.

He drove more slowly, and went by a roundabout route. He had a new notion, and one which might work. It came quietly and insistently into his mind. Loftus suspected Iris of a part in the Red plot; that she had really worked with Milanov. Milanov had committed suicide. If Iris did the same, and Annie disappeared, then the immediate risks would be past.

He'd have to decide quickly.

If Iris 'killed herself'—a suicide would be fairly easy to fake, and the ostensible reason for it would be that she knew she had been watched and was in acute danger—what about Annie? Once the police were in the house, making inquiries, there was little doubt that the maid would talk, and once she started, she would leave nothing out. Both women had to be silenced, but—supposing Annie *disappeared.* Supposing both she and her Tom were missing, wouldn't the obvious conclusion be reached? That they, too, were in the plot, and knowing that Iris had been driven to suicide, wasn't it natural for them to disappear?

How could he get rid of Annie?

He laughed aloud, and a passer-by looked at him curiously. Corliss didn't notice that. Getting Annie away from the house would be the easiest thing in the world. If he sent her a faked message, that she would see her Tom if she went to a certain place, she would go. Her mistress could go to blazes, nothing would keep Annie away from Tom.

He pulled up outside a telephone kiosk at a corner, and, without a quiver, dialled 'their' number. For once, he was answered quickly.

"Corliss."

"Yes."

"There will be another parcel, a lively one, to take care of soon."

"Yes."

"Can *she* be met at the same place as yesterday?"

"Yes."

"She's a middle-aged woman, five feet four or five, grey-haired, thin, flat breasted. I shall tell her to look for a man wearing a Homburg hat and carrying a newspaper under his right arm. Is that all right?"

"Yes."

"She's very interested in the first parcel and her interest might be fatal."

"Very well," said the man at the other end of the line. "You will be careful."

Corliss laughed.

He waited for thirty seconds after ringing off, and then put in a call to Iris's house. He watched the traffic moving along the street and saw two young women, yellow-haired, smartly dressed, walking towards him. They were brisk and vivacious, more than normally attractive. The ringing sound was in his ears.

"Hallo?" It was Annie herself.

"Annie?" The two women drew nearer and looked at him as women always did; even framed in a telephone kiosk, he drew their attention.

"Yes, who is that?" demanded Annie.

"Now listen to me carefully. I have news of Tom. It isn't—"

"Are you *sure?*"

"Yes, be quiet. It isn't what you thought. He's in trouble. I want to help if I can, but you have to be careful. He'll be waiting for you, in an hour's time. Go to the railway bridge at Barnes Common. Tom won't be visible, but a friend of his will be standing near a car, wearing a Homburg hat—you know what a Homburg looks like, don't you?"

"*Yes!*" she hissed.

"He'll also be carrying a folded newspaper under his right arm. He'll take you to Tom, but—"

"Yes?"

"Don't talk to anyone on the way. I shouldn't tell Miss Grahame, until you know what Tom's done. I can't promise that I can do anything about it, but if you'll do exactly what I tell you, I may be able to help."

"I see," she said. "Barnes Common ..."

He hung about the telephone kiosk for a few minutes and then drove towards Iris's house by a roundabout route. When he came within sight of the house, he pulled up and waited to see whether Annie appeared. He gave her ten minutes, and there was no sign of her. She would be gone by now. It cleared the ground beautifully. Iris—that problem remained. How would she commit suicide? Shoot herself? She wasn't likely to have a gun in the house. Hang herself? That would probably be best. He let his mind roam over the difficulties. Police surgeons and pathologists were experts, they would soon pick out marks of hand-strangulation. But if Iris were near him, he could slip a noose over her neck and draw it tight before she realised what was happening. Then he'd string her up somewhere.

He'd need a rope.

Even that was easy; he had one in the back of the car! He got out and lifted up the boot; yes, there it was, a fairly long piece and new, he'd bought it some weeks ago, to secure excess luggage. He didn't need too much of it. He cut it in half, and made a note in his mind to get rid of the other half.

Then he drove to the house.

He felt fine, this morning; the climax was really over, this was chicken feed to what had happened last night. There was no likelihood of Iris suspecting what was about to happen. She would open the door herself, and she would probably be worried because Annie had gone off in a hurry; unless Annie had told her. That was a flaw in his arrangements but he would be able to cope, if the need arose.

He was quite calm.

He drove straight up to the house, hurried out of the car and rang the bell, but the door opened before his finger had left the push.

Iris looked—superb.

21

THE NOOSE

"Come in, Charles."

He took her hands and held them tightly, smiled in a way he knew was warming and reassuring, then put his arm round her waist and went indoors.

"How is she?" he asked.

"She would have been all right if that policeman hadn't called," said Iris. "She has this silly idea that every policeman ought to know about it, if you've put out the general call you said you had."

"The chap probably does know," said Corliss. Hadn't Annie left, after all? That now familiar suffocating feeling came over him. "Where is she?"

"In the kitchen, washing up," said Iris.

If Annie hadn't gone, she hadn't believed him. If she were still in the kitchen, she would surely have told Iris about the call; which meant that Iris was fooling him. He looked at her, sharply. She was a little ahead of him, now, leading the way to the kitchen. She seemed quite calm. She turned her head a little at the door and he could see her profile at its best; it did not matter how you looked at Iris Grahame, she was beautiful.

She opened a door.

"Annie, here's Mr.—"

She broke off, as if in surprise. The big kitchen, half-tiled and painted bright cream, was empty. On the two draining boards were piles of glasses and plates. A dozen or so glasses stood upturned on a tray on the square, deal-topped table; they had been washed. The window was open, and a gentle breeze blew in.

"Annie!" called Iris.

"She'll be here in a minute," Corliss said. He wiped his forehead, then took out his cigarette-case. His fingers touched the coil of rope, which bulged in his pocket. He patted it down, but couldn't hide the bulge altogether. "Cigarette?"

"Not now, thanks. I could have sworn she would be here. I've been upstairs, and came down when I saw you drive in. *Annie!*"

There was no answer.

"Her coat's gone!" Iris exclaimed. "She always keeps it behind the door, in case she had to hurry off to the shops. Her hat—it's absurd, Charles."

She looked astounded, and kept glancing round the kitchen, as if Annie might pop up from beneath the sink or in through the back door.

"Well, she's probably remembered something she wants from the shops, and hurried off to get it."

"But she would have told me she was going out."

Charles shrugged. "Forget it. Iris, I—"

"But I can't just shrug it off like that. It doesn't make sense. There was a telephone call, and I asked her to answer it. I was in the bathroom. She shouted up to say it was the grocer. I could have sworn—"

228

"He was offering her some prize tit-bit and she dashed off to get it," said Corliss. "Don't worry about it."

"You don't know Annie!" Iris turned and led the way into the little morning-room. She was agitated—more so than the circumstances seemed to warrant. She wasn't really the same woman as she had been last night. He had pictured her being in exactly the same mood as when she had asked him to take her for a drive, but that had gone. A pity. She sat heavily on the arm of a chair. She wore a two-piece suit, greeny grey in colour, and a white blouse. By coincidence, the blouse had a V neck. It wasn't cut low; but it showed her neck in all its slender loveliness.

"May I have that cigarette now?"

"Of course." He lit it for her. "Did you have a good night?"

"Not bad. I'm not sleeping too well, these days. Charles, have you any news of Tom?"

He shook his head.

"Anything?"

"Well—"

"Don't keep anything back."

He said easily but with a low-pitched voice which suggested that he hated what he had to tell her: "There is some news, my dear."

"About what?"

"The death of that man in the theatre. We've managed to get hold of one of the cleaners, who was there late—she'd stayed to see the rehearsals. Quite a fan of yours, she thinks everything you do is wonderful, *and* I don't blame her! Apparently she left a bucket of water at the back of the stalls, and went to get it after the rehearsal was over. She saw—"

"André?"

"Yes. He was talking to a little man. We had quite a spot of bother with her." The lies gave birth to more so beautifully and easily, and the absolute faith which Iris showed in him made him feel like an artist at the job; it was a form of acting, she was really no better than he. He went on: "This woman had refused to volunteer a statement because she knew that you and André were fond of each other, and she didn't want to say anything which would make difficulties for you. The most unlikely people become fond of you, don't they?"

Iris didn't speak.

"Of course, it was pretty obvious from the beginning that André had killed him. It's no use mincing words. Once you know the truth, you'll be able to start seriously on the job of getting him out of your system."

"Do you know for certain what work André was doing, yet?"

"I don't. My chief probably does—I'm only a very small cog in a very large wheel. I can tell you that my people seem to think that the show will soon be over. There won't be anything much about it in the newspapers, of course, it's very hush-hush. But at least you needn't worry any more."

"Last night you said—"

"Last night was last night. The house was watching. Two men tried to break in, but were caught before they'd really started. They were at the back of the house. They've confessed that they had orders to prevent you from talking. And they worked with André. There's no doubt that his employers were afraid that he'd talked too freely to you, and you know how ruthless they are. But I don't think they'll be able to do anything else. Most of them are either caught or next door to it."

Iris said: "Oh. And you—"

"My turn for a spot of leave!" He laughed. "How's this play of yours going?"

"Quite well."

"No hope that it'll be a short run, and we could have a week or two in the country, just amusing ourselves?"

"No, Charles. I wish there were, but—"

He crossed to her side, and sat down on the sofa resting a hand on her arm. Looking up at her, he saw that everything he had thought about her before was true; you could look at her from any angle, and she was beautiful. It was a thousand pities that what had to be, would be. As he smiled gently up at her, his thoughts ran smoothly. Annie would not come back. By mid-day, perhaps earlier, Iris would be really anxious. There were already doubts in her mind; the coming of that policeman had implanted them. She would probably insist on reporting Annie's disappearance herself. There was no way of letting her escape and remaining safe, and too much was at stake to allow any risks.

He looked round the room.

There was nothing to fasten the rope to, here, but he had noticed a hook in the kitchen ceiling. It would be easy to carry her along the passage. He would have to make sure that the door and windows were closed in this room and in the kitchen; it would be necessary to get her to move. She was sitting too high, at the moment, and might be visible from a side window of the house next door.

He gripped her arm more tightly.

"You need a rest, you know."

"I shall be all right."

"Is there anything at all that I can do?"

"Not now. I hardly feel anything, I'm just numbed, everything's gone wrong." She looked at André's photograph, jumped up and crossed to it. Damn her! He had wanted her to sit down, to collapse into his arms, he had expected that she would. She was frightened and taut inside and fighting against collapse, she wouldn't want to break down in front of him.

He stood up, and moved behind her. She studied the photograph, intently. He put his hand to his pocket and felt the rope. The knot of the noose ran between his fingers. He began to pull it out.

She swung round.

Here was the moment for collapse—

No; she dropped on to the piano stool, flung up the lid of the piano with a crash, and began to play. He hadn't known that she could play so well. She chose a thing of Tchaikovsky's which rippled, welled out, grew into a furious medley, a reflection of her troubled spirit. Her shoulders moved, her fingers sped over the keys, the room resounded to the burst of music.

She could not be seen from the house alongside.

He stood behind her, and placed his left hand on her shoulder. She did not seem to notice it. He slid his hand slowly downwards, to the gentle rise of her breast, and she went on playing. He took his right hand out of his pocket and held the rope. He glanced down. His heart began to pump and his head seemed to swell. He stood quite still; he mustn't get a dizzy spell, now. The attack only threatened and he felt all right; she still played and still ignored his hand, which rested lightly yet possessively. He fingered the noose, which was large enough to slip over her head without any difficulty. He raised it; she was more than halfway through the piece and wouldn't stop until it had ended; wouldn't stop of her own volition.

He took his left hand away, and drew back.

It was a pity that he had to use the rope; his hands were much more capable and swift, but Loftus would know in a moment if he broke her neck, and he still had to fool Loftus. He held the noose lightly in his two hands and raised it. He caught his breath. The music welled up, reaching a wild, almost frenzied note. He held the noose over her head and poised it there.

He slipped it down!

It caught against her nose, and she faltered. Next moment it was round her neck and he was drawing it tight. The music stopped, her hands rippled raggedly over the keys as she turned round, half rising from her stool. He tugged at the rope with one hand and pushed her down with the other. The horror in her eyes had to be seen to be believed.

"Char—"

The rope caught her throat and choked the word. She snatched at his hands but could not do a thing, already the rope was embedded in her creamy white flesh. He grinned at her. He didn't speak but pulled the noose tight and there was a gurgling sound in her throat. Her eyes took on a silvery glitter, as if she knew that death was coming and dreaded it. Yes, she was frightened now, and there was absolutely nothing she could do about it.

And then the door opened.

2 2

THE EMPTY ROOM

Corliss dropped the rope and spun round, his right hand moving towards his pocket. Iris fell backwards. The door hit the wall and swung back as *Wilson* came in.

It was Wilson, but he'd never looked like this before. His eyes were glittering and there was cold hatred on his face. He came forward like a shot from a gun, and reached Corliss before Corliss could raise the automatic inside his pocket.

Wilson hit him.

It was a smashing blow on the side of the chin, and seemed to split the bone. Corliss shot backwards, crashed and hit the side of the sofa, but he wasn't knocked out. Blind rage merged with desperate fear. His right hand was still at his pocket, his right side towards Wilson. He groped for the trigger.

Wilson came at him. Corliss felt the trigger, but before he could squeeze it or train the gun, Wilson gripped his wrist. Agony shot through his forearm and travelled like a flash up to his shoulder. He grunted with pain and his fingers came away from the gun. Wilson pulled his hand out of his pocket, took the gun out, and for a moment levelled it towards Corliss's head.

Death sneered at Corliss.

Wilson's eyes flamed at him.

Then Wilson checked himself. Corliss saw him turn the gun and hold it by the barrel. Corliss tried to back away, but Wilson struck him on the temple, twice. Pain went through his head, dizziness came more swiftly and more painfully than he had ever known it. He felt himself slump forward. A third blow descended on the back of his neck, and he felt as if something snapped; he lost consciousness.

He did not know where he was when he first came round. He was conscious only of pain which filled his head and his right hand and arm; and of sickness. He lay absolutely still. When he tried to open his eyes, there was a roaring sound in his ears, and a red mist all about him; his forehead felt pulpy, as if it were all cracked and mangled.

He remembered Abbott.

Then, slowly, he remembered everything.

He was in too much pain to move, but could think; and he knew that this was the finish. Wilson—that babbling fool!—had suspected him. That was probably why Wilson had spent the night at the flat. Never mind why—where was he lying? What could he do?

He tried to move his hands, but couldn't; so they were tied. He couldn't open his eyes because of pain. He was lying flat, on something hard; it wasn't a bed. He knew that it was still daylight. After a long time, he dared to try to open his eyes and the pain was like fire. He gasped aloud. That was the first sound he had heard since coming round. No one spoke. Was he alone in this room?

Where was he?

He tried to open his eyes again and succeeded, but couldn't

really see; his eyes seemed to be on fire and the light was too bright. He lay still but his mind kept working although he didn't want to think; thinking hurt with almost physical force. He was lying on his side and his knees were bent. The pain in his right arm wasn't because of Wilson's vicious twist at his wrist, but because he was lying on his arm. The position was awkward, the pain was a combination of pins and needles and a gnawing ache. He tried to ease his position, but it hurt too much.

He wriggled his fingers.

He could just touch the rope which bound his wrists; it was a rope with a rather rough surface—like the rope of which he had made the noose. He felt the knot.

Could he—*undo* it?

He tensed himself to try, but it hurt too much at first. He rested, and opened his eyes again. It was a little easier to see and he was able to keep them open for a few seconds. He was still in the morning-room, lying by the side of the sofa; he could see the feet of the stool and the bottom of the piano.

He heard voices, as if a long way off. Were they coming for him?

It was easy to imagine what had happened. Wilson had telephoned Loftus or one of the other agents, several of them would soon be here. If Loftus were back from the Midlands he would come himself—and how he would gloat.

Well, the gloating wouldn't be all on one side. Nothing could undo the success of the raid on the Department. By now, those photographs of the precious records were on their way by air to a place where full use would be made of them. 'They' would soon know exactly what Loftus and the Department knew about the Red cells in Britain; and they would be able to give orders for the cells to break up, and reform. It would be a deadly blow at British Intelligence. No, Loftus wouldn't be the only one who would gloat, but—that didn't help.

If he could get away—

Would 'they' rescue him? He'd done enough to be sure that they would help all they could, he deserved help as few others could deserve it. If he could get away, reach headquarters, get inside and find sanctuary, he would be all right. They' would smuggle him out of the country.

He began to pluck at the cords again.

The voices were nearer.

"Sure you're all right?" That was Wilson.

"Yes, darling, thanks." She'd said 'darling'; and although her voice sounded husky it was unmistakably Iris's. "No need to worry, now."

"No. When Bill's had a go at young Mr. Corliss, he'll know a thing or two. But I don't want to go through that again. The swine moved so fast."

Corliss found himself straining his ears to listen, and stopping his work at the rope. The knot seemed a trifle looser. He started afresh. The others were either just outside the door or in the next room with the door open; he could hear every word, now.

"I wonder what got into him," Iris said.

"It's hard to say. He should have been all right. Loftus thinks he's a psychopathic case."

'Loftus thinks'—the *devil*! So they thought he was mad. That was the excuse Loftus made for his own bad judgment; *mad.* He'd show them all whether he was mad or not!

"There were times when he almost fooled me, darling."

"He had most of us guessing."

He'd had them *all* guessing. And—the knot was a little looser, he could move his wrists fairly freely. Once he could get his wrists free, he would be able to untie the rope at his ankles. Give him another quarter of an hour, and he would do plenty of damage yet.

"You had to work on a precious pair. Which did you prefer?" Wilson said. What did he mean?

Corliss stopped working again. He felt sick, but not with pain. The words went round and round in his mind, together with their implication.

Iris had worked on a precious pair—

Iris was one of the Department's agents.

"Oh, Milanov," she answered quite firmly.

"The continental, eh? I am to inform you, here and now, Miss Grahame, that I shall in future be wildly jealous of every man who kisses even your hand."

Iris laughed. "Idiot!"

"Seriously, you've done quite a job," said Wilson. "Craigie isn't keen on using women, as you know, but he had to break into the theatrical cell in the West End, and he believed me when I said no one could do it better than you. It's broken up, by the way—one of the little things that have been happening. We've got tabs on all of the people concerned. No big shots. The known Red sympathisers are only with Moscow in theory. Milanov was the contact man, and kept trying to get some of the big names to sell their souls. No luck. By obligingly falling for you, Milanov—"

"Darling, could *any* man resist me if I set my cap at him?"

Wilson laughed, but there was an edge to his voice.

"Yes, my sweet. One did. Mr. Corliss wasn't so overcome by your charms that he was prepared to take you and leave the others. I ought to have broken his neck!"

Corliss clenched his teeth. He had stopped working at the rope, he couldn't think or move because of the blind rage which shook him. They had fooled him completely. The woman was in the Department, she had worked first against

Milanov and then, because he had been suspected, against him. Loftus had known all the time; or at least been suspicious, but—Loftus had made that crazy mistake. He had let Corliss get into the office of the Department: it hadn't been more than suspicion then, just another kind of test.

Was the aeroplane with the prints anywhere near Russia, yet? It was sure to be.

Someone walked along the passage.

"Excuse me, Miss Iris, but will you have some coffee?"

That was *Annie.* Corliss felt as if he were choking.

"Not a bad idea," said Wilson.

"Yes, Annie, thanks."

So she had been in the house all the time. She had told Iris about the message, Iris had realised that it was false—Iris must have known all the time that he had made no report about Tom. Loftus had known that Tom was missing, from the first. They'd strung him along, but they'd underestimated him. They hadn't thought he'd the nerve to break into the office.

He hated their guts; if he could only get free he'd finish them off yet. If he could only get his hands round Loftus's neck—

Annie passed the door again.

Corliss felt a cold sweat break out all over him; it wasn't any use lying there and breathing vengeance. He couldn't do anything, now, except—save himself. If he could only get to headquarters he would be safe. He mustn't listen to what the couple were saying, he must get *free.*

He began to work at the cords again. It was surprisingly easy. His wrists had plenty of room in which to move.

The rope fell aside.

Corliss stood up, but had to lean against the sofa to keep his balance. But his wrists and ankles were free, a few minutes' massage at his ankles and he would be able to move about.

Mechanically, his hand went to his pocket and groped; the gun wasn't there, of course. What about the second gun? He moved his hand swiftly to his hip pocket. It was empty, except for his keys, they'd taken that and his pen-knife.

He looked round the room. The door was open. There were poker and tongs in a small stand in the fireplace; it wasn't much of a poker, but he could do some damage with it at close quarters. He moved slowly and bent down to pick it up. The blood went to his head, which still felt pulpy, but he had been able to move without holding on to anything.

He took a deep breath.

Then, very slowly, he began to walk round the room. He gave the tables and chairs a wide berth, lest he should stumble and knock into one and raise the alarm. He kept clear of them all. When he had made a circuit of the room three times, he knew that his legs would carry him. He had given up all thoughts of revenge. The window was actually open a few inches at the bottom. If he could get out, reach the main road, getting to Feltham Street would become a possibility. He went to the window, rubbing at his wrists, which were ridged where the cord had bitten into the flesh. They were hot and painful. He put his fingers beneath the window and pushed it up gently; he scarcely dared breathe.

He slipped behind the curtain as Annie walked along the passage, and cups chinked together on a tray; what wouldn't he give for a cup of coffee? His mouth was like sandpaper.

The window moved two or three inches and didn't make any noise. The three in the next room were talking. He eased the window up—and it squeaked. He snatched his hands away, grabbed the poker, and turned to stare towards the doorway. The others went on talking.

He pushed at the window again, until it was open nearly eighteen inches.

Was there a window in the next room overlooking this narrow stretch of garden? If so, he couldn't get past without being seen, and Wilson wouldn't hesitate to shoot. Corliss looked out of the window; no, there wasn't another, the next room faced the front garden.

He climbed out; no one was in sight.

He put the poker inside his trouser waistband as he stood upright, glancing both ways. If he walked along the front garden he would certainly be seen, and there was no back entrance. But alongside was the wall dividing the two gardens; six feet of brick and mortar. Near it was a garden seat.

He could climb over the wall.

He stood on the seat and hauled himself to the top of the wall. He was in sight of anyone who happened to glance out of a top floor window or from the house next door. No one had called out. He sat on the wall, gasping for breath. His head felt like a balloon again, and his wrists were on fire. But he couldn't stay there. He dropped down. He fell into a bush and the rustling seemed loud. Leaves quivered, a spiky branch stuck into his wrist, cutting like a knife. But he was hidden from Iris's house and from that next door; there was a long shrubbery and he thought it stretched from here to the front of the garden.

Crouching low, he made his way along, careful not to brush past bushes. Over-confidence was the Department's besetting sin. When Loftus arrived, Wilson would take him into the room and—what a shock! It was difficult not to laugh at the thought of their faces. But he mustn't get over-confident himself. The shadow of fear lay over him, heavy and oppressive. He could not walk quickly, because his ankles hurt; it seemed an age before he reached the front of the garden. Once there, he was near the double gates, which stood open.

Now, he had to show himself.

He stepped on to the pavement. Two or three people were within sight, none of them near him. He smoothed down his hair and straightened his clothes. He must look as if he'd just come from a fight. Anyone who passed him would stop and stare. If he ran into a policeman, he would be questioned. The thing he most feared at that moment was a London peeler.

There was a taxi!

He flung up his hand, to signal to it. The taxi was moving at a good speed, he thought it was going to pass him. Then the driver caught sight of him, and pulled in towards the kerb.

"Cab, sir?" the cabby asked.

"Yes." Corliss got in and almost fell on to the seat. The driver looked through the partition, but seemed uninterested in Corliss's condition.

"Where to?"

"Feltham Place."

"*Where?*"

"Feltham Place, Kensington."

"Fel—okay, I know it." The cab moved swiftly away from the kerb, and Corliss leaned back in a corner and closed his eyes. He was as safe here as anywhere. Wilson had made a complete fool of himself, but he was in no mood to gloat over Wilson. Would 'they' get him out of the country? Surely they wouldn't fail him.

He needn't tell them that Iris had completely deceived him. He could just say that he was suspected, had been accused, had—never mind what to tell them, he'd think of something when he got there.

23

REWARD

F eltham Place was empty.

The cab drew near the telephone kiosk, and Corliss said huskily: "Turn right into Feltham Street—the house at the end." He remembered Abbott lurking at the porch, and realised that the place had been watched for some time, but once he was through that doorway, he would find sanctuary.

The cab stopped opposite the door from which he had seen Abbott. The house was tall, narrow and of red brick—and there were heavy curtains at the windows. He paid the man off, and said:

"Wait two minutes, will you?"

He wanted to be hidden from anyone who happened to look towards the cab. He got out and stumbled up the three steps leading to the porch. The cab hid him from view, because he crouched down. He pressed the bell. He couldn't hear it ringing.

"Okay?" asked the driver.

"One minute, please."

He heard nothing, but the door opened. He didn't recognise the man who stood there, but the fellow was dressed in the dark uniform of all the servants at this house and of His Excellency. He pushed past the man.

"Close the door!"

The servant obeyed; street and cab disappeared from sight. The quiet house looked much the same as by night, because of the dark curtains and the need for electric light. Now that Corliss was here, he did not know what to say to the silent man who stood waiting for him to speak.

"I have to see—His Excellency. It is an urgent matter."

"Yes, sir. If you will please follow me."

No trouble!

The man led the way along the now familiar passages, but did not go downstairs. Instead, he stopped at a door which Corliss had always passed, and tapped. There was no audible answer, but he opened the door at once, and stood aside. Corliss hurried in.

There was no portrait in this smaller room, but His Excellency was there with the faded woman who had talked the night before. They sat at the same desk, a large one with ample room for them both. The walls were plain; there was no map, no picture or portrait of any kind; and there were no windows. His Excellency looked up, and the light above his head cast shadows over the lower part of his face and gave him a saturnine appearance. The woman just looked—drab.

"Why have you come here?" The man's voice was sharp.

"It's urgent," said Corliss. He felt as he had done when he had first seen the man; that the other would know immediately he told a lie. "Loftus—knows who did it last night."

His Excellency did not speak. The woman drew in a sharp breath, and dropped the pen she had in her hand. Corliss licked his lips.

"He tried to—make me confess. I got away. I had nowhere to go, so—"

"You came *here*," breathed the woman.

Corliss turned on her. "Where else could I go? I had to escape. I must get out of the country. You can arrange it for me, it's easy enough, but I couldn't do it for myself." Although he spoke rapidly, his tongue clung to the roof of his mouth every now and again, making him slur the words. "I've done the big job for you, you owe me plenty."

His Excellency did not speak.

Corliss cried: "Well? What about it? Don't you? Didn't I work a miracle for you? Don't sit there staring at me, don't—"

His Excellency stood up, and Corliss stopped. He was panting for breath; this was not at all what he had expected. He felt the hostility in the gaze of both the man and the woman.

"Yes, you did well," His Excellency said. "A great many men do good work, Corliss, but only the weaklings come *here* when they are in trouble. Had you telephoned—"

"I hadn't time! I was on the run!"

"Yes, I understand that," said His Excellency. "And you did not pause to think that you might be followed. To try to save your own life, you have risked the safety of our organisation here. That isn't the act of a reliable man, Corliss. You have not, in fact, been as good as you imagine. You did many foolish things, but you were the one hope of finding the headquarters of Department Z, the one possible way we could get what we wanted, and we were long-suffering."

Corliss shouted: "You told a different tale last night! You would have given me the world!"

"That was excellent," said His Excellency, "but understand, Corliss, that there is a time when every man finishes both his work and his usefulness. Had you not come here—" he shrugged. "We could perhaps have helped you. But this display of cowardice—"

"Cowardice!"

"Don't raise your voice! We cannot help you. We shall send you from here. You can have some money. You must do the best you can, there is nothing else we are able to do."

Corliss didn't speak.

He saw the man open a drawer and saw notes appear in his right hand, but he knew that he would never use those notes. The tone in the man's voice told him that 'they' had finished with him. He knew what had happened to Milanov and to others. They would not risk his being free and able to betray them. They would kill him—oh, not here, but they would kill him. They would probably hide his body.

He jumped at His Excellency.

He grabbed the man's throat and his fingers took tight hold before he could get away. The woman cried out. Corliss felt his fingers press into the lean neck. One twist, and it would be over. One sharp twist was all that stood between this man and death. He tried to twist; his wrists felt on fire and there was no strength in them. He heard himself panting for breath, the face of the man seemed to go round and round in ever widening circles.

Then he heard the roar, as of an explosion.

He felt sharp pain in his side; it seemed to break him in two. His hands dropped away from the other's neck and he staggered to one side. He saw the gun in the woman's hand, levelled towards him.

Then a door opened and a man called: "Whoa back!"

The woman spun round, the bullet missed Corliss by a yard.

The man at the desk snatched at the drawer, but before he

could take out a gun, men streamed into the room. There seemed to be dozens of them, and at their head was Loftus.

Corliss knew that he would die from his wound. He was in no pain, but that was because they had pumped a drug into him. He was in the private ward of a hospital, but did not remember being brought there. His mind was quite clear, but he felt no emotion—it was as if he had lost the capacity to feel. The last thing he remembered vividly was the quick struggle between Loftus and his men and the couple in the room. There had been more shooting, and he did not know whether anyone else had been hurt.

The door opened and Loftus limped in, alone. He came across and pulled up a chair by Corliss's side. His eyes were bloodshot and he looked tired but he was massively calm. Corliss's hatred for him had dimmed; it drained out of him with his life's blood.

Loftus spoke quietly.

"Why did you do it, Corliss?"

Corliss didn't answer.

"There's nothing to be gained by keeping silent," Loftus said. "Days ago we suspected that you were working with them. We've been trying to get their leader over here for a long time, and we thought you might help. We hadn't any doubt, of course, from the time you lied to Iris Grahame about Tom. But—why did you do this?"

Corliss said: "What does it matter? I fooled you long enough to get those records." He was neither proud nor ashamed of that, now.

Loftus shook his head.

"You didn't, old chap. They were faked records. We had a mass of old stuff put into the files, there wasn't a single piece of useful information in those you photographed."

Corliss felt a stirring of resentment; as a child who had been cheated.

"That's not true, it can't be true. You didn't expect me, you wouldn't have let me kill—"

Loftus pulled at his underlip.

"Remember the man who invited *you* to kill him? He didn't mind dying for what he thought was the just cause. We have— our heroes." The word was uttered softly, almost reverently. "Beresford, the man you shot in the office, knew what might happen. In fact, he didn't greatly mind. He was suffering from an incurable disease, his life was measured in months, anyhow. He volunteered to take his chance. Everything was set for you, everything made easy. But you were being watched, all the time. We had to let you go on as long as we could, we wanted to catch you at the headquarters. We drove you there. The taxi driver was one of us."

It was absurd. Corliss felt almost like crying, but it wasn't worth the trouble. Loftus was cleverer than he thought; much cleverer.

"We've been ready to raid the place for some time," Loftus went on, "but we needed conclusive proof of what was being done there. We knew the other people had a nearly perfect system of destroying all records if they were raided, we had to catch them on the hop. We let them think they'd got away with everything and that there was no danger. Because they weren't raided immediately after you handed over your negatives last night, they felt secure."

"Oh," said Corliss blankly.

"They're good," Loftus said; he seemed to speak with an effort. "'His Excellency' is a brilliant organiser here on a special mission for the *Communist International.* We've broken up the big spy ring and we've been able to break up hundreds of Red cells throughout the country, but we haven't provoked an international incident." Every word came out slowly and deliberately. "Did you hear Wilson and Miss Grahame talking at her house?"

Corliss nodded.

"Then you know she was working with us all the time."

"You've said that before."

Loftus looked at him, with a half frown, half smile; and then he nodded slowly.

"Yes, that's right. I'm tired and repeating myself. I'll grant you this, it's been a strain. There was a spot of trouble in the Midlands last night, a nice distraction arranged by your friends, and I had to go up there. It didn't really interfere with our plans, but—" He broke off, and shrugged. "We've discovered plenty, at Feltham Street, and one or two of the minor officials have talked. We know that you were trying to find out what steps we were taking against the Red cells and we know that they were strong and powerful, almost ready to make a widespread attack on industry and commerce—all the plans were drawn up for major and other troubles. Well, they'll have to build afresh, Corliss, this round was easily ours. Thanks to you."

That didn't hurt.

"Why did you do it?" Loftus asked quietly.

Corliss said: "You know so much, how is it that you don't know that? From the time my father died, when he was sent out to his death—"

"*So that's it.*"

"That's it."

Loftus said: "It's a hell of a business. You fight one war that really starts the next. You use a man with all the courage in the world who tackles one enemy and it makes another. Spying's a deadly, dangerous business and the odds are always against you. And there's little decency in it. Black becomes white. I'll tell you the truth about your father, Corliss. He got through and did a fine job, fooling the Nazis. He'd gone to get information they had about the Russians. He got it, but the Russians reached Berlin too soon. They caught and tortured him—"

Corliss gasped: "No! No, that's a lie, that's a lie!"

"It's true," Loftus said. "Here's a note, written by your father before he died, smuggled out of Berlin. Read it."

Corliss began to shiver, but made himself read. There wasn't any doubt of the truth. The Russians, not the Nazis, had tortured and killed his father.

Loftus said: "That's spying, Corliss, and they had to make him talk, as I've made people talk a dozen times."

Corliss kept on shivering.

"The enemy within is always more dangerous than the enemy outside," said Loftus—and suddenly, he smiled. "I'm getting prosy! That's one of the things you've always disliked about me, isn't it? I won't go on, but you ought to know this, Corliss. We've an Intelligence Service with agents who will take any risk, all the time, to make sure that we aren't beaten by that enemy within. There's a cock-eyed notion in a lot of people's minds that we only play at the business. Well, we don't. There are people several thousand miles away who are really beginning to realise that, now."

He stood up.

"Anything you'd like to say?"

"To hell with the Reds," said Corliss brokenly. "To hell with them! If I could—"

He broke off, wincing with sudden pain.

Loftus entered the Whitehall office as Craigie put down the telephone. Wilson and Iris, in the two armchairs, jumped up.

Craigie said: "Hallo, Bill," and came across to the fireplace.

"Have you seen him?" Iris asked Loftus.

"Yes."

"I've just had word from the hospital," said Craigie. "He died ten minutes after you left, Bill."

"Oh. Best thing." Loftus leaned against the mantelpiece. "He'd gone sour on us, blamed us for killing his father. It was a simple question of a form of mental breakdown, and it turned him bad. He could have been a first-class man. Well! He didn't repent but he didn't boast about anything. I don't think he gave anything much thought. He knew he'd had it, and wasn't worrying. Anything fresh from Feltham Street, Gordon?"

"Odds and ends," said Craigie. "They hadn't sent any dispatches across about this office, we can still use the old methods. For safety's sake we'll make some improvement on our reverse spelling code—"

Loftus chuckled. "Hark at him! He loves his magician's wand and swears by *abracadabra!*"

"It works," said Iris, spiritedly.

"Oh, yes. Well, then—all that left the country were the photographs of the fake records. Not *bad*. But it's cost us plenty." He was no longer smiling, looked sombre. "Hilde Hansson—Abbott—Beresford. Be warned, Iris. There's no need for you to carry on with it."

Iris said slowly: "I've only just realised that you hate doing it, Bill. That Reggie does, too. When I started it was a kind of adventure, almost romantic, but now—whenever I see Annie brooding I'll think of Tom, Abby, Beresford, Hilde—"

"You'll get over that side of it," Loftus said. "We all do. But remember anytime you want to drop out, say so."

"I'll tell you," Iris promised. She swung round. "Reggie, do we have to stay here now? Can we go out? There's time for a run somewhere in the car. I need a breath of fresh air."

Craigie said: "Off with you!"

Wilson jumped up. "All right, my sweet, we'll blow the

cobwebs away. No matinée today, is there? I—oh, yes. Satur-
day. Oh, well. Nothing more you want me for now, Gordon?"

"No."

"Send me a postcard when anything crops up," said Wilson
brightly.

ABOUT THE AUTHOR

John Creasey, born in 1908, was a paramount English crime and science fiction writer who used myriad pseudonyms for more than six hundred novels. He founded the UK Crime Writers' Association in 1953. In 1962, his book *Gideon's Fire* received the Edgar Award for Best Novel from the Mystery Writers of America. Many of the characters featured in Creasey's titles became popular, including George Gideon of Scotland Yard, who was the basis for a subsequent television series and film. Creasey died in Salisbury, UK, in 1973.

DEPARTMENT Z

FROM OPEN ROAD MEDIA

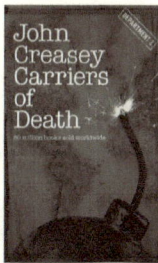  

 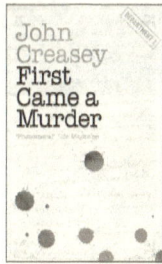 

OPEN ROAD
INTEGRATED MEDIA

www.ingramcontent.com/pod-product-compliance
Lightning Source LLC
Chambersburg PA
CBHW020357030726
47496CB00007B/2189